"Just for the record, Kelly Jean, you were the one who came to me. Remember?"

"How do you know my middle name is Jean?"

"I checked you out," he admitted.

"It wasn't enough that you staked out the newspaper?" she choked. "You investigated me?"

" *'Investigated'* isn't the right word."

"Didn't you ever hear of invasion of privacy, Lieutenant?"

"It wasn't like that, damn it. I only wanted—"

She spun around furiously. "You only wanted what? And make it good, Ethan, because I don't swallow just every hook, line and sinker that comes along, only the best."

The night was electrified with emotions.

"You," he said at last, and wished there had been no shock value attached. "I wanted you."

Dear Reader,

Once again Intimate Moments is offering you a month filled with terrific books, starting right off with Kathleen Korbel's American Hero title, *A Walk on the Wild Side*. J. P. O'Neill is an undercover agent for the DEA, but when he's framed for the murder of his partner, he realizes his own agency has set him up. The only thing to do is take off in search of the truth himself, and the only way to escape is in the company of his lawyer—who's handcuffed to his arm! Theirs is a rocky beginning, but the end will be terrific—if only they can live that long!

In *The Hell-Raiser,* author Dallas Schulze pens a powerful tale of lovers reunited after ten long years. Jenny had always been the proverbial good girl and Mitch the bad boy, but now he feels it's time for her to let go of the guilts of the past and let him take her for a whirl through life.

Linda Shaw's *Indian Summer* takes a hero and heroine from feuding families and forces them into an alliance that is at first just business but eventually becomes something far more: love. As always, Linda plumbs the depths of her characters' hearts—and souls.

In *Run to the Moon,* talented Sandy Steen puts her own unique spin on the ever-popular "secret baby" plot, while Catherine Palmer's *Red Hot* takes you to chile farm country for a steamy marriage-of-convenience story. Finally, let new author Julia Quinn tell you about *Wade Conner's Revenge.* Driven from town by suspicion and unprovable accusations, betrayed by the silence of the woman he loved, Wade Conner returns with a score to settle. But suspicion begins to follow him once again, and now he needs the help of a woman he no longer trusts—to keep a murder charge at bay.

I think you'll enjoy each and every one of these terrific books, as well as all the exciting novels we have in store for you in months to come—books by such favorites as Rachel Lee, Marilyn Pappano, Paula Detmer Riggs and Justine Davis, to name only a few. Meanwhile, happy reading!

Yours,

Leslie J. Wainger
Senior Editor and Editorial Coordinator

INDIAN SUMMER

Linda Shaw

Silhouette® INTIMATE MOMENTS®

Published by Silhouette Books New York

America's Publisher of Contemporary Romance

SILHOUETTE BOOKS
300 East 42nd St., New York, N.Y. 10017

INDIAN SUMMER

Copyright © 1992 by Linda Shaw

ISBN: 0-373-07458-1

First Silhouette Books printing November 1992

All the characters in this book have no existence
outside the imagination of the author and have
no relation whatsoever to anyone bearing the same
name or names. They are not even distantly
inspired by any individual known or unknown
to the author, and all incidents are pure invention.

®: Trademark used under license and
registered in the United States Patent and
Trademark Office and in other countries.

Printed in the U.S.A.

LINDA SHAW

saw years of hard work come to fruition during the 1980s with the publication of numerous contemporary and historical novels. A decade of writing is now behind her, a decade in which she defined her style and won many loyal fans. She lives with her husband in Keene, Texas, where she surrounds herself with her children and three young grandchildren.

To Sue Harrold, The Bookworm Bookstore, and Ada Paravicini, the Coosa-Alabama River Improvement, for generously answering my questions about Montgomery.

Chapter 1

Kelly Madison had not been in the publishing business long enough to be known as a dragon lady. She was hardly in the business at all, having inherited the *Montgomery Daily Mirror* when it was in the final throes of a death rattle.

So when Albert Russo strolled into her late father's office, deposited himself into Vincent's exhausted chair, drew his palm over a scalp where hair had once been and offered her a bribe, she knew she had made a mistake in coming back to Montgomery.

"Mr. Russo," she said, and turned from where she'd been packing her father's things. "In the first place, I'm not your *honey*. And in the second, I'm not for sale, sir. Not even to you."

The executive drew in his paunch in a very corporate pose, ostensibly horrified.

"Why, Miss Madison," he gasped, "what an uncharitable thing to say."

"Yes, well—" she gave him a thin, cardboard smile "—that's the nice thing about watching your father's work go down the tubes. You can be as uncharitable as you want."

Kelly removed three framed photographs from the faded office wall, including the one that revealed the crack that splayed crazily in what, as a child, she had thought was a granddaddy longlegs.

She wrapped each picture in a sheet of newsprint—images of Vincent Madison and his reporters posing outside a younger Redmond Building, Vincent and his three blond-haired girls with waist-long braids and black patent shoes with lacy white anklets.

Albert Russo wasn't appreciative of the nostalgia. His company was based in Schenectady, New York, and he traveled around the country taking over old hospitals, hiring and firing, making lucrative deals with insurance and pharmaceutical companies to create a sort of one-stop, we-have-it-all health-care shopping mall.

Back in the days when Montgomery had been the first Confederate capital, the Albert Russos had come south on horseback—wheeler-dealers following the Chattahoochee River. During Reconstruction they had come by train, lugging their carpetbags. Now they arrived at the airport in corporate jets and were met by stretch limousines with TVs and bars.

Russo slipped a breath mint into his mouth and worked it briefly with his tongue.

"Your inheritance, Miss Madison, is not my problem. Your headlines, on the other hand, are very much my problem. Take this as a warning, my dear—if my name appears in print one more time, I will be upset. You don't want to see me upset." He worked his neck against his stiff collar. "Bribery, indeed."

She should have stayed in Virginia with her aunt Eunice, Kelly thought as sweat drizzled down her sides. She should be planning her strategy of climbing up in the world—finding the ambitious husband and the dream house, a live-in maid and a Porsche 911 SC Targa, meaningful hobbies, a son and a daughter.

"Well, what do you expect, Mr. Russo?" She taped the box and placed it on the floor with the others. "You march into this office and say, 'There are things you could do to make your life easier, Miss Madison. Things don't have to be so hard, Miss Madison.' What am I supposed to think? That you're inviting me to two-step?"

Behind his tiny lashes, Russo was drawing a bead from the top of her pulled-back hair to her ringless hands to her plain, flat-heeled loafers. He was seeing her shapeless jumper and knit top with the sleeves pushed to her elbows. He was thinking she was a frustrated, twenty-eight-year-old woman working on spinsterhood.

There might be a grain of truth to that assumption, she thought grimly.

"I was merely trying to point out, Miss Madison," he said with a weariness reserved for fools, "that the *Tribune*'s subscription rate is ten-to-one what the *Mirror*'s is. The *Tribune* is also enjoying a nice, new facility while you're rotting away in this firetrap. Doesn't that tell you anything? Doesn't it make you stop and think? Aren't you wondering if perhaps you aren't doing something wrong?"

Kelly found it extremely difficult to look the man in the eye, for what he said was true.

"It tells me that if you want a successful newspaper in Montgomery, it helps to be Mayor Georgia Chase. Ambitions to be the next governor don't hurt, either, I suppose." She flicked him a glance of dismissal. "Now, if you'll excuse me..."

"For the record, Maxwell runs the paper these days, not Georgia. If you wouldn't mind some advice—"

"I do mind!"

"Why don't you come into the nineties with the rest of us, Miss Madison? The world happens to run by making a profit. The first rule is, don't mess with another man's profit. If you find that unappealing, perhaps you should take your Barbie doll and go into somebody else's backyard."

The anger that reddened Kelly's cheeks was part righteousness and part embarrassment. She readily admitted her naiveté in the modern business world, but her love for Vincent had not ended with his death. If the *Mirror* were following him to the grave, by heaven, it was going to receive a decent burial!

In a bluff that couldn't match his, but was the best she could do, she reached into a drawer and brought out a tape recorder. She placed the microphone before him and brazenly shifted it to a better advantage.

"Taped on April 22," she said, and adjusted the volume with theatric grace. "Albert Russo of Southeast Medical Group has just told me that if I'll stop lambasting his company in the *Mirror*'s op-ed pages, things will be better for me. Is that correct, Mr. Russo? Our subscriptions might even improve. We'd no longer have to work in a...what did you call it? A firetrap? This needs to be exact, you see. The last thing I want to do is misquote you."

An unbecoming purple flush spread above the fold of the CEO's collar. He snatched the microphone from the desk and ripped the cord from its connection, hurling them both to the floor.

From inside his jacket he brought out a leather book with gold-edged pages. He angrily fanned through them as if searching for a list of her sins. Opening to a page, he plucked a pen from her desk.

"Exactly how much do you figure it'll cost to keep your daddy's paper from being buried in the same box?" he asked.

She boldly met his eyes and searched for a glimmer of human compassion. Finding none, she dispiritedly shook her head.

"I think we're finished here, Mr. Russo," she said icily, and was glad for once of her five feet ten inches. She was taller than he.

With a hiss of breath Russo replaced the leather book to his pocket. With a crunch of his breath mint, he rose and stepped through the open door.

"I was wrong about you, Miss Madison," he said, and considered the *Mirror*'s staff of a baker's dozen who sat beyond them at their desks, watching and listening as they pretended to work. "I thought you were smarter than this."

Kelly, too, glanced over the room. Why didn't one of the editors speak out? The old-timers? Fred Woodson? Ann Jacobs? Or Jerome, the photographer who looked like a bearded exclamation point?

Even I-was-the-first-person-your-father-hired Leah Blankenship was silent. What were they thinking? Kelly wondered. That she had some magical power to wield against this corporate Goliath in behalf of their pensions?

They merely looked at the front of the building where, at the old brassbound revolving door, two black women were entering to make an uncertain search of the newsroom. May Segue was clutching the hand of a small, wide-eyed girl, and Delia was gripping a cheap vinyl bag. On their faces was the bleak futility of being black and poor in the Deep South.

The women had been here before. They lived on the opposite side of Montgomery County—out near the Pierce Creek landfill that Southeast Medical had built—and their problem had never had much chance of being solved. It had less chance now.

"I don't suppose you know these two ladies?" Kelly challenged Russo's back.

He faced her before reaching the door. His voice could be heard over the ringing telephone and the muted voice that answered it.

"I'm not God, Miss Madison," he proclaimed in sonorous tones. "Despite rumors to the contrary."

"Well, those ladies certainly know you, sir."

He struck the pose of a guardian of the people, caressing his cuffs and adjusting his tie as he gave them momentary consideration.

"The daughters of those two women attend Pierce Elementary near your landfill, sir. They're eleven years old and have just been diagnosed as having infectious hepatitis."

The newsroom grew so still, a low-pitched television was perfectly audible. This premise had been kicked around in the story conference for days but had been discarded as a possible exposé due to lack of hard evidence.

Now the editors were exchanging fish-lipped looks in agreement: *She's gone and done it now. In a week we'll be on unemployment.*

Another telephone rang. *"Daily Mirror,"* someone said impatiently.

Albert Russo shot the two women a less respectful look. "If they said that, *they're* lying."

"If anyone's lying, it's you, sir!" Kelly hardly believed the words coming out of her mouth.

"I beg your par—"

"When you built the new hospital for Montgomery County, Mr. Russo, you failed to mention a few pertinent facts—that a furnace would burn day and night and spew bad things into our air. You forgot to tell us that you wouldn't be burning only our own waste, that you'd be bringing it in from New York and Connecticut. And Texas!" She threw back her head in dramatic horror. "We won't even talk about Texas—Houston, Beaumont, Galveston, La Porte. We have more Texas waste here than Texas has!''

So furious that his scalp was red, Russo stepped into the door. Kelly ran after him.

''We've taken samples!'' she shouted recklessly.

Behind her, Leah Blankenship whispered shrilly, ''Your father is turning over in his grave!''

''Butt out, Leah!'' Kelly snapped.

As his temper changed Russo from a suave executive into a shark, his eyes grew small with calculation and he stepped back into the room, circling for the kill.

''I'd think about what I was doing,'' he warned quietly, and pointed a finger. ''If you think Montgomery County is going to stand by while you jeopardize twelve hundred jobs and tax breaks and a new highway simply for the sake of a soapbox, you're dead wrong. And you know what? People don't want to know about biological waste, Miss Madison. They want jobs and food on their tables at night. There are trade-offs in everything. If your father were alive, he'd tell you that he'd made a few himself. Talk to Mayor Chase before you get the city tied up in a snarl of lawsuits. Learn how the game is played.''

Having badly overdrawn her courage account, Kelly sagged against Leah's desk as the man made his exit.

Nothing was more pathetic than the person who didn't know when an argument was over, she thought. Why hadn't she been a little more clever, pretending to agree with the man, then doing what she wanted? Who had dubbed her Joan of Arc?

But he was wrong on one count. Vincent Madison had never made a deal in his life. Russo hadn't been there when a fourteen-year-old boy had packed a ratty valise and left a shotgun house that squatted beside the railroad tracks, hitchhiking along Highway 80 beneath a cruel sun and come to Montgomery, where he got a job pushing a broom in this very Redmond Building.

Years later he had bought the building and started the *Mirror*. When Caroline Weathers, a blue-blooded but penniless Virginia woman, married him, they had moved into the big Victorian house on Ferris Street and raised three green-eyed girls who took piano lessons and wore organdy dresses with eyelet embroidery on the collars.

A stone lay in Kelly's chest now, cold as her father's misplaced dreams. Dreading the accusing eyes of the staff, she squared her shoulders and lifted her chin.

With a dignity she couldn't have imagined of herself, she made her way to the shabby office at the opposite end of the newsroom. There she sank into Vincent's chair and weakly waved for May and Delia to follow.

Leah Blankenship preceded them—a witch on a broomstick.

"You have a call on line two," she said haughtily, and added before flying away, "In all his years, your father never angered the business community. Not once."

Before the paper went under for the third time, there was one thing she owed herself, Kelly thought, and covered the telephone receiver with a palm. She was going to fire the old biddy!

No wonder Russo considered the *Mirror* a third-rate rag. Look at the way Leah was dressed with a skirt drooping to her ankles and her smock buttoned to her neck, a Price Masters crime novel poking out of her left pocket so that it sagged five inches lower than the right.

Motioning for May and Delia to find chairs, Kelly pushed a blinking button on her telephone and swiveled around, glimpsing her own reflection in the glass that separated her desk from the others.

She didn't believe what she saw. She saw herself— No! She imagined she saw herself in Leah Blankenship's body, sitting in Vincent's chair, drab and plain as a post!

"Kelly Madison," she whispered as she peered down at her jumper, so remarkably like one Leah would have worn. Good grief!

"Kelly?" Hite Pritchard's voice drifted over the line. "What's up? Ready to set the wedding date?"

Hite was her dearest friend. His great-grandmother had been an Alibamu Indian, and his father had found his way into the same world that Vincent had aspired to. Except that now Irwin Pritchard was the reigning judge of the state.

Following the Pritchard tradition, Hite was, at thirty-nine, the assistant attorney general of Alabama. On an awful night a dozen years ago, he had been the one who'd taken her to his own house instead of the police station. When she'd clung and begged him not to tell his father or her own, he had held her and understood why she couldn't bear being dragged through the courts. No one believed when a woman was raped, she'd wept.

Now she wished Hite were holding her again so she could rage and despair about this newspaper that could not be saved.

"What's up, did you say?" She reached back and savagely pulled the rubber band from her hair, releasing a mane of ash blond waves to tumble down her back. "Oh, nothing much. The zoning commission is giving us a fit about turning some of these empty east-side buildings into lower-income dwellings. The paper's going under, but that's old news. I just had a visit from the CEO of Southeast Medical, and he practically threatened to sue me because of the landfill articles. Other than that, my day's been just great. How's yours?"

Familiar laughter exploded in her ear. "I guess that means it isn't a good time to ask you to meet me at Mendino's Friday night."

Kelly started to fit her glasses on her face but focused on her reflection again and laid them down. Instead, she arranged the sleeves of her knit top and fluffed her hair.

"Six-thirty?" he asked.

"Perfect. I'll have time to powder my nose after work."

"What a relief. I really get upset over unpowdered noses."

Laughing, Kelly started to hang up, but twirled her chair discreetly around and cupped the mouthpiece. "Hite?"

"What?"

"Would you tell me the truth about something?"

"Sure."

"Do I look like Leah?"

His laughter was the best denial possible. "If anybody accuses you of looking like Leah Blankenship, darling, send 'em to me."

"Dear man. It's easy to see why you're so successful. I'll see you at Mendino's, day after tomorrow."

"Be sweet."

"Aren't I always?"

"No."

Smiling, she dropped the receiver into its cradle and paused for a moment to try to remember who she was. Kelly Jean Madison: schoolteacher, champion of lost causes, disenchanted Cinderella.

Rising, she clasped Delia's hand. "I'm so glad you stopped by, Delia—you and May. I've been thinking about you a lot."

"I know it's a bad time." The woman indicated the clock on the newsroom wall. "Me and May could come back another day if you'd druther."

"Nonsense." Stooping, Kelly straightened the collar of a shy girl who was hiding in her mother's skirt. "Seika, you are absolutely stunning in red. Don't wear any other color."

Delia said, "We left kids in the car, Miss Madison. We can't stay long."

"Then why don't you walk me to the parking lot and tell me everything?" Kelly suggested. "I was going to take off early, anyway. Just let me gather a few things...."

She stuffed her briefcase with the take-home work that had kept her up past midnight for weeks. Motioning the women to follow, she paused at Leah's desk to say she would not be back today.

Leah glanced at the clock, and Kelly was certain she made a note of the time.

The four of them walked onto the Redmond parking lot, where April sunshine sent their shadows jitterbugging over the broken concrete.

"Tell me," Kelly said, "what did the mayor have to offer?"

"That woman!" Delia snorted with contempt. "She said she'd look into it, but when we called back, her secretary said Miz Lah-te-dah Georgia didn't have nothin' for us. She wouldn't even put us through."

"Well—" Kelly shaded her eyes against the sun while her briefcase bumped her knees "—you and the whole world heard what Albert Russo had to say about the landfill. He didn't even bother to deny that they're trucking the stuff in. But doing something about it..."

"Is hopeless," Delia finished.

Kelly cursed her impotence but added the useless encouragement that she would have wanted to hear. "But we can't give up, Delia. We can't ever stop fighting."

The look passing between the two women was one of battle fatigue.

Kelly grasped May's shoulder. "I know it looks grim right now, but you have to keep calling officials, May. Complain to everyone until they're sick of the sound of your voice."

"The doctor thinks we're crazy."

"The doctor is afraid of getting sued if he opens his mouth."

"Isn't everyone?"

No! Kelly wanted to snap. *I could get sued fighting for you!*

They stopped walking. May's children were hanging out of a dilapidated sedan, waving and making comical faces.

"Keep comparing notes with the other mothers at the school," Kelly said on a sigh. "Call them over and over. Keep me informed of anything—any pattern, any lead. If several students come down with a stomachache at the same time or a runny nose, let me know."

They agreed they would do what they could, but it was apparent as they got into their car and disappeared in a cloud of exhaust that they had come expecting *her* to give them the solution.

But she was only one woman. She was fighting a losing battle against recession, and she was going to battle with a powerful executive who had Born To Win stamped on his forehead. She could wind up with enough court costs to put her under for life!

Reaching her own rattling Ford, she peered back at the Redmond Building. Once upon a time, Mimosa Street had been in the middle of a thriving commercial section that stretched all the way to Edlestein Parkway. Almost without anyone noticing, the interstate highway had gone in, and Egan's Office Supply at the end of the block had become Allen's Paint & Body Shop. Valentine's Florist was now an all-night laundromat where the homeless congregated in bad weather. Now the empty warehouses down by the highway lured crack manufacturers. Underprivileged children played in stripped cars on the street while their unemployed parents sat on the stoops and smoked. Their faces were as gaunt and hopeless as May's and Delia's.

Kelly unlocked her car and tossed her briefcase haphazardly into the back seat. Climbing in, she rolled down the windows and turned the key in the ignition.

Click. Dropping her head to the steering wheel, she groaned beneath the weight of the last backbreaking straw. "Not now, please."

Cursing the wretched machine, she glanced around the parking lot for someone to help, but no one was in sight, not even a mugger. She was damned if she'd go back inside for Fred Woodson!

Again she turned the key. The machine mocked her with another *click.*

She knew only too well about the sticking solenoid; she still owed money to the mechanic who had explained how the starter, like the *Mirror,* was fast approaching its demise.

She snatched open the glove compartment and rummaged to find a special wrench she kept for this occasion. Pronouncing a lengthy stream of anathemas upon all machines, she climbed out and scrunched beneath the fender until the starter was visible.

Drawing back, she struck the end of it a blow that sent pain shooting to her wrist.

"I ought to beat you to death," she grumbled.

Crawfishing out from under the car, she scrambled up, dusted off her jumper and slumped with relief as she turned the key and the engine sputtered, then fired.

She sat revving the motor, not daring to let it die. She negligently tossed the wrench to the floor, prepared to drive off the lot. Then the envelope caught her eye.

With puzzled brows she drew out a bulging, brown mailing bag that she'd never seen before. Sealed, it bore no markings on the outside. As the engine warmed, she turned it over, searching for a clue. Finding none, she slipped her fingertip beneath the flap and ripped.

To her disbelief, a river of one-hundred-dollar bills flowed into her lap.

"What in the..." She scooped them into a pile and slid weakly down in her seat, trying to catch her breath so the adrenaline would stop shooting through her. How much money was here? What was going on?

With trembling fingers she collected the bills and counted them. Eighty! Eighty one-hundred-dollar bills! Eight thousand dollars!

Suddenly wanting to get as far from the parking lot as possible, she tried to stuff the bills back into the envelope as if they were germs of some deadly epidemic that must be contained to save the world. But her fingers were thumbs. By the time she finally got the money back inside and shoved the envelope beneath her seat, she was shivering. Locking the doors, she crouched with her arms folded over her abdomen.

When she had stopped shaking, she inched upward several inches until her eyebrows were on a level with the window.

She scanned the parking lot, whispering a litany of self-reinforcement through gritted teeth: "Don't panic, don't panic. You can do this. You can handle this. Think, think."

But the truth created intense pressure beneath her skull. Her car had been locked. Someone had forced their way inside.

Russo! Albert Russo was making good on his bribe. Maybe he was photographing her at this very moment. Maybe the car was bugged.

"Oh, God!"

She unlocked the car and jumped frantically outside, darting across the parking lot. What should she do now? Find the man and throw his tainted money back in his face?

No. She should get calmly back into the car, go home and call Morris Cavanaugh, the lawyer who had advised her father whenever sticky subjects came up. But Morris, if she could reach him at all, would hem and haw and wear her down, and she would never learn what had happened. She had do do something *now!*

Raking hair from her eyes, she furtively scanned the lot and climbed back into the car, then slipped it in gear. She nosed cautiously out onto Mimosa Street, keeping a constant look in her rearview mirror to see if she were being followed. She wasn't reassured when she saw no one; they could be watching from blocks away.

She drove without any purpose. She stopped at traffic lights. She used her brake and her blinker, all without consciously realizing it. She turned on Ferris Street, homing instincts drawing her to the two-story house that had seen the best and the worst of her. But Caroline, her mother, would be no help. The worst possible thing she could do would be to take the money into the house. It would be like accepting the bribe.

The police! If she went to them now, no one would be able to say later that she'd behaved unethically.

She whipped the car around and broke the speed limit reaching the municipal building downtown. Cars were parked in the city lot, most of them marked police units. She was sweating when she finally stuffed the packet into her briefcase and went inside.

The police dispatcher's window was thick, bulletproof glass. A woman her own age sat before a complicated console, a transmitter positioned before her.

Through a circular opening, she told the woman, "I'm Kelly Madison from the *Mirror*."

Sue Mendoza looked up, her nameplate clearly visible. "Ma'am?"

"I need to see . . ." At a loss, Kelly shrugged. "Ah, Chief Felker, I suppose."

"You're from the *Mirror*, you say?" Sue Mendoza looked Kelly up and down as if suspecting a concealed weapon. "The chief doesn't give interviews without an appointment."

"This isn't an interview."

Sue stabbed a ballpoint pen into her curls and scratched. "He's gone for the day."

"Could I see his assistant?"

"Don's gone home, too. The evening shift has come on."

"A detective, then," Kelly said tightly, beginning to dislike the woman intensely. "*Any* detective."

Sue skimmed a list and reached for the telephone. "Lieutenant Chase hasn't clocked out."

"Chase?"

With no warning, a domino in Kelly's mind toppled and bumped another domino, then another and another as a chain reaction brought the memories full circle.

"*Ethan* Chase?" she stupidly echoed as the memories came full circle. "Georgia and Maxwell . . ."

"Yes. Look, do you want to see a detective or not?"

"But I thought . . . I mean, Mr. Chase, uh, Lieutenant Chase, I mean, I didn't think he lived in Montgomery anymore."

"He came back."

"Oh."

The woman's expression was one of I-haven't-got-all-night-lady.

Beyond Kelly, double doors opened. Sounds of rush-hour traffic spilled inside—honking and brakes squealing, voices clashing as two uniformed officers brought in a handcuffed youngster.

As she numbly looked on, she saw, not the boy's sullen shuffle, but a faraway image like a peeling, sepia-toned photograph—a twelve-year-old girl huddled in a football stadium with her father on a cold Thanksgiving as a crowd roared with victory.

A muddy quarterback had been walking off the field that day. Fans were going wild, screaming, pouring out of the bleachers. A girl, a cheerleader, was fighting her way through the throng to hurl herself into the arms of the quarterback. Silhouetted by the cold sunshine, the quarterback bent his head and kissed the girl.

Kelly had never consciously selected that moment to epitomize her romantic girlish dreams. Ethan Chase, the quarterback, had simply been there—Prince Charming at the moment when Nature was quickening her inside, and when the rest of the world didn't know she existed.

Over the years, of course, Ethan had faded from the memory, but the golden prince remained. When friends had been hard to come by, he was her friend, the one person she told everything to. The prince learned all about her mysteriously blooming body. His golden, bending head was proof that love really did exist. No matter how ugly the world became or how hopeless, he would come for her someday, and they would live happily ever after.

"Ma'am?"

Starting, Kelly blushed and cleared her throat. "Isn't there anyone else I could see?"

Much put-upon, Sue Mendoza pushed a button. "Detective Fisher. Second door on your left down the hall." A buzzer purred on the console. "Police station . . ."

The heels of Kelly's loafers scuffed a warning as she dejectedly made her way to Detective Fisher's office. Growing more bleak by the moment, she found the second door on the left and peered inside.

She was confronted by a room full of desks and heavy steel filing cabinets, glaring fluorescent lights and ringing telephones. Here and there, holstered revolvers were riding polyestered hips. Men in plainclothes were sprinkled around. At the entrance, a light was flickering from a short.

A man looked up from his desk. "Yes?"

"Detective Fisher," Kelly said as her briefcase bumped her knees.

"See the partition at the back of the room?"

"Yes."

"That's him."

"Thank you."

As Kelly approached the barricade that was nothing more than a folding screen of carpet, she was about to check the posted nameplates when a tiny mewling caught her by surprise.

A smile curved her lips. A kitten? At the police station?

She laughed softly. Well, maybe Montgomery's finest had a mouse problem.

The mewling was followed by the sharp shatter of breaking glass. Kelly stepped around the partial wall without being invited. At a glance she saw two city-issued desks, one of them agonizingly neat with a perfect outgoing-mail tray next to a polished bronze name plaque: John Fisher.

The chair behind the desk was empty.

The other desk was buried beneath an explosion of papers, file folders, used paper cups, empty bottles of mineral water, two finger-stained volumes of Yellow Pages, a carton of Marlboros spilling packs of cigarettes and a football trophy with a gold-plated man mounted on the top in the process of throwing a pass.

Good cop, bad cop, she thought as the image of a quarterback kissing a girl brought her to a sharp standstill.

Swinging from the statue's arm was a gold chain to which a tiny plastic banana was attached—a notable irony, but no more so than the sign taped above a large box against the wall where three fluffy kittens were attempting to scale the top: Take Me And Deduct $5 On Your Income Tax.

The kittens had managed to climb a distance, but their new claws gave way. They dropped back into the box again.

Except for one of them—a tiger-striped charmer who finally reached the precarious edge and blinked down at a human being, six feet of hunkered-down male as it navigated around a desk to collect shards of broken glass.

Kelly felt as if she had been walking in her sleep. The man's trim hips were jutting back to the scuffed heels of Western boots. His starched jeans were strained to the limit. The tail of a khaki shirt was pulling free of a leather belt. The point of a tie was sweeping the floor, and the leather holster riding his shoulders made everything legal.

Her jaw dropped as she finally registered the spiky brush of black hair. *Black* hair? But that was all wrong! It wasn't the way the story went! His hair wasn't supposed to be *black!*

He rose up under the edge of his desk and cracked his head with a *thunk* and dropped to his knees again. Slivers of glass fell, tinkling, to the floor.

He blinked sympathetically at a bleeding, crescent-shaped wound in his palm.

"Shh—t!" he muttered in disgust.

Chapter 2

Kelly felt foolish and brutally tricked.

Life wasn't to be trusted. It lied and played a person false. This man, this once-upon-a-time quarterback, Ethan Chase, who was shocking her with his outlaw sexuality, wasn't golden at all! He wasn't a prince, and he wasn't her friend. He was simply a man who had lived forty-odd years the hard way and knew he must make the best of what was left.

"Is there something I can help you with, ma'am?"

"Pardon?" A voice at Kelly's back brought her spinning around.

She took two steps that placed her outside the partition again. There she confronted one of the most handsome black men she'd ever seen. A badge was clipped to his suit, but not just *any* suit. Gabardine, hand tailored, it could have walked off the gorgeous body of Denzel Washington and straight onto his. John Fisher, the ID said.

"N-no, thank you," she managed to stammer. Russo had been right about one thing; it was time to leave the playhouse behind. Great causes demanded great champions.

"If you came to see Lieutenant Chase—" his smile was sympathetic as he nodded toward the strange goings-on behind the wall "—he hasn't left yet."

"I—"

"Hey, Top Gun!" he bawled. "You got a visitor."

There were more sounds of shuffling, and then a body emerged.

Ethan Chase was considerably taller than Kelly's own five feet ten. Now that she faced him straight on and he was blocking out the office with his shoulders, she realized his nose had been broken. More than once, apparently, for it created a sort of Harrison Ford look to his face. His mouth was wide and mobile, and the lines framing it were permanent. His eyes, a cutting-torch blue, were capable of terrible ironies.

A tough guy, she thought with a jerking pulse. He was a burned-out tough guy.

"Well, well," he drawled as he lifted black brows to scan the whole of her. "You're in luck. We're having a two-for-one special on kittens. For the next hour, double value for your money. Incidentally, we deliver."

Kelly inched backward, searching helplessly for John Fisher.

The detective had disappeared.

"Oh, no." She shook her head. "I live with my mother."

He grinned. "Wonderful. Take an extra one for her."

"What I meant was, she has two cats already. If I brought home another . . ."

The edges of his mouth twitched with a satanic form of amusement. Kelly wished she could turn around and dash out, but she couldn't. Nor did she hold out much hope that in the next two seconds she would faint or die or melt into the floor and leave nothing but her shoes.

"Okay, okay, okay," he said more congenially. "*Three* kittens for the price of one, but that's the absolute limit I can go. You've really got me over a barrel."

The tiger-striped kitten, having mastered the slippery cliff of the box, finally dropped to the tile floor and skidded puffily to Kelly's feet. Grateful for any distraction, she dropped her briefcase to the floor and knelt, scooping up the furry animal.

"Well, hello, there," she murmured, "aren't you the adventurous one?" The kit promptly burrowed beneath her hair, and she laughingly attempted to retrieve it. "Don't try to seduce *me*. It won't work."

"A pity," the lieutenant murmured.

Reaching back over her head for the frightened kitten, Kelly came to her feet in the same motion. She would find another way to deal with Albert Russo. She didn't have to stay here and feel stupid!

She stepped to the box and tried to free herself of twenty determined little claws.

The feline, however, had his own problems, and she had as much chance of ridding herself of him as a bushel of grass burrs. He was pulling her hair out by its roots!

"Oh!" Unexpected pain put her through a contortionist's routine. "Come here, you little monster. *Ow!*"

"Oh-oh," John Fisher said as he returned to grasp the situation. "Trouble, right here in the heart of the Confederacy."

Before Kelly could retort to Detective Fisher that if he thought he had trouble, he should try living in *her* shoes for a second, she abruptly found herself cocooned by Ethan Chase.

There was no time to find his approach improper. His hands were everywhere at once—in her hair, on her neck, skimming her shoulders, colliding with her hands, burrowing to free her from the kitten and the kitten from her.

"Easy, hang on," he gruffly encouraged.

"Hurry, hurry!" Her wail was muffled by the wall of his chest.

Freeing her was like unsnarling a backlash from a fishing line. The more afraid the kitten became, the more tenaciously he clung.

"Stop wiggling," he ordered. "It makes things worse. There, gotcha, you little devil. Saved from the claws of death!"

Envisioning herself killing this man, for *he* was the enemy now, not the terrified kitten, Kelly collapsed against him.

"Okay." His murmur was startlingly intimate against her hair as his arms circled her waist. "You're okay now. Everything will be okay."

You're okay now. Everything will be okay.

Though the entire incident had lasted no more than a few seconds, they were enough for Kelly to see herself descending the stairs of the big Victorian house on Ferris Street, wearing the prom dress Caroline had lovingly sewed. The tulle skirt floated layer upon layer until she could have lifted her arms and drifted through the air like a fairy.

Vincent had stood at the bottom of the steps that day and told her how beautiful she was. She *was* pretty. For once she was as pretty as her two older sisters, and at the dance Terry Benedict had swept her into his arms and twirled her onto the glittering floor.

She had believed his lies with an aching desperation. How could she not? His tuxedo was so splendid, and he smelled so good. He was the first boy to ever ask her to dance, and when she laid her head dizzily upon his shoulder, it was much the same as now, as she was leaning upon Ethan Chase.

At eighteen she hadn't known to be afraid when Terry took her home and stopped to pick up his older brother. Very little of that night had survived the distortion of years, and only later did she remember gritting her teeth and closing her eyes and transporting herself into the arms of this very detective who was kissing her before the eyes of the world as he walked her off the football field.

Even later, as she wept in Hite Pritchard's arms, it was her golden idol who had held her and whispered against her tear-streaked cheek, *You're okay now. Everything will be okay.*

"Wait a minute!" she cried, and suddenly thrust free of the detective's hands, not knowing what she really fought, the past or the present. "Just . . . wait a minute!"

Behind her, the small office was abruptly silent. It was so still that Kelly was certain they had heard her thoughts.

Feeling ridiculous, she stood to her full height and brushed her jumper into place. She lifted her head and smoothed her hair in a parody of poise.

She echoed her own words, "Wait a minute, please. I need . . . a minute."

The yowling had brought the mother cat loping back into the office, and while Kelly grappled with her scattered composure, the cat zipped between her legs, panicked at the fate of her offspring in the hands of humans.

John Fisher located a chair and pushed it behind Kelly. His partner, with amazing tenderness—did she actually hear a murmur of baby talk?—placed the kitten back into the box. He located a felt-tip pen and stalked back to the sign, where he slashed through the $5 and replaced it with $3.

"I think we lost a sale, Top Gun," Fisher said, laughing. "We'll be lucky if she doesn't sue the city for damages. Here, miss, catch your breath."

"Thank you." Kelly dropped gratefully onto the chair.

"I tried to talk him out of bringing those beasts in here," Fisher told her with a chuckle. "But there they were, in an abandoned Mazda, blinking at us with those eyes and twitching those little tufted ears. I think it was the ears that got us. Now the place smells like tuna fish."

"That smell," the lieutenant rumbled, "is your lunch, Fisherman."

"You'll have to forgive us, miss." Fisher glared at his sulking partner. "It's the end of a very hard day. It would help if you came to give blood." Grinning, he pointed to Ethan's bloodstained hand. "I'd offer him some of mine, but... well, you understand."

Roaring with merriment at his own joke, he gave Kelly a smart salute, sauntered around the corner of the partition and disappeared.

Kelly found herself abruptly alone with the brooding lieutenant who was lowering himself into a swivel chair and poking through the rubble on his desk. Finding a pack of cigarettes, he lipped one from the pack and held it between his teeth, unlit, as he spun around and punched a button on the computer terminal.

"Since you didn't come for a kitten—" his words around the cigarette were all but unintelligible "—bargain though it is, what can the city of Montgomery do for you today, Miss... Ms...."

His glacier blue eyes flicked to her ring finger. As automatically, Kelly saw that he wasn't wearing a wedding band, either.

Did that mean he hadn't married the homecoming queen? Or had he married her and divorced? Or was he still married and wasn't wearing a ring?

"Madison," she said with a terseness that prompted the sides of his mouth to curl unpleasantly downward. "*Miss* Kelly Madison."

Placing the unsmoked cigarette behind his left ear in a ruffle of black hair, he turned to the keyboard and typed her name, whistling tunelessly between his teeth. "M-a-d-i-s-o-n."

On the wall above him were framed certificates of achievement, Kelly saw, along with various poses of him with government officials she didn't recognize. He didn't appear impressed with them or himself.

"I get the distinct impression, Miss Madison," he said, typing without looking up, "that you were expecting someone else."

Mercy! Could the man read minds, too?

"No," she hastily lied. "I wasn't expecting anything, I mean any*one*."

She sighed.

He swung around and unbuttoned the cuff above his bandaged hand, rolling it back to reveal a tanned, muscled forearm. He repeated the routine with the other cuff, his brows so dour that Kelly lifted her briefcase to her lap and hugged it like a shield of protective armor.

At length he looked up and sat without moving, peeling her back like layers of an onion. He steepled the fingers of his bandaged hand with those of the other.

"Have we ever met, Miss Madison?" he asked.

"Of course not!" Kelly broke into a nervous sweat—hot, then cold. "Rather, I mean, not exactly."

"Interesting way of putting it."

"Actually I did see you play football once."

He laughed bitterly. "You must've been in diapers. Excuse me," he added when he saw her stiffen. "That was unprofessional, wasn't it? You must have been in..." He shrugged. "What? Preschool?"

That did it! Kelly sprang from her chair. "I was twelve, Lieutenant. Look, I hate to be rude, but is this going anywhere? If it's not, I have a lot of things pressing me."

He gave her an oh-really look and spun around to his terminal. "Yes, well, at my age, Miss Madison, twelve *is* preschool. Your address, please?"

Grudgingly Kelly gave the house number on Ferris Street and her phone number. As he typed, she crossed and uncrossed her legs. She fidgeted with her briefcase and idly memorized the label on a parcel that formed a plateau on a mountain of his desk's disorder—from the Book of the Month. Attn, the mailing label said, Price Masters.

Irony tickled the back of her throat. Maybe this man would like her better if she were Leah Blankenship!

He brusquely pulled the parcel from view, tossing it to the floor behind his chair. "You probably read William F. Buckley, Jr."

Kelly wanted, suddenly, to jab him. Hard. She curled her lip. "I certainly don't read that trash."

His parry was to consider her voluminous jumper and sagging stockings that she hadn't hiked up after her bout with the kitten.

He grinned. *It figures.*

You bastard!

Detective Fisher returned with foam cups of steaming coffee. Oblivious to the dangerous tension, he offered Kelly one with the remark that the city hadn't yet reached an acceptable environmental consciousness regarding foam.

Kelly shook her head, certain that she would throw up if she tried to swallow a drop.

"Miss Madison was just about to give her statement," the surly lieutenant said.

Fisher took his seat. "Madison..." he mused, first with puzzlement and then astonishment as he pointed a finger. "You're not the Madison who—"

"I publish the *Mirror,* yes," Kelly said. "Rather, I took over when my father died. I came back to try to keep it from going under, but—"

"Came back?" Ethan interrupted. "Back from where?"

Did it matter? "Virginia," she said. "I lived with my aunt and got my degree there. I was teaching seventh grade when—"

It was none of his business that Vincent had sent her to live with his sister Eunice because he wanted to spare her the pain of bobbing along in the wake of her own sisters—two of the most popular beauty queens Montgomery had ever produced.

"I read your paper, Miss Madison," Fisher was saying. "I apologize for not making the connection before. You must know Ethan, here. His family owns the *Tribune*. Georgia Chase, his mother, is the mayor of our fair city."

If he'd been on his toes, Ethan thought, he would have known at once who Kelly Madison was. Vaguely, in the complicated fretwork of his past, he could place her older sister—a real looker, as he recalled. Monica? No, Melissa. Yes, Melissa Madison. M&M, they'd teased her, because she was so delicious to the taste. And most every guy he knew had tasted her. Not him, of course, because he'd had eyes only for Patty then.

But there was nothing vague in his memory of Vincent Madison. Did this youngest daughter of Vincent's know as much about his own parents as he knew about hers?

Don't cast me in the same lot with my mother, he wanted to tell her, but her mouth was tightening with a distaste that he found strangely personal and irksome.

He spun the cap from his bottled water and tipped back his head. Liquid sluiced down his throat. Swiping his mouth, he lifted the bottle in a mock toast.

"Miss Madison and I haven't met since she was out of Huggies," he told Fisher with his best son-of-a-bitch arrogance.

Her glare could have incinerated him, and Ethan took another shot of water, just in case.

"I found this in my car this afternoon," she told Fisher with such a sharp dismissal that Ethan sprawled back in his chair.

She told about someone named Albert Russo, and Ethan couldn't place the man. He didn't sweat it. Fisher was taking copious notes.

"It's my opinion," she was saying, "that the money was Russo's way of insuring that I don't print any more embarrassing questions about his company. If I'd known what was in the envelope, I wouldn't have opened it. As it is, I suppose I ruined the fingerprints."

She glanced over her shoulder, and an irrational charge jolted Ethan.

More gruffly than he intended, he said, "It's doubtful that Russo has fingerprints on file, Miss Madison. That isn't to say we couldn't get them, but the fact is, you didn't really see him place the money in your car, did you?"

Slowly, confronting him the way an actress assumes her place in the center of the stage, she came fully around and let the beats fall with flawless timing.

"You're one of them, aren't you?" she said as she looked him up and down, her emerald irises shot with fire. "You're one of those lawmen who won't believe a murder threat's been made until the victim is dead."

"Oh, brother," Ethan mumbled, and rolled his eyes dramatically.

"You're welcome to file a complaint with the city attorney, Miss Madison," Fisher tactfully suggested.

But he could have been talking to one of the kittens. She was seething righteous rancor now, and she underscored her accusations with short, explosive slashes of her hand.

"Does a woman have to have stab wounds before you'll believe she's been raped, Lieutenant Chase?" she challenged. "Are you one of those men who gets a woman on the witness stand and asks, 'Didn't you want it just a little? Hmm? Didn't you like it? Come on and tell the truth. Just a little?'"

God, what a tongue! He struck the floor so hard with his feet that his skull absorbed the shock.

"That isn't what I said, Miss Madison!" he angrily declared as he lunged half across his desk.

"Then I might as well go home." She put a waspish sting into each syllable as they stood nose to nose, and her slim fingers clutched the envelope of money. "There's obviously nothing I can do here."

"Russo has to be *accused* of something, damn it!"

Fisher was sending horrified signals to remain professional, which Ethan ignored.

"I just did accuse him!" she snapped. "And you refuse to even approach him."

"It won't do any good." Ethan jabbed rudely at the inches between them and was directed by Fisher, who was frantically waving his arms. He wound down, mumbling, "He'd just say you misinterpreted his remarks."

"Who told you that, Lieutenant?" She feistily thrust her chin. "The detective fairy?"

Ethan flushed like a high school boy caught kissing the girl when the porch light comes on. He was so near her, he could feel the heat of her rushing blood. He could smell the residue of some dark, sweet perfume, and he irrationally wanted to bury his hand in her hair and coil it around his wound and place his face into the silk of it.

"You've got a big mouth," he growled.

"And you've got a big ego!" She struck the corner of his desk with the envelope. "You know, Russo was right on target. Your family's newspaper really has been bought off."

Ethan bared his teeth. "I don't think I like you, Miss Madison."

Her frigid smile, ironically, was beautiful. "No, but I'll bet your mother likes *you*. There's nothing like having someone down at city hall, is there? But then, Georgia *is* city hall. How very lucky for her."

Before either man could say a word, she spun around and jerked up her briefcase. It occurred to Ethan as he watched her that his mouth was open, and Fisher, for once, was speechless.

Weariness dragged at her shoulders as she moved a few paces, yet her head was erect with a certainty that right was on her side.

"Good day, gentlemen," she said huskily as she reached the partition, hesitated, then disappeared without a backward look. "You're right. There's nothing you can do for me."

Chapter 3

Ethan Chase hadn't been born a son of a bitch. He liked to say it just sort of happened. Gradually, like termite infestation or the formation of black holes.

As the first child of Georgia and Maxwell Chase, people said he was born under a lucky star. Perhaps he was. The church where Georgia and Maxwell were married was certainly beneath one. During the Northern occupation of Montgomery, it had been saved by the same federal officer who had been bent on destroying it. Recognizing St. John's bishop, Hamner Cobbs, as his own minister in Cincinnati, the officer had ended up ordering a special guard placed around it.

Later, when life became an enemy, Ethan wondered how differently fate might have been had Bishop Cobbs never come from Cincinnati to Montgomery. Would he, Ethan, the firstborn son, have been destined to assume the publishing of the family newspaper? To carry on the grand tradition of the *Tribune* started by his mother's grandfather in

1888? Would he, at twenty, have married Patty Lomax, marring Georgia's perfect plans?

To Ethan, a football scholarship to the college of his choice was merely incidental. He wanted nothing more than to get his hands on the *Tribune,* put it into the respected ranks of the *Washington Post* and *New York Times* and expose injustice throughout the world. Football, though he happily accepted its fringe benefits, was for sissies.

Unfortunately Patty Lomax was not the debutante everyone expected him to marry. Raised by an aunt whose résumé was the Atlanta police docket, Patty was, in Georgia's words, "not worth twittering about."

Looking back, Ethan admitted he'd been abysmally naive. He should have known he would never be able to find Patty once she disappeared. He should have seen that money like Georgia's had long arms. The twenty thousand dollars she gave to Patty's whorish aunt had taken them far away.

His first retaliation at his mother was to drop out of college. Though he argued and pleaded, Maxwell could say nothing to dissuade Ethan. As the weeks and months went by, Ethan functioned in two modes: anxiety and depression. Finally he tried to climb inside a bottle of tequila and play dead.

It was on a rainy November night as he was backing his low-slung Corvette out of the garage that Maxwell ran out of the house and waved both arms. What son, Ethan asked himself later, could drive away and leave his father standing in the rain?

Though he stunned Maxwell with his haggard, shell-shocked state, he refused to let his father drive. He had heard all the arguments before. Why shouldn't he speed like a madman along Highway 143 toward the Alabama River? Wasn't it his right after being treated so badly?

Why couldn't Ethan accept the way things were? Maxwell shouted in a burst of paternal desperation. Patty would not be found. She didn't want to be found!

Knowing somewhere in his crazed mind that his father was right, Ethan was consumed by a defeat too large for his young heart. He began to weep as he drove. His face twisted as great, racking sobs tore from his chest.

Maxwell attempted to apply logic to the evil of what Georgia had done. "Can't you see that it's all for the best? You'll move beyond this, son. One day you'll see how your life was made better, despite the way it happened."

Afterward Ethan questioned if he hadn't subconsciously tried to destroy them both that night. The tragedy was, they had both lived.

Too young then for the wisdom of hindsight, his last weapon, his trump card, was to refuse to ever go near Georgia's beloved *Tribune*. That done, he frosted the cake; he became a common man. Leaving Montgomery, he joined the police in Jackson, Mississippi. For nearly twenty years he saw his family only on rare, painful holidays. At twenty-two he hadn't known how to repair the breach; now, at forty, it didn't seem worth the effort.

Ethan had been back in Montgomery a month. He had seen his mother twice. He had not picked up his old life and friends. His father would never walk again, and he was true to the son-of-a-bitch code he lived by. If a woman, any woman, made the mistake of venturing close enough to chip through the aching husk that encased him, she wouldn't try but once.

There was a part of him, though, that still retained a faint heartbeat of creativity. Behind his badge, the soul of a writer still lived. To him it was a perfect, perfect irony that he wrote in secret and only for money—pulp fiction, gritty, purple-prosed crime novels under the name Price Masters.

And all this because, once upon a time, a federal officer had recognized Bishop Hamner Cobbs standing on the steps of St. John's Church in Montgomery, Alabama.

As Ethan watched Kelly Madison's obstinate little gait as she left the squad room, the game he played was a reflex action. He saw a woman as Price Masters would have seen a woman on a steamy, sultry night.

She was one of the classiest broads I'd seen in a long time. You know the kind—one of those really sad faces that looks down at you from the window of a passing train.

But I'd been at the game a long time. I knew she was trouble, big-time. So I played tough. From my door she turned back a final time, peering at me from beneath her hat that left only her nose and chin visible, and hair the shade of blond created to make a man sin.

"Are you sure you won't take the case?" she begged, and reached out with her small pink tongue to wet her lips. "I'm desperate, Mr. Masters. Tell me what you want."

What she didn't know was that third-rate gumshoes like me don't wind up with dames like her, so I said, "No can do, angel. Take it downtown. They'll take good care of you down there."

Fourteen-carat tears spilled to her cheeks. She didn't say a word, and I lit up a Camel as her heels clicked down the hall. With smoke burning my eyes I watched her climb into her car where the driver would take her back to her safe world beyond the neon lights and gasoline fumes and murdered John Does that filled my own nights.

There goes trouble, I thought sadly. But she was still the classiest broad I'd seen in a long time.

"What was that all about?" Fisher asked, and gave Ethan a start.

With a snort more jaded than that of his lonely doppelgänger, Price Masters, Ethan plowed through his hair with the fingers of his sound hand.

"Nothing," he said dully, and looked at the space where Kelly had been.

Fisher fetched the leather duffel that he carried to the gym three times a week. There he would meet his live-in lover, Fancy Auletta—a woman as vivacious as her name.

He and Fancy had bought a prestigious old house in Willow Park. Twice a week they played racquetball with the president of the yacht club or the vice president of the First National Bank—anyone whose name was glitzy enough to make a proper social rung on their way up. John and Fancy had their whole lives color coordinated and planned to the minute.

"Give me the envelope, then," he told Ethan. "I'll lock up the money. Tomorrow we'll process Russo. Who knows? Maybe we'll get lucky and come up with something that'll verify the woman's story."

Ethan was poking among the papers and file folders on his desk, the used paper cups and empty bottles of mineral water. He looked beneath the Yellow Pages and pushed aside the football trophy from a Thanksgiving Day game he'd played back in the Stone Age. He tripped on the Book of the Month parcel and hurled it vehemently into his chair.

He pinched the bridge of his nose in bafflement. "It's not here," he said.

"You mean, you've lost it?"

"It's not lost. I saw her put it right here, on the desk."

"Somebody's child could be lost on that desk, Chase, and we wouldn't know until it was old enough to vote."

Both their heads lifted at the same time. Fisher stared at Ethan in amazement, and Ethan's nerves went dead like a throw switch.

"I'll be damned," he said with a low whistle. "She took the money."

With a happy-go-lucky chuckle, Fisher scooped up his duffel and tossed it across his shoulder.

"No money, no bribe. I'm outta here, pal." He made a backhand pass at an imaginary ball and executed a graceful balletic sidestep. "Yessiree, I do feel lucky tonight. Ethan, you should take up a sport. You used to be athletic, didn't you? Put some zing back in your life, man."

Ethan pulled a face, not so much in mock of his partner but for his own bruised ego that now wished, kidlike, that Kelly Madison had been more like the woman of Price Masters's world. She could at least have been a little more impressed with the hero he'd once been.

"You wanna know what I think?" Fisher said as he paused at the partition.

"No," Ethan grumbled.

"I think she got to you."

"Who?"

"Who do you think? Cute Little Miss Newspaper."

Ethan glared at his friend. Kelly? Kelly Madison was everything a man disliked in a woman. She was too opinionated, too outspoken and too independent. When a man wanted a woman, he wanted a Georgia peach, all ripe and juicy, not some ice queen with a tongue of high-tensile steel.

"Yeah, she got t'me," he groused, "like a blasted thorn in my foot."

Fisher laughed merrily as he walked backward through the rows of desks to the front door of the room.

"It's not too late, Top Gun," he bellowed, cupping his mouth. "You could buy yourself some decent clothes, go to some of those self-improvement classes, start taking vitamins and quit smoking. Hey, you could even work out at the gym once in a while.''

Heads turned. Fondly insulting leers found Ethan.

"Get outta here," Ethan said, and waved him on.

Left alone with his troubled musings, Ethan removed his corduroy jacket from the back of his chair and slapped halfheartedly at the creases and wrinkles. He glanced down at his jeans and scuffed Western boots. He straightened his bandage and tucked in his shirt and aligned his tie.

Was Fisher right? Would a woman . . .

"Hellfire!"

He stuffed the pack of cigarettes into his inside pocket and opened the drawer of a filing cabinet and took out his Stetson and fit it on his head. He shrugged against the holster riding his shoulders.

It wasn't really possible that Albert Russo *had* gotten to Georgia, was it? Wouldn't that be something?

Returning to his telephone, he dialed Georgia's office. After letting it ring four times, he dialed the big house in the country where he'd spent his childhood.

Priscilla, his mother's personal maid on a staff of eight, answered. "They've both gone out for the evening, Mr. Chase," she said politely. "Is there a message?"

"No message, Prissie. I'll catch her later."

"Yes, sir."

Squinting, he found Kelly Madison's telephone number in the report he'd typed. He memorized it, punched in the numbers and stood working his knuckles against the handkerchief binding his hand.

After the second ring, a woman's voice answered.

"Kelly Madison, please," he said.

"Hite?"

Ethan experienced one of Price Masters's nuclear-device pauses. Hite Pritchard? His old fraternity brother? Good God!

"No," he told the woman. "Ah, look, I'll catch Kelly another time. No message. Thanks."

He let his hand rest a moment on the receiver after hanging up, oddly troubled. Shrugging off his strange mood, he switched off the light over his desk and scooped up the Book of the Month Club parcel his agent, Jake Schimmerman, had sent just today. He hadn't even had a chance to see his latest piece of published trash.

He squinted fiercely at the kittens, who were now full and sleepy.

"And I don't need any literary flak from you four, either," he told them sternly. "Now stop that whimpering, or I'll drive you out on some dark farm road."

There! He guessed he'd showed them who was boss. "Did you get that?"

They got it.

"I'm not giving her another thought, either," he added, "and that's that."

No one dared argue with him.

But Ethan did give Kelly another thought. Though he would not admit an obsession with her, for the next two days she would not leave the margins of his mind. On Friday, as the April morning began to heat up and the smog spread its hydrocarbon haze over the city, he finally gave in and drove over to Edlestein Parkway.

He drew his pickup alongside a *Mirror* vending machine in front of the all-night laundromat on Mimosa Street. Leaning out the window, he aimed a quarter at the slot, missed, swore and aimed another that connected with the change box.

He drew out a morning edition. The horn of a passing car blared as it passed.

"Okay, okay," he said irritably.

After parking across from the Redmond parking lot, he dropped more coins in the meter, raised the hood of the truck and slouched for a few minutes against the front left fender with the brim of his Stetson low, like a spy.

He pushed dark glasses up over the bumpy cartilage on his nose and acted as if he were waiting for a mechanic. With the hip pockets of his new jeans against the chrome strip on his fender, he began to read.

There. In the lower left corner of the paper was the masthead and her name: Editor, Kelly J. Madison.

A confused mixture of emotions filled him. He reminded himself for the millionth time that he was Price Masters, not the CEO of the *Tribune*'s board of directors. Thousands of writers would kill to have what he had. Why wasn't he happy?

Happiness had little to do with anything. He ripped off the masthead and folded it carefully, tucking it inside his jacket pocket like a treasure he would take out later and consider.

On the *Mirror*'s front page was a photograph of approximately fifty citizens who had gathered on the same lot that faced him from across the street.

Neighbors Band To Salvage East Side, the caption read.

The paper, it seemed, was spearheading a drive to clean up the streets east of Edlestein Parkway and restore some of the older buildings rather than tear them down.

"Operation Bootstrap," city news editor, Ann Jacobs, had written. "Local residents mean to make a show of good faith. They appealed to the city to help get drugs off the streets. 'We want the crack houses cleaned out so we can send our children to school without worrying if they're going to get there.'"

The next paragraph was about street repair and the planned construction of a park. Nurseries civic-minded enough to donate greenery were offered a phone number to call.

The small project was admirable, yes, even noble, but Kelly Madison didn't have the capital to undertake such a task. The *Mirror*'s sales couldn't possibly generate the kind of money necessary.

The skin of Ethan's skull tightened. *Kelly, please tell me you haven't used Russo's eight thousand dollars for this.*

Which meant, of course, that he believed her charge against Russo. Now he was going to have to start thinking about her in an altogether different way. Hell, he would probably be forced to end up liking her, and that would damage his son-of-a-bitch status.

Why had she come charging into his office, anyway, getting herself tangled up with a kitten and under his skin at the same time?

"Price, old buddy," he said with more than a scoop of self-mockery as he tossed the paper into his pickup, "you just thought you got rid of trouble. She's back in town."

Getting on the police radio, he had Sue patch him in to Fisher, who was at the courthouse.

"What're you doing on that side of town?" Fisher sharply demanded when he came to the phone. "You were supposed to—"

"I'm checking out some crack houses. Get your butt over here."

"Can't. Judge Pritchard's court is clogged up like a kitchen sink."

Great. Well, he might as well go in and get to work on the twenty case files that were piled on his desk.

Ethan slammed the door of his truck. As he was reaching for the key, a Montgomery County Electric truck crept onto the Redmond lot. The man who got out could have been a bodybuilder right off the pages of Joe Weider's muscle magazine—a hunk, Hollywood-style.

He shouldered his way through the building's revolving door. When he hadn't come out after ten minutes, Ethan swore and pushed his seat back to stretch out his legs. He turned up George Strait on the radio and smoked half a pack of cigarettes, one after the other.

"What I need to know," Kelly told the electrician, Carl Hennessey, as he was finishing his assessment of the fourth story above the *Mirror* offices, "is if the wiring is sound."

Having arrived a few minutes before the muscle-bound utility man, her sister Debbie and the twins were also wandering through the warehouse-size space.

After sharing her plans to salvage the old building, Debbie had volunteered her opinion of whether the place was worth pouring the remainder of Kelly's inheritance into it— a gesture Kelly didn't have the bad manners to refuse.

"I'll just poke my head in," Debbie had said with a laugh from her place at Caroline's Sunday dinner table, "just to make sure Carl quotes you a good price. Since I recommended him and all."

Now that she'd seen Carl, Kelly understood her glamorous sister's sudden interest in remodeling. The man's T-shirt showed muscles she didn't know the names of.

"I'd forgotten how roomy it is up here, Kell," Debbie was bubbling as she collared one of the twins when he skidded past with a shriek of sneakers on the hardwood floor. "I could put my whole house in here."

Vincent had never partitioned the upper floor, and it was perfect for a loft apartment, except for a bothersome lack of plumbing. The skylights didn't leak, and six arched windows looked down onto Mimosa Street, dismal though it was. Four great support pillars were aligned through the center.

"Stop running, Edward," Debbie shouted to her other son, as he, too, skidded past, "or no swimming for either of you! That's an order!"

"Aw, Mom," wailed a singsong duet.

Catching the mischievous Edward and wrapping him in an aunt's fond embrace, Kelly whispered, "Mind your mother. One day soon I'll bring you and Theo up here with your skateboards. If that's not good enough, we'll hose the whole place down and turn it into a skating rink. Now, gimme five."

She and Edward went through the ritual they'd been going through since the twins had realized she was a pushover for kids.

"*No problemo,* gorgeous," he chirped, and with a terrible imitation of an Austrian accent added to his mother, "Ah'll be back." He bounced away on thin, springy legs. "Hey, Theo! Wait up!"

Seeing the boys reminded Kelly of how close to thirty she was and still without her own family. "You've got to make those boys stop watching *The Terminator,* Deb."

Her sister groaned. "You think I like having people know that my six-year-olds' favorite thing is wall-to-wall Schwarzenegger? You're a worse problem. You spoil them rotten."

As she talked, Debbie was hungrily watching Carl move through the place. "You inherited all the mothering genes in our family, Kell. Can you believe that Melissa's working on her third husband and I'm hanging on to my second by the hair of its chinny-chin-chin? While you—"

"I'm an old-maid schoolteacher, Deb. No more, no less."

Having found her reflection in one of the windows, Debbie drew in her stomach and struck a pose, so pleased with her image that Kelly suddenly felt dowdy, despite the fact that she was wearing her prettiest floral-print dress with taupe shoes and stockings.

"What I want to know is," Kelly briskly changed the subject, "where did you find Mr. Olympia over there?"

Debbie looked furtively over her shoulder and said from the corner of her mouth, "Remember that trip to Des Moines that Jack made last year?"

With a horror that wasn't altogether mock, Kelly rolled her eyes to the top of her head.

Debbie busily repaired a lock of her hair, consulting her reflection again. "Kell, why are you so dead set on fixing up this firetrap, anyway?"

"Don't call it a firetrap."

"Do you remember the money pit that Tom Hanks and Shelley Long—"

"I saw that movie."

Debbie giggled, and Kelly, tired of watching Mr. Olympia strut and her sister primp, walked over to the window and looked down at the street. A typical dull day. Women were doing laundry and Alex Allen was banging dents out of a Honda Civic. A pickup had stalled in the street, and its hood was raised. A man got out of it and poked his head beneath it.

She turned away, then jerked back. There was something strangely familiar....

"I have to do something with my share of Daddy's money," she said absently, and rubbed a circle in the filmy glass for a better look. "I thought I'd make myself an apartment up here."

"You could live at home with Mother for free."

The ranginess of the man fascinated Kelly, and his long trim legs, his neat rear. "Would you really want to live at home?" she half mused. "Even for free?"

"Oh, God," Debbie groaned.

Like a crack of lightning, Kelly snapped spine-straight at the window. Emerging from the hood and turning to face the street was Ethan Chase.

He was wearing a linen jacket with his jeans, no less. He reached into his truck and brought out a Western hat that he shoved jauntily back on his head, then pushed a pair of sunglasses higher on his nose.

He drew back his cuff to consult his wristwatch as if he were in a hurry. He ran a sharp eye over the Redmond Building and the parking lot, down the street, everywhere but up.

Kelly's heart made a wild leap in her breast. He was spying on her, the villain! How dare he?

Some inner radar appeared to guide him, or perhaps it was her movement behind the glass. His dark head tipped up, and he found her, almost as if it were the action out of some rehearsed play from a long time ago.

For the second time in her life, Kelly felt herself invaded by the man, except now he was real. His virility attacked her senses, and a very real pressure started to build inside, spreading outward to her breasts, her knees, the tips of her fingers, the wellspring at the back of her eyes.

But he had been rude to her. He had failed her. And now he had spied on her.

"Carl," she said over her shoulder, "could you tell me what this is?"

Carl walked to the window in his gorgeous jeans and snowy T-shirt. "What?"

With her father's quick eye for a caption, Kelly saw herself with Carl as Ethan would see them, her face tipped beneath that of the gorgeous man, her blond hair catching the morning sunshine, her head framed by her lacy collar.

Kelly Madison, she mentally dashed off, *is seen enjoying the company of Carl Hennessey. She is wearing a lovely dress that she purchased specifically to attend her nephews' sixth birthday party earlier in the spring. Also to wear to Mendino's tonight, where she will spend the evening with Mr. Hite Pritchard. See how unlike Leah Blankenship Miss*

Madison is. See how unattainable to obnoxious police lieu-tenants who don't believe her when she walks into their office with eight thousand dollars.

"This is a telephone line, Miss Madison," Carl politely explained. "But you'll want to replace it, I expect."

"Hmm," Kelly said, and winced as Ethan, below her, wiped his hand over his jaws. "Are you sure, Carl?"

"Positive, ma'am."

With a sense of continuing drama, Kelly rose up on her toes. "Oops, you have a bit of caulk in your hair, Carl."

With a boldness that was totally unlike her, she reached up to the man's flawless brown waves and brushed away an imaginary shred of debris. "There, gone now. Good as new."

Are you watching, Ethan Chase? Are you seeing that you made a mistake with me?

She gave Carl a swimming smile. "I really appreciate you coming by this morning, Carl. I know it was an inconvenience."

The man grinned. He was accustomed to women behaving like idiots over him. "No problem, Miss Madison."

The tiny theatric left Kelly at a loss of what to do next. She wondered why she was stooping to such second-rate tricks. It was something Debbie would do. Why didn't she simply go downstairs and walk across the street to speak to Ethan? Why couldn't she be a grown, mature woman for once? Didn't she really, in her woman's heart, want to see the man? Didn't she owe it to herself to try one more time, for the years she'd invested, dreaming about him?

Yes!

Suffused with purpose, she whirled around. "Would you excuse me a minute?" she asked Carl and Debbie in a voice she hardly recognized.

"Of course," Debbie said eagerly as she eyed Carl. "There's no rush, Kell, no rush at all."

Kelly couldn't get to the door quickly enough. Heads lifted as she dashed through the newsroom, the hem of her dress swishing, and for once she didn't care that the editors would gossip once she was out of sight. Her whole life was unexpectedly dangling before her, needing only to be picked like a prize pear.

With pulses slamming, she rehearsed what she would say when she faced Ethan: *I know we got off to a bad start before. I'm sorry.*

Or, *Ever since I can remember, I've had this terrible crush on you.* Scratch that one.

Or, *Have you had time to think about Albert Russo? Can you help me?*

A stitch was in her side by the time she stepped around the corner into full view of Allen's Paint & Body Shop and the Laundromat. Her heart was a trip-hammer, battering at the memories inside so that she felt exhilaratingly free of her past.

It was abrupt, as if she had walked into the middle of a strange movie. There was nothing but a vacant space by the parking meter, and she stopped stone still and lifted her balled fist to her lips, squeezing her eyes against the pressure of tears.

"What a little fool you are," she cursed herself, and backed to the building, where she slumped weakly against the bricks. "What a stupid, stupid little idiot."

Hadn't the past years taught her anything? Was there anything so sad as a woman who deceived herself into believing she had the means to attract a man? Must she learn the same lesson over and over?

Now she must go back inside and bear the looks of the people who had worked for her father, and if she wanted to sleep tonight, she would do it with a dignity that would put gossip to rest before it started.

She swiped savagely at her cheeks and, sniffing, threw back her head. She drew on a facade that was as familiar as an old coat, and she fashioned a smile much different from the one when she'd posed before this very building with her sisters over twenty years before, wearing new black patent shoes and lacy anklets.

What she would not give for that happy innocence again. She wished Vincent were alive. She wished she could help him keep the paper afloat. She could make a difference now.

But those days were gone. She wasn't a twelve-year-old girl dreaming about some golden hero who would scoop her up on his white charger and thunder into never-never land.

"One thing I would not do, Daddy," she said with a hard resolve, "is go with you to a football game on a cold Thanksgiving Day."

Chapter 4

Fancy Auletta was the kind of woman they had invented the phrase "black is beautiful" for.

"She's also the perfect wife," John Fisher liked to tell Ethan. "Or she would be if we could ever find time to get married."

Shortly after hiring on at Channel 13 as a lowly typist, Fancy's frenetic energy had landed her the job of anchoring the local news. Her incredible face was now plastered on billboards and the sides of mass-transit buses. Fancy Auletta was definitely on her way up. Everyone knew it. She was a real take-charge lady.

No sooner had Ethan returned to his office and grumpily placed a curse on all electricians who spent their spare time in the gym and laundering their T-shirts, then Fancy breezed in.

She wore a suit the color of sunshine, and its skintight skirt struck her thighs at their most luscious midpoint. She had in tow a gangly black youth in knee jams and sneakers who was lugging three plastic pet caddies.

Friendly whistles followed Fancy from the front door back to the partition of carpet.

"Give 'em hell, Fancy!" someone yelled.

"You can eat crackers in my bed anytime, Fancy!"

"Wa-hoo! The South's gonna do it agin!"

John Fisher had just returned from Irwin Pritchard's sluggish court, and his mood was listing dangerously into the red zone.

Sweeping augustly around the partition, Fancy marched straight to the box of kittens.

"Lieutenant Chase," she purred as she picked up one of the kittens and nuzzled it. "John told me that you two were playing father to triplets. Unfortunately he's also been sneezing his head off for the past week. I decided it was time to act."

Ethan distorted his face in a lazy grimace. "Hi, Fancy, glad you could drop by. But lay off my cats, will ya? Hey, what's that kid doin'?"

Fancy fluttered her scarlet nails at the boy who was torn between depositing the kittens in one of the boxes and spread-eagling himself against the wall.

"Never mind him, Petey," Fancy blithely consoled. "Actually, Ethan, I have wonderful news. I've found the little darlings a home. No, no, don't bother to thank me. He's a lovely Farmer Jones type with two gigantic dairy barns, and he swore to me on his sainted Aunt Sophie that if he never fed these cats a drop of food, they would thrive for the rest of their nine lives. Isn't that right, John?"

John walked in, a steaming cup of coffee in each hand. He spied the boy packing up the kittens and shrugged sheepishly at Ethan.

"I meant to tell you, partner," he explained. "Allerest's stock went up two points last week, thanks to those damn cats."

He tried unsuccessfully to find a clean space on Ethan's desk, then gave the second cup of coffee to Fancy instead. "Well," he asked in a surreptitious undertone, "is he going to go out with her?"

"Shh! I haven't gotten to that yet."

A buzzer went off in Ethan's head, and his feet struck the floor with a jolt that sent Fancy's young helper on a wild search for an escape.

"What?" he barked. "Go out with who? What's going on here?"

"Whom, Ethan," Fancy cheerfully corrected. "And you're going to love her."

The look Ethan shot his partner would have melted steel. "No, no." He waved his arms. "Oh, no. Take my cats if you have to, Fancy, but no blind dates. A thousand times no."

Fisher had seated himself at his own desk and was placing a napkin neatly beneath his cup. He positioned a spoon on the napkin and tore open a packet of artificial sweetener.

"I told you he wouldn't go," he said, and dropped the empty packet into the wastebasket and brushed stray particles of sweetener from the desk top.

"Ethan," Fancy insisted, "this woman is exactly your type."

"Then I know I don't want to go out with her."

"I told you so," Fisher chanted.

Fancy refused to admit defeat. She circumvented Ethan's desk. "I heard all about you, Lieutenant—up there at Jackson, offending every woman who looked at you twice. Well, it won't work with me. I happen to believe in blind dates. John met me on a blind date."

Balancing his hips on the edge of his desk and crossing his ankles, Ethan shook with laughter. "My point exactly."

Fisher said, "Darling, I think what Top Gun is trying to tell you is that he already has a lady."

"Fisherman," Ethan warned on an ascending note, glaring.

Undaunted, Fancy plucked a piece of lint from Ethan's linen jacket, which was draped over the back of his chair. "Shame on you. I swear, Ethan, you're enough to put gray hairs in a woman's head."

"Fancy—" Ethan laughingly folded his arms across his chest "—you don't really think I'd be crazy enough to bite on that one, do you?"

She smiled her famous smile. "But you will. Oh yes, you will."

Petey had finished caging the kittens and mother cat. Fancy picked up one of the caddies and shooed the boy out of the office.

On her way around the partition, she leaned back to tell John, "See that you don't forget."

As the chorus of friendly teases followed her through the squad room, the two men looked at each other with sighs that meant different things but were all of a piece.

John found his desk and nervously stirred his coffee for a moment. Swinging his chair around, he opened a drawer of his filing cabinet. Without leaving the chair, he skimmed across the floor and came to a stop beside Ethan's desk.

He leaned over and slipped something into the breast pocket of Ethan's linen jacket. As he sped away, Ethan fished through the pocket and brought out a packet of condoms.

"Oh, brother," he groaned.

"I don't want to hear it," the black man said as he began typing a report of Irwin Pritchard's verdict. "I've got to live with the woman, so don't say a dad-gummed word."

* * *

When all the upwardly mobile people had moved from Mimosa Street, Mendino's stayed.

Two blocks from the Redmond Building, it had survived the black eye of Allen's Paint & Body Shop and the all-night laundromat. It retained its appeal to Montgomery's intelligentsia despite the stripped cars littering the curbs. It even continued to attract a few yuppies who hadn't investment-banked and takeover-lawyered themselves out of existence.

Pat and Quentin Mendino had been Kelly's father's best friends as long as Kelly could remember. As much as she enjoyed seeing them, her ordeal with Ethan made her wish she was back at home, huddled in her bed.

She arrived at the height of Mendino's happy hour. Entering, she handed over her raincoat and umbrella to the doorman and struck her breeziest, most lying pose.

"You can start the party now, Uncle Jack," she brightly announced. "I'm here! And I intend to dance the Charleston on the tabletop!"

Jack Hawley, the black doorman, had been taking coats at Mendino's since the dinosaurs died. Stars of silent movies had given him their wraps.

His seamed face was a map when he laughed. "Why, Miss Kelly, that would be some sight to see, I reckon. What a picture you've done gone and turned into. Jus' like your pretty ma."

Not particularly fond of having people assume she had to work her fingers to the bone just to look nice, Kelly accepted the compliment. Her creamy blouse was especially feminine, lying in liquid folds of silk over her breasts. The sleeves, lusciously long and full, folded back in French cuffs fastened with pearl-button studs.

Her tight, short skirt, powder blue, was belted by a gold chain, and her needle-thin high heels and stockings matched the cream of her blouse. Since her legs were the only truly remarkable thing about her, why not display them to good advantage?

"You can't fool me," she teased, and tweaked the red bow tie at Jack's collar. "You have a crush on my mother."

The old man chortled, and Kelly drew the chain strap of her beaded evening bag over her shoulder, discreetly making sure the clasp was secure on Albert Russo's eight thousand dollars.

"I jus' meant we don't see much of Miss Caroline these days," he said as she wandered to the entrance of the dining area and peered inside.

"She'll be delighted you asked. When Hite gets here, tell him that I and my cranberry juice are at the bar."

"I'll do that very thing, Miss Kelly."

From the street, Mendino's made a person think twice about the wisdom of going in. Yet, once inside, people found themselves treated to a vintage history of Montgomery.

On the old walls were tacked hundreds of photographs. They were stapled and glued: paratroopers from the two Air Force bases, Maxwell and Gunter, posing before their bombers with their arms draped around their buddies.

At high noon, the capitol gleamed proudly from Goat Hill. There were lithographs of the War Between the States, Abram Mordicai's first cotton gin, railroads, packing plants, furniture and concrete factories, lumber mills, Lehman Brothers dry-goods business after they left Bavaria in the middle of the nineteenth century, Governor George Wallace, John Dabney Murchison completing his flight training, Martin Luther King and the bus boycotters and, of course, John F. Kennedy and Robert.

Kelly didn't give them a passing glance as she headed straight for Miriam Goodson, who was emptying a tray of dirty glasses into a sink behind the bar.

A dyed-in-the-wool survivor of the sixties, Miriam was still a flower child. Her braid of flaming red hair reached her knees, and she boldly wore tie-dyed T-shirts without a bra. If Quentin Mendino wouldn't have put his foot down, she would have worked barefoot.

When Miriam spotted Kelly's short skirt, she reared back and comically fanned herself with her towel.

"Don't start with me, Miriam," Kelly warned, and tossed back a froth of curls that she'd laboriously wound on heated rollers and sprayed.

From a faraway table where she was chatting with guests, Pat Mendino had also seen Kelly enter.

Pat's great talent, Kelly had always thought, was in knowing where her strengths lay. The woman's face was a disaster, but she cleverly drew attention from it by draping herself in outlandish caftans and fastening ethnic jewelry from every conceivable place. The strange part was, it worked.

"Now *this* is more like it!" the woman boomed as she bulldozed her way through her guests and grabbed Kelly's hands to drag her from the bar stool.

She turned Kelly in a pivot as if she were a rack of lamb on a rotisserie.

"If you would dress like this all the time, my precious cherub—" she effusively caught Kelly's left hand and angled it to the light "—we'd get a ring on that finger. Quentin, have you seen this beautiful child?"

Beginning to wish she'd worn her usual slacks and pullover cotton top, Kelly pulled her face out of shape.

"Do something, Quentin," she wailed playfully to Pat's husband, who was officiating behind the bar. "Control this woman."

Quentin scratched the razor-sharp part of his hair. "Woman? What woman?"

Pat struck the shoulder of her husband of forty years. "Pay no mind to this brute."

Miriam emerged from behind the bar with a laden tray. "The reason Kelly isn't married, Pat—" her braid bounced sassily "—is your own fault. How do you expect anyone to conduct a romance to Bach and Mozart? Now, if you want Kelly to *really* get serious, put on some Creedence Clearwater Revival."

"Creedence Clearwater Revival!" Pat parodied a grotesque gag. "What's romantic about 'Suzie Q,' for heaven's sake?"

Miriam was already moving away and calling back, "Where do you think the baby boomers came from, Pat-Q?"

Quentin Mendino grinned as he placed a glass before Kelly. "Cranberry juice on the rocks. Don't get drunk on me, now. I promised your father I'd look after you. If I don't, he'll come back to haunt me."

Kelly had to remind herself to smile. She wondered if Ethan were going out tonight with a beautiful lady on his arm. Were they with friends? Were they laughing? Were they listening to music or dancing?

"Quentin," she said as jealousy raveled her composure, "what do you know about Ethan Chase?"

The bartender stopped pouring, his round face furrowing with concern. "You're not going to do another piece on Mayor Chase, are you?"

"Georgia's fair game."

"We both know why you keep going after her, kiddo. You know, it won't bring back your daddy."

"Nonsense. She's about to announce her candidacy for governor. I was thinking of a different angle, a sort of family-behind-the-woman thing."

Sighing as he retreated into his usual cave of neutrality, Quentin aimed the flip of his towel at the front door. "There's the man you need to talk to about that."

In the mirror behind Quentin's head, between the decanter of Scotch and a tier of long-stemmed glasses, was the reflection of Hite's father, Judge Irwin Pritchard.

Irwin was an imposing man, simply elegant with Brillo-pad hair springing vigorously from his scalp. He was nearing retirement age now, but his eyes could still make a strong man shiver.

Pleasure blinked briefly on his face when he saw Kelly, and he disregarded the deference of people who called out to him as he walked toward her.

"My dear," he said, and took her hand, drawing her to her feet, "how lovely you are this evening."

"I was obliged to dress up tonight, Your Honor," she said with a cheeriness more suited to a dental appointment. "Guess who I'm having dinner with? A hint—he's tall, dark and handsome, the spitting image of his father."

"Give this young woman another of whatever she's drinking," Irwin told Quentin. "Now, Kelly, tell me, when are you and Hite going to settle down and make me a grandfather?"

Quentin placed the usual glass of blended whiskey on the napkin before the old man, freshened Kelly's juice and scooped up the judge's tip. "Kelly was asking what I knew about Ethan Chase. I said she should ask you, Judge."

Kelly could have punched Quentin's big mouth. "I was inquiring as a journalist, naturally."

"Naturally." The judge's hawkish eyes locked with Kelly's in the mirror. "Actually I haven't seen Ethan in years. He's back in town, I've heard."

Kelly made her face as guileless as possible. "I heard that, too."

"Working for the city, if my memory doesn't fail me."

"Yes, I believe you're right."

Sighing, he touched his black tie. "Rather disappointing, all around. A waste of good talent."

"Really?"

"You didn't know that Ethan was to have taken over the publishing of the *Tribune?* Then there was that dreadful accident that put Maxwell into a wheelchair. Not exactly the best time for Ethan to turn stubborn and run off to God-knows-where, all because of some woman who wasn't worth—"

She'd known it! In the marrow of her bones, she'd known that bitterness like Ethan's could have been rooted only in failed love.

"I understand," she lied.

"She came from nowhere and went to nowhere, as I understand it. Ethan, the scrapper, should have gotten down on his knees and thanked his mother for saving him, but what did he do? He alienated everyone. Irreparably, I'm afraid. Now, nearly two decades later, he turns up a detective or some ghastly..."

Unable to remember Hite's father so passionate about anything, Kelly kept her silence and smiled blandly when he murmured, "Unfortunately our children don't always plan their lives around our wishes."

"Mmm." She hid behind the lip of her juice glass.

"You, on the other hand—" Pritchard tossed down his drink and snapped the glass on the bar "—should know better."

"Sir?"

"I've been following your editorial page with interest." His shrewd brain was again at the top of its form, and his smile one of massive irony. "I would be amiss if I didn't admit that you surprise me, Kelly."

Be amiss, be amiss, please! "I—"

"Why are you coming on so strongly about this landfill thing? Why the campaign against Albert Russo? Have you ever met the man?"

"Actually—"

"One doesn't get ahead by taking on issues that have the blessing of the city fathers, my dear. I learned a long time ago that it's better to swallow a few things you may not like for the greater good. Do you get my drift?"

Kelly wasn't sure exactly what she would have told the man if "Suzie Q" hadn't suddenly thundered over the sound system.

Judge Pritchard shot up from his bar stool as if a cannon had fired. "Damn it, Mendino! Are you trying to give me a heart attack?"

Grinning, Quentin directed Kelly's attention to Miriam, who was on the opposite side of the room, waving both her arms in victory like a signal corpsman.

Pritchard sheepishly recovered his poise by extending a parchment-thin hand to Kelly.

"Come, my dear," he said. "When the music reverts to the natives, it's time for history."

The photographs that Pritchard pointed out to Kelly covered a wall she might have passed a hundred times and would have sworn she knew well. But when the magistrate tapped his yellowed fingernail on several of the peeling images, she leaned closer and squinted to discern the faces.

"These tell a fairly good account of the Chase family," he said, and swiveled around as a small stir occurred at the entry.

Over Kelly's shoulder, Georgia Chase posed at the front entrance, drawing off a swirling crimson cape and thrusting it carelessly toward Jack. Pritchard laid his hand upon Kelly's arm in a tactful pause.

"Look," she said, eager to be alone, "I appreciate this, sir, more than I can tell you. Why don't you leave me to browse until Hite gets here?"

"Of course, of course."

Just as he turned to go and Kelly thought she was about to escape further inquisition, he shifted his attention briefly from the mayor to her.

"You have an opportunity before you, Kelly Madison," he said with a surprising intensity.

"Pardon?"

"You're a clever young woman. Actually you're smarter than your father was. Use your head, Kelly. Be smart. If you're careful, things can go well for you."

Somewhere in Kelly's mind, a key slipped into a lock and twisted. First Russo, now Judge Pritchard! Surely the two instances were not connected, for Russo was a slime, and her admiration for Hite's father was second to that for her own father. But he was pressuring her, and she was powerless to let his remark go as she had been to call Russo's hand.

She gathered straggling threads of her courage. "You wouldn't be referring to the First Amendment, would you, sir?"

Voices crowded around them as Irwin Pritchard drew to his full height.

"You misunderstand me," he said in his voice that was famous for turning cold and deadly. "I was speaking as a friend. You may someday be a member of my family. Try to not make too many enemies along the way."

Albert Russo definitely had a friend in Irwin Pritchard, Kelly thought, bruised with disappointment.

"I'll remember that, sir," she mumbled.

Satisfied, he closed her hand in both his own. "And if you ever need some assistance, I'm sure that Georgia wouldn't hesitate—"

She nodded briskly. "I'll be fine, sir. Really. Have a pleasant evening."

Before he could reply, she closed her hand upon his hand and, shaking vigorously, slipped free of him.

"Thank you," she said again at the risk of appearing too hasty to leave. "Thank you very much."

He had already forgotten her as he moved toward the vivacious, charismatic woman in her early sixties who, together with the nine carats of diamonds about her neck, was attracting a small crowd of sycophants.

For a woman Georgia's age, she was remarkably preserved. Her skin was exceptionally smooth and clear. Laughing, she lifted her impeccably rouged cheek for Pritchard's kiss and whispered something in his ear that made him laugh.

At that moment, over Irwin's shoulder, Georgia's eyes made contact with Kelly's—radar finding its target. The bitter anger in those eyes made Kelly's skull thrum with a fine, keening pitch: *You can't hide from me, Miss Schoolteacher-Playing-at-Publishing. I know every move you make.*

Kelly gripped her handbag where Albert Russo's eight thousand dollars were tucked like dynamite needing only a fuse. She didn't understand how the *Mirror* was a threat worthy of such venom.

Before she could turn her back on the woman, Georgia shut her out by moving toward the press of people inside. She hesitated before entering, staring at them as a mongoose might size up a cobra.

She tipped back her beautiful head and, laughing, moved inside.

Kelly was left abruptly alone with snapshots that, except for Ethan, now held little interest for her. Fishing her reading glasses from her beaded bag, she held them to her eyes and leaned closer. Ethan! She recognized him now. How very young he was, so sweet and innocent as he posed with his father before Maxwell had lost the use of his legs.

Other pictures cluttered the wall: Georgia when she was working herself up through the political chain of the city; football poses with Ethan one-half inch high, uniformed and kneeling, a forearm braced cockily across his knee; Ethan running; Ethan tank-topped and wearing shorts, even then tall and muscular, the dark hair on his legs curling up into his shorts, his shoulders powerful.

She hungrily touched the glossy reproductions of Ethan's face and felt, she thought, a feeble pulse beat of life in her old dream. How had Ethan done it? Dragged her, kicking and clawing, out of the isolated shell in which she'd learned to live? He had made her remember a desire she had locked up with great care, and he made her wonder if there was still time for her to have the love and motherhood and family that so many women took for granted. If she could live that hour in his office over...

"Kelly!"

Kelly found Hite gracefully seeking a way to detach himself from his father and Georgia Chase, and the laughing salute he flipped them was graceful and handsome and debonair. Her heart felt ready to break. Life was so unfair. Why couldn't the compassion she felt for Hite pass as love? She knew lots of marriages built on less than what he and she felt for each other.

She went willingly into his quick, hard hug.

"God, you're a sight for sore eyes," he exclaimed as his kiss found her swirling hair. "Mmm, you smell good, too. I've been looking forward to this for days. What a week!"

"I know," she whispered against his shoulder, and squeezed her eyes tightly shut so that the image of her prince could not intrude. "It wore me out."

* * *

Ethan had to duck when he walked through Mendino's door. He paused there a moment—more Price Masters than Man Behind the Badge.

He nodded briefly to the hat-check man, removed his Stetson but carried it with him into the restaurant. His internal radar pointed him immediately at his oldest friend not too far away. Hite was wrapping his arms about Kelly Madison.

They were, he had to admit, a perfect couple. Hite with his thousand-dollar suit and flawless Windsor-knotted tie, his spit-shined Ferragamos, was a dashing counterpoint to Kelly.

She looked different tonight. Her hair, which had been unexceptional when she'd come to his office, was now a cloud of spun gold floating about her shoulders. Funny how he hadn't noticed before how tall and slender, taller than Hite by an inch or so, and in high heels . . .

A visceral resentment for Hite twisted in his gut. The judge's son had come out the winner again; not only was Hite the pride of the city, basking in the pleasure of his parents, he was the man with everything to gain, and Kelly Madison was on his arm.

He strode to the bar.

"You look pretty Indian for an Anglo," Hite had once teased when they were going through the finger-pricking routine of blood brotherhood.

At the time, he *had* looked Indian. He and Hite had sneaked off to have their heads sheared in matching Mohawk cuts, which had earned him a month's grounding from his mother.

Furtively watching Hite and Kelly in the mirror behind the bartender now, Ethan thought he should have done more than just call Hite on the phone a few weeks ago and bluntly announce, "I'm back."

"A double vodka," he told the bartender.

The man gave him a strange double take, as if they had met in another lifetime. Ethan tossed down the drink and slapped his tip to the mahogany surface.

Rising, he made his way toward the table where Kelly and Hite were deep in conversation, their heads nearly touching. He had either underestimated Kelly or had misjudged how much he had changed; she had gone straight to his head like the vodka.

She was talking earnestly. Her legs were crossed beneath the table, and her hands were curled about a small beaded purse. As she leaned forward, her skirt rode high on her thighs. He saw himself running his lips along the inside of those sleek thighs.

Hite reached for her handbag, and she quickly drew it into her lap beneath the table.

Son of a bitch! She was telling him about the money! He had been right all along! Kelly had decided to keep the eight thousand and use it for the *Mirror*'s community project!

"Sir?" a waitress said as she hurried up to him in protest. "Do you have a reservation?"

"I'm meeting someone," he snapped, and elbowed his way to the table as Kelly was saying, "Don't be stupid, Hite. Fair is fair!"

It occurred to Ethan as he walked into their lives that, whether any of them intended it or not, they would now be the eternal triangle. It wasn't a thing he had imagined for himself.

He came up behind Hite and laid his hands upon his old friend's shoulders, physically forming the triad.

"This man stupid?" he said, and looked over the top of Hite's head to lock his eyes with Kelly's wide, startled ones. "Hite Pritchard is the smartest man I know, Miss Madison. And he's pretty, too. Why, just look at him. Hite's what every man wants to be. Hell, I'd like to be Hite myself."

Kelly's lips compressed irritably, and Hite's chair scraped across the floor. He lunged out of it, his hand thrust in greeting. "Damn it, man—"

"Hello, Hite." Ethan's grin slid off one side of his mouth as he shook the hand of his friend. "Sorry to crash your party."

"Hey, you know better than that."

The two men, it occurred to Kelly, were awkward as boys as they shook hands then dispensed with the formality and wrapped their arms around each other, laughing and slapping the other's back. The reunion was so intimately personal, she felt like a Peeping Tom and tried to discreetly focus on the Western hat in Ethan's left hand.

But she couldn't help but see how wonderful Ethan looked in his creased jeans and crisp Western shirt tucked in, the linen jacket in much better condition than the corduroy one.

Compared to Hite, however, Ethan was too roughly hewn to be called handsome. His hair was too blackly rebellious with its sprigged crown and the forelock that kept tumbling across his brow. His nose was too mangled, and where Hite's jaws were beautiful and in proportion to his mouth, Ethan's were craggy.

But handsome or not, Ethan's magnetism was formidable. Across the restaurant people were taking a second look, and though she could have punched him, she was drawn into his force field along with everyone else.

Again Ethan found her over Hite's shoulder, his look as physical as an embrace.

You hurt me, she snappingly accused, remembering her mad dash through the newsroom.

Regret softened the angles of his face. *I know.*

But she was determined to sound casual. She murmured, "I wasn't aware that you and Hite knew each other."

Ethan's smile belonged to her, not Hite, as they released each other. "Hite and I go way back."

"Would that be one generation or two before me?"

"Ouch!" Hite laughed.

The crowd suddenly ceased to exist for Kelly. She and Ethan were the only two people left in the whole world. But she would not make another mistake with him. She would be a real woman this time.

He was reaching for a chair.

"You were smart to stay in Montgomery, Hite," he said, and sprawled across the chair, hooking his thumbs in his belt and smiling at everything but Kelly. "A man misses a lot when he strays too far. Take it from the perennial prodigal son."

Hite pushed his chair closer to Kelly, and she hoped dizzily that he would lay his arm on the back of her chair in a symbol of possession.

But he didn't so much as touch the cuff of her blouse or graze her elbow.

"Oh, it's not so bad, Ethan," he said with ebbing enthusiasm as he looked from Ethan to her and from her back to Ethan. "You know who the fatted calf was killed for."

Ethan pulled a smile that Kelly was beginning to recognize now as a counterfeit.

"Yeah..." His drawl was silky and disturbing. "But you got the girl, Hite. It doesn't come any better than that, buddy."

Chapter 5

Since the first day when he walked into the locker room of the boys' gym at Eastman High School, Hite Pritchard had been eating Ethan's dust.

That day had marked the beginning of a long love-hate relationship—more love than hate as Fate would have it, for Ethan had turned out to be his best friend.

But not without a struggle. There was a certain defeat in being the best friend of everyone's hero. Ethan was the star, the class comedian, the center of the show, the Romeo who had every girl dreaming of moonlight and parked cars, most particularly the girls whom *he*, Hite, had worked up the courage to speak to.

So they were like star-crossed lovers, he and Ethan. Irwin Pritchard's career was entwined with that of Mayor Chase and Maxwell. Their families went to the same church and belonged to the same clubs. Day after day, year after year, he and Ethan were the opposite sides of the same coin.

Now Kelly was staring at Ethan in a way he, Hite, had always wanted her to look at him. She had laid her purse on the table, and while he and Ethan exchanged their awkward hellos, she had plucked at the tiny beads until he expected her whole handbag to go scattering over the room like fallout.

It wasn't fair that Ethan could drop back into Montgomery's mainstream so easily. Where had he been, damn him, when Kelly was hysterical after that grisly rape? Weeping for days until he feared she would crawl into a hole and never come out.

Then a turning. It had happened the night he'd waited so long in the hospital corridor. Ethan, already looking like hell from his recent divorce, was hunkered against the wall outside the emergency room door. As ravaged as Hite had ever seen a man, Ethan was rocking back and forth on the balls of his feet.

"Ethan?" Hite had whispered in shocked surprise.

When Ethan didn't respond, he had squatted down beside the same wall. Maxwell was in emergency surgery. Georgia, out of town, had been called by his own father.

"God, it came from out of nowhere, Hite." Ethan's throat was knotted with grief. "One of those big semi rigs, forcing me into the wrong lane . . ."

"Forcing *you,* Ethan? What're you talking about?"

Ethan had escaped the wreckage with only a bruise upon his shoulder and a few popped buttons, torn clothing.

"I was driving," he'd groaned, and buried his face in his hands.

Hite had draped his arms around the shoulders of his friend, and they clung as they had not clung before or since. "Hey, man . . ."

"Oh, God, I was driving, I was driving."

During his sophomore year in college, Ethan had sent Georgia over the edge by marrying Patty Lomax. Hite had been too discreet to gloat that his friend was finally out of the marriage market, and he'd actually liked Ethan more after that.

With no warning, at least to outsiders, Patty had suddenly left Montgomery. Ethan had gone a little crazy after that. He shut himself off from everyone, dropped out of college altogether.

Then the accident had happened, and after a string of surgeries the doctors finally gave up on Maxwell. Something in Ethan had died when Patty left, but seeing his father put in a wheelchair for the rest of his life made him into a shadow of what he once had been. More and more he stopped functioning. A few months later he'd thrown his suitcases into the back of his '74 Ford pickup and, with hardly a word to anyone, moved to Jackson, Mississippi.

Now, after nearly two decades, he was back in town—no longer the wonder boy but a silent, hard-bitten man whose blue eyes were almost painful to look at. Time had not been kind to the son of Georgia and Maxwell Chase.

But battered men had a way of bringing out the maternal nature of women, Hite supposed. And a deaf, dumb and blind person couldn't have missed the tension between Kelly and Ethan. Even their silences throbbed.

Breezing by the table, Miriam paused to chew her gum in time to the rock and roll while she waited to take Ethan's order. Ethan was oblivious, and Miriam's look found Kelly, then the tables behind her where a hundred glasses were lifting to a hundred lips, then Kelly again.

She flipped over a clean page of her order pad. "Would you like me to come back later?"

Ethan continued his lost perusal of Kelly. Miriam leaned forward and murmured to Kelly as if the two of them were part of a conspiracy, "Uh, Kelly, should I tell Pat to play Beethoven?"

Hite smiled as Kelly flinched.

"Miriam! Oh, I'm sorry." Her smile was quick and apologetic. "The Beethoven is perfect."

Too late she realized her mistake and lowered her lashes to commence picking at the loose thread on her purse again.

Ethan looked around as if he suddenly realized where he was.

Miriam pounced. "Sir?"

"Coffee," Ethan mumbled. "Black and lots of it."

Miriam scribbled the order on her pad, gave Hite a look of sympathy and sailed away just as ZZ Top was beginning "Sharp Dressed Man."

Hite turned back in time to see Kelly snap the thread so that beads went skimming across the tabletop. The three of them made a grab for the colorful baubles, and Kelly's insistence that they were worthless fell on deaf ears.

"I do believe you're falling apart, Miss Madison," Ethan quipped as he scooped up several and caught Kelly's hand to drop them into her palm. "Not that I hold such things against people."

Witty, Ethan, Hite thought sourly. Very witty. Yet Kelly *was* falling apart, right before their eyes. Her compulsive attempt to repair her purse seemed to push her even closer to the edge of some deep, personal abyss.

"It's fine, it's fine," she insisted, and fished out her glasses and put them on in an attempt to tie the culprit thread in the dim light.

Ethan blandly offered, "Here, let me do that for you."

"No, no. I'm getting it." She wet her fingertip and drew it along the slippery thread to make a knot. "All I have to do is catch this—"

"That's good," Ethan said. "One can't be too careful when carrying a large sum of money, can one?"

At the words "large sum of money," Kelly lifted her head and pushed a fallen wisp of hair from her eyes. Her mouth was too tightly compressed, Hite thought, and her sweep of the raveling purse to her bosom was too extravagant.

"Hite?" she said.

Hite spread both his hands like a priest absolving himself of guilt. "Leave me out of this, Kelly."

Ethan was circling Kelly now. "You do have a large sum of money in your purse, don't you, Miss Madison?"

Kelly again consulted Hite, and Hite, wanting to pinch her and punch Ethan, muttered, "Damn it, Kelly."

"I don't suppose it's fitting to plead the Fifth Amendment, is it?" she said with a flippancy that wasn't at all like her.

Hite snorted his contempt. "I don't know about you, but I refuse to answer on the grounds that it might incriminate *me.*"

No one was smiling now—no one except Ethan, if a person could call the way his lips were drawn back from his teeth a smile.

"You know, Miss Madison—" he retrieved several more beads and placed them into a collection in the ashtray "—I once had a great-grandmother."

"How lucky for you." Kelly jerked the glasses from her face.

Ethan's frown was a warning that he was still sworn to enforce the law. "She was the most paranoid woman I ever knew. We're talking major suspicion here."

"I can see where your genes come from."

"She didn't trust the law and she didn't trust banks. To protect her money, she sewed her own slips and put a little pocket right in the front. You know, right here, close to her heart. She put her money in there and fastened it with a safety pin."

He stared luridly at Kelly's breasts until Hite envisioned himself blackening both the man's blue eyes.

She lowered her purse and leaned forward. "Look here, Ethan—"

"Just a suggestion, of course," he added, grinning. "For all I know, you detest sewing."

"You'd be surprised what I detest, Lieutenant."

Ethan did not reply. He patted his pockets for a slender cigar, which he brought out and stripped of its wrapping. Reconsidering, he drew out another and offered it to Hite.

When Hite shook his head, Ethan teasingly made the same offer to Kelly before shrugging and replacing it. He sat inhaling the tobacco blend.

"Well, Hite," he said at length, and his heartiness was like a needle in Hite's ribs, "is the food still as good here as it used to be?"

Blood rose slowly to Hite's face. "It depends on what your taste is these days, Ethan."

"It hasn't changed too much." Ethan included everything and everyone in his sweeping gesture. "This place has, though."

"In some ways."

"Great music."

"I liked the old music."

Kelly, Hite realized, had noticed that she had been excluded from the conversation, and she was thrashing around in an attempt to understand. For once he wished she was more like her sisters. Debbie or Melissa wouldn't have lost their sense of place.

Kelly's sisters would, with some chess player's coolness, have kept tabs on everything that was being said and what it meant. Then they would have run it through a diagnostic test of their own and would have come to the conclusion that he and Ethan were only doing what came naturally to the male of the species—scrapping over the female. They would then have performed their Scarlett O'Hara trick and pitted one man against the other.

But Kelly's eyes only widened with distaste. She pushed back her chair and muttered something about being certain that they would excuse her, that they would have no trouble finding another piece of horseflesh to place their bets on.

No sooner was she gripping the edge of the table than Ethan's fingers were banding her wrist.

"By the way, Miss Madison—" his drawl sliced like a blade "—I might mention in passing that a certain piece of evidence came into my office the other evening but strangely waltzed right out again. I haven't slept a wink, wondering how that could have happened. I don't suppose you'd happen to know anything about it."

Kelly looked from Ethan to Hite and back to Ethan. "I might. If you happened to have any knowledge of someone parking outside my place of business, spying on me."

Hite raised his brows. "Ethan, did you do that?"

"This man staked me out," Kelly said.

If he had more Indian blood in him, Hite thought, this would be the time to put on the war paint and beat the drum to that mystical singsong chant.

But he asked in the voice of his father, "Has Kelly committed some crime, Ethan?"

Ethan had leaned back in his chair and was casually touching the end of his nose with the cigar. Hite could remember the very football game when it had first been broken.

"If a person reaches the age of six, Hite," he drawled, "he's committed a crime."

"What's my crime?" Kelly snapped. "Eating potato chips in my bed?"

"You eat potato chips in bed?" Hite quipped.

"I like potato chips in bed," Kelly shot back.

Laughing, Ethan placed the cylinder of tobacco between his teeth and promptly removed it. "I read your paper this morning, Kelly," he said. "This project you're undertaking—it sounds expensive."

Not understanding his point, Kelly shrugged. "In some ways it will be, yes."

"The *Mirror*'s also having financial difficulty. That's no secret."

"I don't get the point, Lieutenant."

"Please don't call me that, Kelly."

The way Ethan's tone softened when he said her name, the gentle murmur of an old friend, or even of a lover, made Hite see the mistakes he had made with Kelly. He had misjudged her, and now she was looking at him, Hite, with a hurt so pure that he died a tiny death.

"Hite," she said as her her voice cracked, "consider yourself hired as my attorney. I want you to file a lawsuit against this man for defamation of character."

He should have asked her to marry him years ago, Hite thought. "What *are* you going to do with the money, Kell?"

The color drained from her face, and her eyes sparkled with angry, unshed tears. *Et tu, Brute?*

"I was thinking I would give the money to a couple of deserving women, Hite, whose daughters are very sick. Probably because of the landfill. A nice twist of justice, don't you think? Give me your best shot. Could the good lieutenant here arrest me if I made a public ceremony of the gift? Oh, I'd be careful not to defame Mr. Russo's good name. I realize that *your* father and *his* mother are most anxious that not a smudge of scandal stain the man. So tell me, would I be okay or should I pick out the color I'd like to paint my jail cell?"

Hite didn't bother with trying to save face. He no longer cared what either of them thought. Or what they did, for that matter.

"Would you two excuse me?" He dropped several crumpled bills on the table.

"No." Kelly reached for his hand, but Hite was already weaving his way through the restaurant.

Knowing precisely whom to blame for this terrible situation, who was to blame for everything that had gone wrong in her entire life, Kelly watched Hite's retreat. Then she riveted her most blistering accusation on Ethan Chase.

But his face was drawn with such unhappiness that her memory, inescapable as a net, made her once again the spectator, high in a crowd of screaming fans.

Rising, he stood beside her chair as if there had never been a question about the evening ending any other way. "I'd like to drive out to the landfill, Kelly."

The words drew themselves along Kelly's senses like a strand of silk.

"Then do it," she whispered.

"I want you to come with me."

Chapter 6

"Don't get the wrong idea about this," Kelly warned as she ducked beneath the bridge of Ethan's arm and swept through Mendino's front entrance to the parking lot outside.

She hurried several paces ahead, too unsure of what had just happened to walk in tandem with the unpredictable lieutenant.

"Kelly," he called after her, "only an orangutan could get the wrong idea about you. And I'm not all that sure about the monkey."

Occupying a quarter-acre of Mimosa Street's depressed real estate, Mendino's was bordered with lacy live oaks that had managed to survive asphalt and tons of spewed carbon monoxide along with drooping electrical wires that brought tree trimmers each season to perform their casual amputations.

The whispered call of their branches was muffled by the sounds of the city beyond the interstate highway. A light rain had fallen. Droplets were jeweled on the cars that filled the lot.

"It was unforgivable, you know," Kelly retorted over her shoulder. "What you did to Hite."

"I didn't do anything to Hite."

"He's your friend, and you hurt his feelings. Why do you think he left?"

"If you think I'm the reason Hite left, my dear—" his laughter caught up with her "—you're more out of touch than I thought. Are you always in this big of a hurry?"

Kelly came to a stop. "Why, I forgot how old and feeble you are, Lieutenant. Maybe we should get you a walker or one of those motorized wheelchairs. Here, take my hand. Let me help you, poor man."

A car, whipping onto the lot, raked them with its halogen beams. Momentarily blinded, Kelly collided with the fender of a Suburban.

"Easy," Ethan murmured as he reached out to keep her from tripping. "You should learn to be more careful, Miss Madison. Otherwise, I'll have no one to take care of me in my old age."

Lifting her chin just to let him know that she wasn't the sister of Debbie and Melissa Madison for nothing, Kelly smiled. "How old are you? Wheelchairs and walkers notwithstanding."

He chuckled, placed the cigar between his teeth and brought out his lighter to cup its dancing flame with his palm. He puffed briefly, then flashed a sparkling smile. "I can still make babies, darlin', if that's what you mean."

"That wasn't—"

"Actually I'm forty. How old are you? Sixteen?"

"I'm old enough to have babies, darlin'," she sassily retorted, "if that's what you mean."

"Come on. Twenty-five?"

"Add three years."

"Twenty-eight?" He reared back in feigned horror. "Gad, you really are a baby."

Kelly wasn't particularly of a mind to laugh, but his grin was too infectious and his appeal too unplanned and natural. She wished she dared reach up to straighten his hair where the wind had rumpled it. Perhaps she might have if Mendino's door hadn't opened to spill a shaft of light and a blast of Miriam's rock and roll.

"Miss Madison, wait! Miss Madison!"

Kelly placed space between herself and Ethan Chase as if she were a child caught snooping in a forbidden drawer. "Uncle Jack!"

The aged doorman moved across the tarmac like a wind-up toy. In his hands were her raincoat and umbrella, which she, in her flurry over Ethan, had forgotten.

"You might nearly slipped by me, Miss Kelly," he said when he caught up and cast a discreet glance at Ethan.

The old man was measuring her, Kelly thought with chagrin, against his old-school code—that a woman wasn't a lady who arrived with one man and left with another. She guessed her cheeks would match the red of his tie.

"Well, Hite left early, Uncle Jack," she mumbled.

"Yes'm."

"So I just..."

"Yes'm."

She smiled thinly and felt that her whole life was spread out on display. "So Lieutenant Chase and I decided to...do you remember Ethan Chase, Uncle Jack?"

"I should say I do." Jack had to look upward to see Ethan. "Hello, Mr. Lieutenant, sir, I recognized you when you come in."

With his cigar anchored between his fingers, Ethan removed his Stetson and offered his hand with a genteel courtesy that pleased the old man.

Kelly huffed a sigh of impatience. Ethan hadn't been so congenial with her, had he? His eyes hadn't danced nearly so generously, nor had his laughter wrapped around her as it was cozily wrapping around Jack.

"Lieutenant Chase and I are driving out to the landfill," she said aridly. "In a professional capacity, you understand."

Inching back in a tactful retreat, Jack touched his head in a salute. "I see. Well, you take care now, Miss Kelly. And you, sir, come and see us now and agin."

"Good night, Jack."

As the man moved away and the shaft of light bore him back inside like Captain Kirk beaming Bones back onto the spaceship *Enterprise,* Kelly tucked the umbrella beneath one arm with her mutilated evening bag and draped her raincoat over the other.

"Now he'll go straight to Pat," she said.

"Really, why?"

Did he honestly think, Kelly wondered, that she would explain that Pat had been waiting years for someone like Ethan to come along? That within a week, everyone who frequented the place would be musing that she and Ethan were "an item"?

"Nothing." Kelly dourly shook out the raincoat with the intention of putting it on.

"That's what I like about you, Kelly," Ethan said. "You really lay it on the line. I guess I'm going to have to get one of those tight muscle shirts and rip out the sleeves. You know the kind I mean, don't you? Or maybe I should just get a job with the electric company."

He attempted to help her with the raincoat. With a retroactive blaze of offense, Kelly snatched her scarf from its pocket and lashed the length of silk at his head like Indiana Jones wielding his bullwhip.

"Do you know I nearly broke my neck trying to get down the stairs to talk to you?" she railed.

His laughter boomed richly over the parking lot and caught the attention of new arrivals, who smiled as they passed.

"Carl Hennessey was there on business, I'll have you know!" Kelly whispered loudly.

"Sure, sure."

But a frisson of satisfaction passed through Kelly, and she flicked the scarf at him again playfully. "Why, Ethan Chase, I do believe you're jealous."

"Damn right I'm jealous." Grinning, he captured the scarf and lassoed her neck, reeling her in. "I can't get my shirts nearly that white."

With a tight fist, Kelly pounded his shoulder. "You're horrible."

"Yeah. I am, aren't I?" Tossing his cigar to the asphalt, he removed his Stetson and placed it on her own head, holding her fast with the silk scarf and plumbing her with an awareness that was much too quick, much too knowing.

His lazy grin continued to chip at her, and his eyes traveled over every inch of her face. "Tell me, Miss Madison. What did you want to say that was so urgent you almost broke your neck getting down the stairs?"

Kelly searched for a reply that was properly lighthearted and coy, but coquettishness refused to come. His gaze moved lower and considered the way their bodies would connect if he moved six inches closer.

Before she thought, Kelly glanced down at the junctured V of his legs.

With an impact more volatile than a physical caress, they were abruptly locked in the confrontation of the ages: *So this is the way it is*. They did not speak but continued to stare and stare and stare. *This is the way it is. Where do we go from here?*

Ethan, wanting this kiss more then he could have imagined wanting anything, seriously debated taking it. She was affecting him in ways he hadn't experienced in years, and he had grown too self-protective with age.

"I know what you're doing," she said with a catch of breath, leaning away.

Ethan watched the way the wind fluttered the collar of her blouse. Her bra didn't cover the tops of her breasts, and he could discern the impression of scalloped lace beneath the silk.

"Ah, cruelty, thy name is woman," he murmured.

"If you really believe that," she managed to parry as she reached up to remove his hat and thrust it into his hands, retrieving her scarf and raincoat with the same movement of finality, "I wouldn't worry too much about making babies, Lieutenant."

He happily took the bait and followed her when she began walking. "Wait a minute, you can't just leave me here, all mangled and bleeding."

"That's not blood, Ethan. You're drooling."

Ethan laughed, fascinated all over again with the way she wore the night, the way the wind was lifting her hair and tossing it about her head in swirling arabesques. It was teasing the hem of her short skirt and molding it even more to the luscious curve of her rear.

He could not count the times he had seen the wind kindle such wantonness in a woman's clothes and felt nothing. Yet each time her dainty high-heeled shoes touched the tarmac, desire spooled inside him.

"Where's your car?" he asked.

She stopped dead in her tracks and faced him. "My car? You're not suggesting we take *my* car?"

"You don't have one?"

"Are you serious?"

"You came in a taxi?"

"I came in my car, Ethan, but that's not the point. Do you know how much gasoline costs these days? Take your own car."

"I don't have one."

Which was a bald-faced lie, obviously—all part of the dangerous game they were playing. If she took *her* car, Ethan could later cajole her, *Would you mind dropping me off?* Then he could say, *Wouldn't you like to see my boat before you drive back? Wouldn't you like a nightcap? A blank check? My head on a platter?*

She began wrapping the scarf around her head like a snood and tossed a trailing end over her shoulder.

"Then how do you ever catch the bad guys?" she purred wickedly. "On a skateboard?"

"Nice of you to worry—" he showed his teeth "—but I catch my share of bad guys."

She turned abruptly, and her heels clicked an unnegotiable staccato.

"So long as you understand this trip is strictly professional." She veered toward a modest blue Ford. "I want to make that perfectly clear."

Nothing could be clearer, honey.

He couldn't help saying when they reached her car, "Just for the record, Kelly Jean, you were the one who came to me. Remember?"

She had opened her bag and was searching for her key. She looked up, her lips pursed in a child's confused moue. "How do you know my middle name is Jean?"

She waited, Ethan thought as the wonderful fragrance of her filled his nostrils, like someone who expected a stone to hit the bottom of a well. He thought of sparing her with a lie, but he didn't want an untruth hanging between them.

"I checked you out," he admitted.

She missed the lock with her key. It struck the door with a tiny ping. Nor could she recover quickly enough to protest when he took the key and unlocked the door.

He swung it open, and she stumbled into the wedge. She stuffed her raincoat and umbrella into a back seat that was crammed full of old newspapers and boxes that were taped closed and labeled.

She hesitated then, her proud back so weighted with defeat, Ethan felt like Jack the Ripper.

"It wasn't enough that you staked out the newspaper?" she choked. "You investigated me?"

"'Investigation' isn't the right word."

"Didn't you ever hear of invasion of privacy, Lieutenant?"

"It wasn't like that, damn it. I only wanted—"

She spun furiously around. "You only wanted what? And make it good, Ethan, because I don't swallow just every hook, line and sinker that comes along. I swallow only the best."

The night was electrified with emotions.

"You," he said at last, and wished there had been no shock value attached. "I wanted you."

Finally! He had finally articulated the thing he had felt from the beginning but could not reconcile with his own self-imposed exile from life. Now that he'd said it, what did he do about Kelly's lips, which were growing slack with amazement? Her head, which was turning, ever so slightly away, in a profile of disbelief?

"You fraud," she said.

"You're right." Before she could get into the car, Ethan placed his foot in the opening of the door. His left arm over the window finished the human barricade. "I am a fraud. But only in part, Kelly. One of the reasons I came looking for you tonight was to find out about the money. I understand what you told Hite about giving the eight thousand to some women, I really do. It's a good idea, but I have to warn you that it could be dangerous farther down the road. It's crucial that you don't spend any of that money without an accounting, Kelly. Not to improve the east side or anything else. Do you understand what I'm saying?''

Two diamond tears trembled on her lashes. Her lips threatened to betray her, and she pressed them together. But her chin quivered uncontrollably, and she blinked rapidly to force back the tears.

"Ah, Kelly,'' he whispered, and hated himself.

In a move that bannered the end of her scarf, she spun around in an attempt to move past. When he refused to step aside, she struck his arm with a fist, glancing it harmlessly.

"Kelly—"

Her outrage, once given expression, was like a tide that could not be turned. With a consuming hurt, she battered his chest with her fists, kicking at his shins and connecting once with such strength, Ethan danced around on one foot.

"Stop it, Kelly," he ordered, and jerked her up as he would have a punk on the street instead of a silk-clad woman with intoxicating green eyes.

He pinned her harshly against the car, and she cried out in a mixture of shock and anger. Immediately he wrapped himself around her—muscle covering bone.

"I'm sorry," he choked, and squeezed his eyes tightly shut as he pressed his face into the scarf, which was sliding low around her throat. "I shouldn't have said it that way. It's all right. Hush now. Hush, Kelly."

"I can't believe you'd think such a thing." Her voice was muffled against his jacket. "How could you believe I'd keep that money for myself?"

"I'm in the suspicion business."

"Well, I'm not your business, Ethan."

"You are very much my business."

As he rocked her back and forth in consolation, Ethan felt as if he'd stumbled headlong into a hole with no bottom. Instinct warned him as he dropped in that most terrible of free-falls that she deserved better than someone like himself. She wasn't a woman for one-night stands, and he was too burned-out, too much of Price Masters to offer her anything lasting.

Defeated, she had let her head go back. The sight of her beautiful throat—so white, so silken—generated a flood of images in the windows of his mind: her, melting out of her silks at the end of the day, appearing to be made of gold as she gathered her hair before a dressing table, watching her own reflection as she weighed her breasts in her palms.

She could not know how close to orgasm she'd brought him with the sweeping ripeness of her body. She could have moved against him, and he would've been damned. She could have crooned him to it.

But his fatal flaw was in always moving too quickly, too rashly. So he took refuge in humor, for shared humor was an implicit assertion of togetherness, and he prayed that she saw the same possibilities for their future that he saw.

"Now that you've heard my apology," he said against her cheek as he ordered his hands to release her, "I'm afraid I'm going to have to arrest you for assaulting an officer."

The silence was their judge and jury. They were tense and unable to be graceful. Her breaths grew quiet and revealed their tattered edges. Ethan didn't breathe at all.

"And if I resist?" she whispered, and lifted her head.

Smiling unhappily, he took a step backward and held up his hands. "I'll chase you down like a mad dog."

Her laughter was a reprieve. It came softly from the back of her throat and possessed the kind of selflessness that a man hears only rarely in his life—as if she were much older than he, much wiser and much more generous. It was a laugh that was in no hurry. It was a laugh that was able to forgive.

"Without a car, Lieutenant?" she said gently.

Ethan considered the fretwork of trees above them and fancied he could hear the leaves unfolding and birds sleeping. His voice was thick with disavowed loneliness.

"I could catch you easily enough, I daresay."

She invited him closer with her eyes of green crystals. "So we must decide, then."

There was no need for her to ask it as a question. They both knew what the next step was. The only thing in question was if they would take it and how.

"It would just be a kiss," he said without apology. "Like they say..."

"A kiss is just a kiss. I don't know if I trust a kiss of yours, Lieutenant."

"Maybe it's your own kiss you don't trust."

"Maybe we'll never know."

"Maybe we must know."

Kelly no longer smiled. She felt outside of herself, gazing down on both of them from a great distance where the past was meeting the future. The quarterback was taking the girl into his arms, and her softer body was fitting to the hard angles of his as if they had done it many times before.

Or was it her own hip that Ethan was closing his hand upon? Was he drawing his palm along the span of *her* ribs? Stroking *her* back and following the curve of *her* spine? Pulling her closer? Taking a breath like a man who has seen a jewel at the bottom of a deep, clear lake and knows there is only one way to get it?

In her center settled a heavy, driving ache. Her right thigh was pressed between his legs, and the hard thrust of him was unmistakable. He moved against her, letting her know the extent of it, but they were both too sophisticated to think that desire did not come without a price.

Part of her was kept in reserve for that price, and she sensed the same caution in him.

"There's someone I need to tell you about," she said against the plane of his jaw. "Someone from the past."

His hands were fastened upon her shoulders. "Hite?"

Kelly did not say Terry Benedict's name. She could not say anything. She wanted only for Ethan's mouth to claim hers before her caution sent her retreating back within her boundaries of safety.

Eve-like, she lifted her lips to his. "Hite and I..."

"I don't care." He caught her with a groan from deep inside, as if he had suffered some fearful pain there for many years.

Kelly twined her arms around his neck as his mouth grazed hers. She rose up on her toes as his lips tested hers in a series of questioning sips. The faint taste of tobacco and coffee, the smells of after-shave and soap and the wind intoxicated her.

His lips clung gently, slanting and hovering as her own flowered. She realized now that she had expected something different. She had imagined that he would devour her, would lose his control so utterly that he would thrust his hand inside her blouse and plunder her mouth with his tongue.

His assault was the subtle way he lifted his head and gazed down into her eyes, searching, she thought, for a deeper truth than she was letting him see. Suddenly she was shy, and he was pleased. He kissed her ear and the back of her neck, the bones of her shoulder. His lashes were a butterfly softness as he closed his teeth upon the lobe of her ear and pierced its shell thrillingly with his tongue.

"Oh," she said with a sigh, and collapsed against him. *Kiss me again—kiss me until I can't breathe.*

But it was too soon, so she closed her fists upon the front of his jacket, content to know she was desired, to realize that he wasn't a marauder.

She hugged him, and as he buried his face into her neck, her hands found the pistol tucked at the base of his spine. The coldness of steel brought reality. Her reality became his reality.

"There are words to be said," he said hoarsely, "but I don't think you'd believe them now. I'm not sure I'd believe them."

Regaining her balance, Kelly pushed gently against him, and he straightened and repaired his clothes and made sure his gun was where he wanted it.

"Hite's in love with you," he said.

There was, Kelly admitted to herself, truth in what he said, but to give the words credence would be to close some door. Her mind was still too drugged with desire to be wise. Better to say nothing at all than the wrong thing.

"If it's convenient for you to think that," she said, not unkindly, "think it."

It was the worst kind of answer. His rough sigh as he moved away from the car, away from her, vindicated his caution and her own reticence.

"I was out of bounds," he said.

Left unsaid was that if *he* were out of bounds, so was she. Kelly sensed him shadowboxing with something he didn't understand, and she wanted to explain, but she stupidly remained mute.

"Okay," he said. Then he repeated with a sigh of finality, "Okay. Do you want to drive or shall I?"

The kiss could have never happened. He walked around her car to her passenger door.

There's still time, she thought with panic. *You can stop everything right here.*

But she didn't stop anything, and he paused before getting inside, considering how best to fit a size-40 body into a size-16 opening.

"This was your idea," she reminded in a tone that was not at all sure of itself.

As she slipped behind the wheel, he went through a series of masculine shifts and turns and compensations that only increased her awareness of how perfect his legs were, his thighs. Once in, he battled briefly with the seat belt, but it was broken and refused to fasten.

Holding it up, he said wryly, "Your list of crimes is growing longer, my darling."

He didn't know the half of it. Kelly turned the key in the ignition and prayed that the solenoid, for once, would not stick.

To her relief, the engine sputtered and coughed and roared to life. The familiar scent of exhaust was thrown back at them, and a cloud of white smoke drifted through the open window.

He coughed.

She gestured that he was still free to call the whole thing off.

"You couldn't drag me out of this car," he said.

When she pulled a more relaxed smirk, he chuckled with slightly less tension than before.

"All right," he said with a policeman's penchant for logic, "let's get this straight. Forget Hite, forget everything. We're two ordinary people going for a pleasant ride. There's a great moon behind all that mist, and we have a vintage car whose back seat is a collector's item. What more could two consenting adults ask for?"

If he had been anyone else, Kelly would have laughed it off, but her memories rewound like a videotape. She was once again in Terry Benedict's car. His brother was holding her hands, and Terry was driving into her with agonizing monotony until she was deliriously counting the dry, brutal strokes until he was spent. Then again with his brother, but she hardly felt anything that time.

"I no longer find anything romantic about the back seat of a car, Lieutenant," she said as if the intimacy of the past ten minutes had never existed. "Nor will I ever again."

Chapter 7

The Southeast Medical landfill was tucked with debatable innocence into the leisurely hills of Montgomery County.

Kelly drove very badly through the tree-lined streets toward it, Ethan thought. Once in traffic, she gathered speed only to nervously apply the brakes at every provocation until he wanted to either shove her foot to the floor or take the keys.

They passed a procession of car lots whose plastic pennants flapped beneath strings of light bulbs. The Wedgwood Theater's main feature had ended, and viewers were streaming out in a wave as they drove by.

Eventually Montgomery was a hazy glow behind them, and the headlights were peeling back the misty night.

Ethan leaned back in the uncomfortable seat and pondered the riddle of Kelly Madison.

There was a danger here that he had not yet articulated, but his senses kept getting lost by the way her hair stole light from the dash and turned to gold, the way she reached up and drew a wisp from her eyes. It was her innocence that bewitched him, he thought—not a naïveté, exactly, more a stubborn refusal to remain unbowed by circumstance. She didn't yet know that life was a hamstringer, lurking in the shadows behind a person, then darting out and grabbing the ankles.

She made him remember lost dreams. She made him ask the saddest question of all: What would he do now if things had been different?

Price Masters, of course, would have had the answer. *I always had been a sucker for innocence, and this woman was no cutie-pie piece of fluff. Looking at her stopped my breath, and I felt my veins swelling—like the day I dived too deep and knew I'd never come up. This is how it felt to die, and I wanted to pray. Please, God, gimme a break, just this once, will you? Let her look at me and not see a loser.*

"What happened to you, Kelly? In the back seat of a car?" He laid his hand upon the headrest of her seat. "What happened?"

Uneasiness shadowed her face, and she shook her head. "I shouldn't have said anything. I never talk about it. I never really think about it anymore. I don't know why I brought it up."

"How old were you?"

"I said I don't talk about it, Ethan."

"Not ever?"

"I talked about it then. That was enough."

"With Hite?"

"Yes."

"And your mother?"

"No."

"Your father?"

"No, Ethan! I didn't tell anyone but Hite."

A voice in Ethan's head, having nothing to do with Price Masters, warned him to be very careful. He was venturing into a part of her that he wasn't sure *she* knew too much about.

"You and your father weren't very close, were you?" he probed cautiously.

She pursed her lips in a frown. "How can you say that? I adored my father. He was my dearest friend in all the world."

"For sending you to live with your aunt in Virginia?"

"If you'd ever met my sisters, you'd know it was an act of love." Her shoulders dropped in a sigh. "Look, Ethan, my father suffered a terrible hurt in his youth, and he wanted more than anything to rise above that. But he was true to his beliefs, even when it wasn't popular, even when it cost him the acceptance he wanted so badly. He was the most courageous, most honorable and caring man I ever knew. So don't you ever cast aspersions on my father."

Ethan's grievance against Vincent Madison wasn't for his strength or weaknesses. It was for brushing Kelly beneath a rug as he had, for deluding her. Her unquestioning trust made him want to come out of his shell, to wrap his arms around her and make up for things she didn't even know she'd been cheated of.

But a man's life formed a circle. He had hurt Patty, and he had hurt Maxwell. Who would protect Kelly from him?

"I wouldn't be so quick to attribute love to Vincent's motives, Kelly," he said, then immediately regretted his statement.

"What's that supposed to mean?"

"Forget it."

"You were the one who brought it up." Her defensiveness was brittle and spiny. "You must be thinking about your own father."

She was tougher than he'd thought. Ethan slapped his pockets for a new cigar and stopped short, hearing the unfamiliar rustle and reaching inside to find Fancy's outrageous packet of condoms. Fancy's matchmaking might not have materialized, but her mothering was remarkably timely.

"For the record—" he heard himself being more honest than he intended "—my father's been a hundred times more than I deserve."

She drew out a thoughtful silence. "I'm sorry."

"Sorry?"

"For the accident."

"So, you've heard the one about how I put him in the wheelchair, eh?"

Ethan realized, finally, why she was quickening his dead heart. Where he had turned bitter and irreverent, she was still forgiving. Where he was hard, she was soft and gentle. When he would crumble, she would be a fortress, and her very resilience, her refusal to break, was why he now said words he had never uttered before, except to his father.

"It, uh... it was my fault. That whole thing." He sank back in his seat as if someone had lifted a ten-ton weight off his back. "I've never forgiven myself." His voice dropped to a whisper meant only for the ears of his private demons. "Never."

He bit the end off his cigar and anchored the cylinder between his teeth. He was shocked by his own hands, shaking. He searched his pockets for a lighter, and when she reached over to stay him, there were no recriminations in her voice.

"I can't have you smoking in my car all the time, Ethan. Besides, you really should quit."

Her words not only implied a future; she was offering admittance into her life. Before he could slip inside, her expression stiffened, as if she were dealing with her own demons.

"You knew my father." Her words were not a question; they were a statement of fact.

Ethan took a moment to absorb his missed chance. "How do you figure that?" he asked, feeling his way with her now, inch by inch like a blind man.

"Don't play games with me, Ethan." Her look searched his. "You knew him."

Ethan considered the rolled tobacco in his fingers. "I really could use this smoke, Kelly."

"You're sidestepping."

This wasn't what he had planned for this evening, Ethan thought with sudden melancholy.

He said morosely, "I used to hear Vincent Madison's name from time to time. I hardly remember those days, so it won't do any good to pick my brain. They were a long time ago, Kelly, and I've got a big mouth."

"You're protesting too much."

"He and my family were in competition. What's the big problem?"

"You're definitely protesting too much."

"Oh, hell."

He turned his face to the wind that whistled through the window. Stars were peeping through the clouds now. Mist hovered over the low places. Patches of woods flitted past, and dark fields. A barn rose up out of nowhere and was, for a moment, transfixed in the corridor of light from the headbeams.

She snatched her attention from the highway to him. *"What did your family have to do with my father?"*

If Ethan had guessed they would quarrel, he would never have spoken Vincent Madison's name, at least not until the truck was past. He looked up to see it thundering toward them, its exhaust pipe spewing hellish red sparks, its headlights glaring, horn blasting, its trailer whipping from side to side like a shark's lethal tail.

A horrible déjà vu took him back eighteen years, and when the force of the big rig sucked the tiny Ford into its vortex, he was caught again in the jaws of death.

"Watch out!" he shouted.

She overcompensated by jerking the wheel so that the right tire was wrenched onto the shoulder. Having lost its traction, the little car was literally blown off the road. The tires went skidding sideways through the loose gravel, and rocks popped beneath the fender like water exploding in a pan of hot fat.

Grabbing the wheel, Ethan held it fast. The tires screamed as the car went slipping, sliding and fishtailing to a stop.

The beams of the lights veered crazily over the edge of the high shoulder into a farmer's pasture. A cow looked up from where it placidly grazed, knee-deep in grass, its horns pearled with dew. It shook its head and lowed in mistrust of humans and their noisy machines.

Ethan was suddenly consumed by a nausea so violent, he kicked the door open and threw himself outside. His feet crunched on the loose gravel, and he braced his hands on his knees and drew in great, steadying gulps of air.

Easy, easy, nothing happened. She's all right. You haven't lost her. She can still walk and run and laugh. She's okay.

A passing car blared its horn until it was a thin, keening wail in the distance.

As he crawled back inside and shut his door, the sight of Kelly's head in her hands dropped an ache into the pit of his belly.

"Kelly..." Pulling her into his arms, he brought her forehead to rest against his own. "It's okay," he muttered as their faces touched and he stroked the back of her wind-blown hair. "It was close, but we're okay."

When she only sniffed, he brushed his lips across her cheek. The fragrance of her skin made him remember days when he could laugh without having to force himself.

"Would you like me to drive?" he asked.

But she was playing out her moment of aggrievement now, squeezing the last drops of injustice from it. "You yelled at me."

Laughter, short and wonderful, made him hug her tightly. "Poor baby. Did I yell at you? Well, give me a good, sound kick in the rear."

Cuffing his shoulder lightly, she nodded yes.

"Does that mean yes, I yelled, or yes, you'll give me a good kick?"

"Both, you brute."

Disengaging herself, she swiftly repaired her hair and smoothed the front of her blouse, touching her own breasts with a thoughtlessness that sent heat rushing into Ethan's blood.

"Someday," he said, and shifted in his seat to ease the growing discomfort in his groin, "when we know each other very well, I'll tell you why I yelled."

Headlights from passersby were capturing their trauma and zooming past. Having recovered, she slipped the car in gear and glanced behind them in her rearview mirror before pulling out onto the highway once more.

"Good," she said. "Then maybe you'll tell me how you knew my father."

"Maybe I will, if you'll tell me what Hite Pritchard has to do with you."

"Hite's my best friend."

"Do you love him?"

The question, Kelly thought after she absorbed the impact of its surprise, was not illogical. But its implication took her a lot further with Ethan Chase than she had been prepared to go.

"Of course I love Hite," she said.

"Come on. You know what I mean. Are you *in* love with him?"

"I don't know what you're talking about."

"Tell me what's between you and Hite, Kelly, so I won't sit here and make a worse ass of myself."

But Kelly could not take the step that would have ended in that terrible honesty of where she truly stood with Ethan—not the golden prince but Ethan Chase, the real man.

He confused her even more when he took her right hand and opened it to place a kiss in the cup of its palm.

"In case you ever need it," he said as the car devoured the highway ribboning into the night.

Only fools believed that total strangers could, in the space of five minutes, fall passionately in love. A perfectly sane person could, however, *think* about falling in love, and she, Kelly thought, had gotten a sixteen-year head start.

She nosed the Ford onto a gravel road that dipped steeply before sweeping up a sharp incline, then spilled onto the lip of an artificially created bowl.

Framed by headlights, the landfill gleamed like a gigantic wounded elbow. A web of chain-link fence surrounded it, topped by strands of barbed wire that bore the familiar logo of hazardous biological waste.

To one side, also surrounded by high chain link, was the furnace where the Southeast Medical waste was burned before being dumped into the fill.

"The melting pot," she said wryly.

"I must be out of touch. This place looks more like a country club than a landfill."

The steep, outer slopes of the bowl had been landscaped. Grassy and artistically planted with young trees whose leaves were now opened to meet the spring, the terrain slid down the hillside to the pooled thickets and timbered hollows of the valley.

At the base of the hills, Pierce Creek stitched through the valley toward the Alabama River.

"It makes for good public relations," she told Ethan. "Russo's a master at public relations."

She pulled to a stop beside a bulldozer and kept her toe on the brake.

With brisk finality, Ethan reached over and turned the key, dousing the lights. Opening the door, he climbed out to light his cigar.

He placed his back to the wind and cupped the lighter's dancing flame. The tobacco burned red.

Fascinated, Kelly watched as he walked with a predatory grace to the edge of the artificial ledge. He seemed taller than before, more lanky, more roughly cut. The skirt of his jacket fluttered in the wind, and his hair was tossed wildly about his head, black as the night. With his hands clasped behind his back, he looked like a troubled general surveying the fate of his armies.

Not completely understanding her own role in this night's drama, Kelly got out of the car.

Her high heels were immediately buried in the loose dirt. "Drat!"

From the back seat she drew an envelope of photographs that Jerome had shot after staking out the dump site for three nights in a row. Slipping out of her shoes and snagging their straps in a finger, she hobbled in stocking feet to where Ethan was.

"We have pictures of trucks coming in here with out-of-state plates," she explained, and opened the packet.

With his cigar anchored between his teeth, he gave the enlargements a token perusal in the darkness. "You're thinking you're going to stop this man on an interstate-commerce detail?"

She shrugged. "Why not?"

"The law says, if the source has no means of taking care of its own hazardous waste, it has the right to ship it across state lines."

"I'm tired of hearing that argument, Ethan. The law is nothing more than a vehicle for the waste companies, and you know it."

"I'm not arguing with you."

"Besides, I don't trust landfills. They have a nasty way of leaking. Did you speak to your mother about Russo's hint that she'd taken a payoff?"

His sigh blended with the lacy susurrus of the wind until he almost seemed part of the night. Kelly knew immediately that he hadn't approached Georgia, and his failure to do so was like a betrayal.

"Actually," he said as he replaced the photographs in the envelope, "I tried a number of times to make an appointment to see her."

She refused to forgive him. "You have to make an appointment to see your own mother?"

"My mother isn't your average, run-of-the-mill parent." Bending, he brought his face closer to hers. "And I don't take lightly to being teased about it, darling."

Though she was the perfect prey to his nearness and bigness, the height of him, the torque, the leverage, the irony, his grin angered her. *It's all a glorious con,* it said. *Welcome to life.*

She held her hair to keep it from being whipped by the wind. "For a tough guy," she mocked, "you're awfully free with your darlings."

He did not pick up her cue to lightness. He rubbed the center of his upper lip and presently ground out his cigar with the toe of his boot.

He kept his eyes fastened on his boot. "You think I'm a tough guy?"

"Aren't you?"

He looked sharply upward, and his gravity went through her like a blade. She took a step backward as her heart knocked at her ribs.

"Look, Ethan—" she combed her hair with her fingers "—I don't know what I think. At this point, I don't really know anything."

In the darkness, his blue eyes were as dark as a gathering storm. "Tell me the truth, Kelly. It's important. More than you know."

Was she always going to miscalculate this man? Kelly licked her lips and tried to swallow, but her mouth was dry as paper.

Moving to a place several feet nearer the landscaped hillside, she hugged herself and stared out at the slumbering city.

"I think you're a fair man, Ethan. One who carries his scars well. You have an uncanny ability to see below the surface of a thing. And you're...surprisingly artistic. I guess that's the right word—artistic. Sometimes you say the most amazing things."

She felt him move to a place just behind her. She flexed her stocking toes against the rough ground and gathered the courage to go on.

"You're a survivor, too," she said. "Overall, a straight shooter." Nervousness prompted her to turn around and laugh thinly at him. "I can picture you living on the prairie in some isolated cabin—no one for miles."

"Skinning buffalo, no doubt," he said with a wry grin. "And reading by firelight."

"Come on."

His chuckle baited her. "You're cute when you're annoyed."

His teasing was intolerable! She worried a strap of her shoe. "We were talking about how I could nail Russo."

She clumsily dropped the shoe and stooped to pick it up.

"You don't need my mother to accomplish that," he said as he reached the shoe before she did, bringing them face-to-face. "Learn from Watergate. Follow the money."

It was on the tip of Kelly's tongue to remind him the money trail was precisely the reason she had come to his office that first evening. But he was drawing her to her feet and peeling out of his jacket, draping it around her shoulders.

Grateful for its warmth but unprepared for the sensuality of being cocooned by something so intimately his, so seductively personal, Kelly burrowed inside until only her eyes were showing. He closed his arms about her, crushing Jerome's photographs between them.

For a moment they stood in their stiff embrace, waiting, but neither knew what they waited for. From somewhere close by, a cicada was churring loudly.

Presently, admitting to herself that it was what she wanted to do, Kelly melted into his side with a sigh, and he pressed his face into her hair, drew the scent from it.

"It's too cold up here." He found her hand beneath the folds of linen. "Let's walk."

He had thrown off his seriousness the way some men would shrug out of a sweater, and Kelly stumbled alongside him for a few steps.

The terrain, however, was rough, and her shoes were in her hand, not on her feet. "Slow down, Ethan," she whimpered after stubbing her toe. "I'm barefooted."

He stopped in midstride to gaze down at her toes. "Well, so you are."

Stooping, he wrapped his arms about her knees like a pirate gathering booty and hoisted her high over his shoulder. Kelly was vaguely aware of the photographs sailing away into the night, for she promptly snapped in the middle and jackknifed over his shoulder.

One shoe slipped from her fingers while the heel of another gouged painfully into her stomach. "Ethan! You barbarian, put me down!"

"Shh, you'll wake the dead." He lightly slapped her rump. "And stop wiggling."

To Kelly's dismay as she struggled to drag the shoe from between them, the clasp of her belt worked free.

The chain spilled in a gold-plated puddle upon the ground. "I'm coming apart!" she railed. "Ethan! *Ethan!* Listen to me, Ethan—"

"I can hardly keep from doing that now, can I?"

A thousand times in the movies she had seen a man thrown over a saddle. It was definitely not what it appeared to be. His jacket was now wadded half beneath her, and her blouse had pulled free. Her ribs were about to crack, perhaps already had, and her skirt was twisted about her waist. Her rear, protected only by panty hose, was disgracefully exposed to the stars and the planets and to whatever extraterrestrials Steven Spielberg and George Lucas had not put on their payrolls.

"I'm going to kill you, Ethan," she promised between gritted teeth. "Very, very dead."

He laughed. "I look forward to it."

Moments later he was dropping her onto a slab of outcropping stone that thrust out of the hillside like a snaggletooth. Its surface was still warm from the day, and if the sun had been shining, Kelly guessed they would have been able to see Pierce Creek.

Maddeningly intact, she found herself sliding the length of Ethan's frame until her toes came to rest on the tops of his boots and she could feel his heart beating in a strong, powerful tide.

When she caught a breath, it was as if he took the breath for her.

"Remind me never to do that again," he said, teasing her with his words but not his eyes. "I think I've injured myself."

"That brings me no end of satisfaction. I'll probably have to have my ribs x-rayed now."

Their sporting, old as time itself, was not something either of them did in ignorance. It was a necessary ritual. They looked deep into the eyes of the other, knew exactly why it was and where it could lead.

Yet it seemed obligatory that their words exist on a level other than what was happening.

"Then kisses will make it all better," he mused, and watched the way her blouse had twisted free of its buttons, the way her lips were parted and her hands were groping for his jacket that was slipping off her shoulders.

"In case you haven't noticed, Ethan," she said, a willing victim of his magnetism, "the era of the caveman is past."

He moistened his lips, still devouring her. "The good old days, all right."

The night was large, and their breaths were rough with emotion. Even the pretense of words was unacceptable now. It was a perfectly logical situation, yet logic had little to do with it.

He wants you, a voice said in Kelly's head. *And you want him. By letting him know, by loving him now, you will exorcise all the demons that haunt you.*

Yet she couldn't bear for him to know how easily she could be taken. She turned her back, and he fit himself to her hips and crossed his hands over her waist.

His lips skimmed her nape beneath the swirling hair. Kelly let her head loll back on his shoulder, offering him more.

"Would you believe it if I said I didn't think I could want a woman this much?" he muttered.

"I'll believe anything you tell me."

His fingers found the last button of her blouse that kept her intact, and it yielded without a struggle. He located the tiny clasp that secured her bra, and it, too, snapped free.

She gazed down at her own breasts gleaming in the pale, silvery moonlight. Turning, she welcomed his bending head, his mouth closing upon the place where all her sensitivities were collected.

For Ethan, the night had suddenly lost its perimeters. He wanted to get down on his knees and thank heaven for sending this woman to him. She had risked much by going this far, and he could feel her desire waging a small war with her inexperience.

If he were an honorable man, he thought, he would ask her to marry him first—the old-fashioned way for an amazingly old-fashioned woman.

But he wasn't that sure of his future. Or his honor. So, as kisses kept them connected, he drew her down to the slab of stone, where she lay back and her hair spilled like a part of the moon fallen to earth. Kneeling, he leaned back on his heels and worshipped her with his eyes.

She was not at ease enough with herself to enjoy being adored so thoroughly. She covered her breasts until he lay down beside her and folded her in his arms.

"What are you thinking?" he asked as he pressed a kiss to her cheek.

She drew his hand to her breast. "I can't think, Ethan. Be glad that I can't think."

What man since Adam had ever been offered a gift so sweet? Her skin was as smooth as cream, and his finesse suddenly ceased to exist. It was easy, he thought vaguely, for a man to possess a sexual technique when it was separate from love, but when a man met his own future in human flesh, he was suddenly as vulnerable as a newborn.

The moonlight had turned her to silver. His hands were shaking as he traced the arch of her brows and her lips.

"This is all backward," he said gruffly as he took her hand and drew it low to the aching part of himself.

"Life is backward," she said. "At least we have it."

Did they?

The kiss between them blurred into another kiss, then another and another, each more urgent and hungry than the first. She moved beneath him and, turning, attempted to help him with her unschooled hands.

Her blouse tore with a rash rending that made him want to beg her pardon, but she was struggling with his zipper. The only poetry left was the hunger that drove them.

Such heat, however, could not long sustain itself. From his consuming lust, Ethan tried to fix in his memory the scent of her so it would be with him always. Already he missed her, and the fear of losing what he'd come this far to find propelled him blindly forward. He feared bruising her against the stone, yet she appeared oblivious.

He pressed his lips against her ear and whispered things that he was certain he would never remember. He found the silky promise of passion between her legs. Yet, as beyond hope as he was, he couldn't place the future at risk, not their future.

Fancy Auletta and her mothering, he thought grimly as he managed to find the tiny packet in his pocket that had such a bad reputation for shattering romance.

"Yes," she said, understanding. "Yes."

She took him in her hands then, guiding him. He hardly moved at all when he entered her, for the tightness was incredible. Then he knew only the insistent forgiveness of her palms on the backs of his hips, pressing him to the reckoning that had been too long denied.

"When I saw this happening in my mind," he grated against her cheek, "it wasn't like this."

It was as if he were made of glass, then—shattering into a million pieces. He was on the wrong side of his own skin. He thought he told her he loved her, but surely that part was a delusion. Though it was true, it wasn't very smart, and he was, above all, an intelligent man.

Afterward, after the blinding, wrenching spasms, when he could speak again, he rolled to his back and gathered her repentantly into his arms.

"Whatever you do, darling girl," he pleaded, "don't be sorry for this."

She was curled into his side, her head tucked trustingly beneath his chin. Her words, when they finally came, did not blame him but were puzzlingly happy.

"I've waited all my life for this, Ethan," she said with mystifying conviction. "I would never be sorry."

As usual, she was wrong. Later, when Kelly was alone in her dark bed and Ethan was a blurring memory left at Mendino's where a lone pickup was waiting for him, she tried to understand what had happened far out in the hills of Montgomery County.

At the moment, when he was kissing her, her love had come from out of nowhere and had been very real. But now it was a mist. She couldn't grab hold of it.

Inside, she was tender and sore. She could touch her body, knowing Ethan had been there, and here. His mouth had been here, and his scent was everywhere. That was the sadness of it, wasn't it, that she would always want him more than he would want her?

The release that had not happened for her when she was with Ethan, was so near the surface that it came as she was soaping herself in the shower.

It was then that she leaned her head against the tile and wept. She had never felt more alone.

Chapter 8

Kelly's habit was to try to reach the kitchen before her mother.

Usually it wasn't hard to do. By the time Caroline floated down the stairs, tall and "Deborah-Kerrish" in one of her filmy, daffodil-colored robes, Kelly had usually tidied the place, fed the cats, Prissy and Mott, read enough of the *Tribune* to be thoroughly intimidated for the day and—most important of all—brewed coffee.

Caroline was a wonderful mother and a remarkable homemaker. She was, or had been, a wonderful hostess and a gracious gentlewoman who could take a plain pear, a glass plate and a linen napkin and create a ceremony worthy of the president and first lady. With a sewing machine and a few yards of chintz, she could decorate a room that vied with those featured in *Southern Living*.

But her coffee was undrinkable. No one had the courage to tell her. So Kelly generally crept down the stairs at the crack of dawn to brew it.

The old house, usually her friend, was different today. Its timbers sighed and creaked around her, threatening to close in like the walls of some crazed director's macabre movie set. She would be trapped forever with thoughts that spun round and round like an old worn-out 78 record: *Now what? Now what? Now what?*

It wasn't the soreness, though she was, inside and out. Though their physical acts had been pretty straightforward, Ethan had nonetheless opened doors that she hadn't looked into for a long time. What disturbed her was that he had created in her a hunger for more, much more.

The rustle of Caroline's gown brought Kelly's head up.

"It's not that you're nearly thirty years old, darling," Caroline said cheerfully as sunshine glided into the room in her wake. "It's your biological clock. It just keeps ticking away. Can't you hear it? I can. Listen."

"Goodness, Mother!" Kelly wondered if she were giving off signals. "What brought all that on?"

As eloquently as a poem, Caroline plucked the unopened tin of coffee from Kelly's hands.

"That was *my* question, dear," she said with a pretty laugh. "I finally had to go to bed, but I fully expected you to knock on my door when you came home and say that Hite had proposed."

The thought of Hite down on one knee prompted Kelly to join her mother's merriment, but she saw to her dismay that Caroline was lethally spooning coffee into the machine and plugging it in.

"Debbie dropped by with the boys," her mother added, "and we watched an Audrey Hepburn movie. All the way through, right up to the part where she said, 'I love you, Tom, Harry...' whatever. You still hadn't come home, so after they left I watched Robert Redford and *The Electric Horse* by myself."

"*The Electric Horseman,* Mother."

"When you weren't home by midnight, I went to bed. You know, dear, Audrey Hepburn always held out for marriage. Old-fashioned ways are still the best."

Rolling her eyes, Kelly could not believe Caroline's exquisite timing. "Mother, I can't think of a single word to say."

"Then come sit down and eat your breakfast, dear."

Kelly watched, fascinated, as Caroline laid out old-fashioned Desert Rose cups and saucers on the place mats. With a grace that was as much a part of her as breathing, she laid out crisp, ironed napkins and placed a sterling-silver spoon into the sugar bowl with a musical *clink*. She poured fresh cream into the pitcher.

With a guilty smile, Kelly pulled out a chair whose cushion had been lovingly covered with a pink-and-green plaid.

A rivulet of coffee streamed from the decanter into her cup as Caroline poured, and Kelly studied the brew with deep suspicion.

"As it worked out," she said as Caroline moved to the refrigerator and brought a wire basket of eggs, "Hite and I didn't have dinner, after all."

"Really?"

Kelly spooned a healthy disguise of cream and sugar into the coffee. Stirring, she lifted the cup to her lips and stifled a shudder.

"Actually," she said quickly, "Ethan Chase and I drove out to the Pierce Creek landfill. I don't suppose you remember Ethan Chase."

Caroline had fetched her mixing bowl and was removing the whisk from a drawer. A tense beat of time passed, and she struck an egg on the rim and spilled its contents.

"Max and Georgia's son?" she asked on a thin spindle of breath.

Kelly focused hard on her cup. "Yes."

"The one who played football?" Caroline cracked another egg. *Crack, crack, splat.*

"The quarterback, yes."

"I thought he moved away."

"He came back."

Caroline's voice was astonishingly hard. "Your father would be alive today if it weren't for Georgia Chase."

"What?" Kelly twisted round, shocked.

"It's true."

"But I don't see—"

Crack, crack, splat. "Of course you don't. You were a child. Children never see."

Desperate now to end the unfortunate track of the conversation, Kelly rose. "It doesn't matter. Just forget I said anything." The grandfather clock chimed from the hallway. "Goodness, would you look at the time! I'm going to be late, and Leah will be mumbling those remarks of hers."

Another egg splattered into the bowl, and Kelly watched as Caroline blinked down in confoundment at a dozen broken eggs.

"Oh, Mother," she whispered, and went to the older woman, "how insensitive I am. A real putz. Come, sit down and have some coffee. It's...delicious! We'll start over from the Audrey Hepburn movie. What does it matter if I am late? I've been wanting a good excuse to fire Leah, anyway. Except that I never fired anyone in my life and would probably end up giving her my car or something."

Caroline didn't rise to the bait of Kelly's feeble humor. She allowed herself to be led to the table, where she took a chair and sat with her beautiful hands clasped over her mouth, rocking slightly with disbelief.

Having come to the inevitable point where the parent becomes the child and the child the parent, Kelly stared at her mother's back.

"Are you going to be all right?" she said.

Caroline didn't look up. "You won't be seeing him again, will you, Kelly?"

Mother, don't do this to me. Can't you see I'm different today, that I'm searching for my own life, that I'm full with the needs of womankind?

But she said, "I don't understand why you're so upset, Mother."

"Georgia Chase ruined our lives."

"How can you say that? Daddy had his chance. He took his best shot. He could've published a paper like the *Tribune* if he'd wanted to, and he could have made the money. But he chose another way, and as it happens, a more noble way. We mustn't forget the proud ideals he had."

With a flash of fury like none Kelly had ever seen in her mother, Caroline jerked around, her lovely features contorted—hard, bitter, unforgiving. She lunged from her chair, striking the dishes in her haste so they crashed to the floor.

Kelly gaped at the mess. "My God!"

"I wouldn't make your father out to be too much of a hero, my dear," Caroline intoned, and waved Kelly back from the shattered glass with a harsh sweep of her hand.

Kelly felt as if she would lose her balance. She didn't recognize the woman whose moves were hard and virulent. "What're you trying to say? Mother, answer me!"

Blinking as if she had awakened from a hypnotic trance and had been told she'd swung from a tree, Caroline touched her lips. She considered the eggs and the broken glass and sighed heavily.

"Pay no mind to me, dear," she said woodenly, as if the life had drained out of her the moment it had surfaced. "It's the rambling of an old woman, nothing more. Goodness, what came over me? The next thing you know, you'll be having to put me in one of those terrible homes where everything smells of cooked cabbage."

But Kelly couldn't whisk the words away as easily as Caroline was sweeping up the broken glass. Her memory banks were calling up all kinds of cross-references, primarily the one that Ethan had kept pussyfooting around the evening before.

There *was* a connection between her father and Georgia Chase! And not just one of competition. It was something more, something . . . ominous, sinister.

She hesitated to leave with things so upset. The sunshine seemed to have disappeared, leaving the kitchen drab and faded. Caroline glanced up from where she knelt with her dustpan, her robe a pool of yellow on the floor.

Kelly was reminded of the first time she'd seen Ethan, down on his hands and knees collecting broken glass. That was an eternity ago. She was not the same woman who had walked into the police station with eight thousand dollars.

"Never forget that your father loved you very much," Caroline said.

Kelly had never known that Vincent's love was in question.

My father was my dearest friend in all the world, she'd told Ethan.

For sending you to live with your aunt in Virginia? he'd said.

"Why do you say that?" she asked.

Caroline did not answer, and Kelly was struck by a horrible thought. Surely Vincent and Georgia had not been lovers? Surely her father had not sent her to live with Aunt Eunice for his own self-interest? Good Lord, what shoddy little secrets was Caroline sitting on?

"Good morning, Montgomery," Lisa James said from her broadcasting booth at WACV radio. "Investigative journalist for the *Daily Mirror*, Fred Woodson, reports in today's issue that in a series of highly charged, closed-door meetings with city officials, Albert Russo has been answering questions about toxic-waste dumping.

"Woodson told WACV that pressure has been mounting because of the aggressive editorials that have appeared in the *Mirror* regarding the Pierce Creek landfill, which is owned by Southeast Medical Group, the conglomerate that built Montgomery's newest hospital.

"When asked by WACV if the city had any plans to investigate the safety of the dump site now called into question, Mayor Georgia Chase said that no investigations were scheduled.

"'The *Mirror* is engaging in sensationalism,' the mayor claimed at a press conference this past evening. 'The paper has taken a decided downhill slide since the death of its previous publisher, Vincent Madison, and this attack upon Southeast Medical is a tactic by Madison's daughter to recoup the *Mirror*'s losses. There's no excuse for going after a person with the credentials of Mr. Russo, especially not in the light of what the medical group has meant to our city.'

"Russo denied to WACV that waste materials placed in the Pierce Creek landfill posed a health hazard for residents. 'That is a trumped-up charge concocted by Ms. Madison to keep the *Mirror* out of bankruptcy,' he said."

The *Great White* was a thirty-two-foot sloop that Ethan had found in dry dock on the Coosa River the day after he moved to Montgomery from Jackson, Mississippi.

He'd bought the boat cheap, then he'd proceeded to pour the royalties of the last three Price Masters novels into restoring it. It was anchored on the Alabama River, northwest of the city, and it was in vintage condition, the teak varnished, the brass gleaming.

Coming home to port at the end of each day had been what sustained him in a job that he was growing more and more disenchanted with. The *Great White* was his inner sanctum. No one had ever been there, not even John and Fancy. Here he could unstrap his gun and stop being a policeman. He could sit down to his word processor and become, if not the editor-in-chief he was meant to be, the author of the current sludge-in-the-making, *Treachery on a Pillow*. Then he could sleep.

Rather, up to now he'd been able to sleep. Now he was aware of Kelly when he slept. He dreamed about her, but it was as if he were dreaming that he would sleep and *knew* he would dream about her. He had no recollection of waking with her on his mind, but there she was—when he lay down and when he got up.

He wasn't particularly proud of himself for leaving Kelly on Mendino's parking lot. Surprisingly they had not kissed goodbye. They had wrapped their arms about each other and simply held on for a long time without speaking.

On his way to work the next morning, Ethan heard Lisa James's broadcast. The minute he reached his desk, he called his father at the *Tribune*.

"Oh, I heard all about that remark on Lisa James's show this morning," Maxwell said after Ethan got around to inquiring exactly how well Georgia knew Albert Russo. "Of course your mother's had dealings with Russo. You aren't inferring that something unethical is actually going on?"

"I'm not inferring anything, Dad, I merely asked a simple question."

"There's nothing simple about that question, son."

Ethan mumbled something about not meaning to upset him, and Maxwell mumbled something about Georgia not being appreciated enough by her constituency.

Maxwell finished up by saying that Georgia, with all her faults and overbearing ways, was not a stupid woman. There was too much current flak about political ethics for Georgia to risk even the faintest smell of scandal.

"I'm not saying Mother did or didn't do anything, Dad." Ethan fished a cigar out of his pocket and sat inhaling it. "The question has been raised, however."

"Gossip always turns to mud during a political campaign."

"It doesn't hurt to second-guess the mudslingers, Dad."

"Well, I'm sure your mother can prove her integrity if she needs to."

"I'm sure she can."

"Come on, Ethan, you don't really want me to spy on your own mother, do you?"

"No one said anything about spying."

"Oh, all right, I'll keep my eyes and ears open, but you're wrong, I tell you. Now, how is everything with you? We don't see enough of you since you came back."

Ethan wished he could tell his father about Kelly. *Look, world, I'm in love!*

"I'll see you soon, Dad," he said, and flicked his lighter and puffed briefly on the cigar. "I promise."

"Sure, see you soon."

Pinching the top of his nose, Ethan immediately dialed the *Mirror.*

"She's not here," someone named Leah Blankenship said. "May I take a message?"

Disappointed, Ethan glanced at Fisher, who was tapping the crystal of his wristwatch in a reminder they were late. "Just tell her that Ethan called."

"Ethan Somebody called," Leah told Kelly as she was plodding through the revolving door.

Kelly's surprise pulled her up short, and she wondered if she hadn't, deep in her heart, been dreading that she would never hear from him again, that everything that had gone before had been a preparation for the worse pain of losing Ethan before she really ever got him.

"Thank you, Leah," Kelly said, and smiled brightly at the disgruntled woman whose inevitable Price Masters novel had been laid open and facedown on her desk.

"He didn't give his last name," she called as Kelly crossed the newsroom.

Kelly's smile broadened to include Ann Jacobs and Fred Woodson, who looked suspiciously up from their clicking keyboards. "That's all right, Leah."

Managing to appear calm and unhurried, Kelly reached her office and lunged for the telephone. Her briefcase dropped to the floor, and she kneed her chair from the desk as she dialed.

Her heart was a thresher as she waited to hear his voice, and she actually heard herself humming and tapping her toe. This was the perfect day to do something special. She would go shopping. She would get her hair cut in a short, professional-looking style.

"He's out," the dispatcher came back on the line to say. "Is it an emergency?"

Her descent to earth was like bailing out without a parachute. She was once again plain Kelly Madison, the proprietress of a dying newspaper.

"Just tell him that Miss Madison returned his call," she said with a sigh.

By the time Ethan checked in from where he and Fisher had gotten tied up with a jumper on Highland Avenue, he was running very late. The *Mirror*'s front desk was no longer answering the phone.

"She's not here," her mother said when he called her house. "Who is this?"

Certain that Caroline Madison knew exactly who he was, he politely replied, "It's Ethan Chase, Mrs. Madison. My mother—"

"I know who your mother is, Mr. Chase. Kelly's still in town, working late, I assume. I can give you the number there."

Ethan had a brief hallucination of the woman being able to see through the telephone and know what he and Kelly had done.

But I love her, he wanted to explain. *If Kelly doesn't love me now, she'll come to. I want us to have a life together. I'll be good to her. I'll take care of her.*

To which she would think, of course, *Sexist! You think she can't take care of herself?*

"Thanks," he said guardedly. "I have the number."

"Good day, Mr. Chase." *Click.*

Ethan felt as if his hands had been rapped sharply with a ruler. He changed into some clothes he kept in his truck and drove across town to pull onto the Redmond parking lot.

He ghosted along the outer fringe, where the antiquity of the Redmond Building was written in the great old maple trees arching overhead, their laced branches interwoven.

At the back door a light fixture was attached to the side of the building, in it an old-fashioned bulb with a tin reflector. Bugs circled and stunned themselves senseless, dropping to the concrete.

The lights of the offices were turned off. Around eleven o'clock, the printer would come in and work until 2:00 or 3:00 a.m. Then the bundles of papers would be placed at a collection site. Delivery people would pick them up and have them in the vending machines and stores by the time people were caffeinated enough to read them the next morning.

The fourth floor, however, was ablaze with light. As Ethan tipped his head to stare at the windows draped with cloths and sheets, he suddenly felt mislaid in the world. Who in the hell was he? Ethan Chase? Price Masters? Kelly Madison's lover? What was he doing here?

A Cindy's Pizza car zoomed onto the lot and screeched to a stop at the side door beneath the bug-infested light. The delivery boy barreled out, adjusting his paper cap to a jaunty angle and sauntered toward the door, where he raised his fist to bang.

"I'll take that," Ethan called out as he strolled toward him.

Spinning around, the youngster bristled with suspicion. He looked Ethan up and down with the arrogance only an eighteen-year-old was capable of.

"Who're you?"

"A friend of the lady who ordered that."

"Wal, I dunno," he hedged. "Gonna take it up? Miz Madison always tips me good." He shook his head. "I better take it up myself."

Grinning, Ethan handed over a five-dollar tip. The youth turned the bills to the light, then pocketed it. He returned to his car but did not leave immediately.

"Tap your horn a couple of times when you pull out," Ethan said.

"You better take it up, mister—" the boy leaned out his window "—or I'll lose my job. Don't you go eatin' it by yourself."

Ethan waved him on. "I take to stealing pizzas, junior, I'll lose *my* job. Now get outta here."

"You got it."

The horn bleeped twice as the car spun in a doughnut turn and blasted off the lot.

The aroma of pizza, having never appealed to Ethan, smelled less appetizing now. He wrinkled his nose.

"I suppose it's better than eating crow," he mumbled.

Balanced precariously on a stepladder at ten o'clock in the evening, whistling tunelessly between her teeth, Kelly dipped her roller into a tray of white paint.

In her mind's eye she could see how pretty the new apartment would be. She could smell the intimate dinners she would prepare for Ethan to be eaten by candlelight and music. He would sit in a chair slipcovered with a Laura Ashley print, and she would bring two glasses of wine and a dish of strawberries on a silver tray.

"You never know when to quit," she warned herself, and stretched as far as the ladder and her aching muscles would allow. "You get a taste, then go all greedy and grasping. That's your problem, Kelly Jean Madison. Greed."

She spread paint onto the last section of wall. Spying a place she had missed on the opposite wall, she climbed down, dipped a brush, repaired the flaw and rotated for a panoramic view of the place whose walls were as white as a bride's wedding cake.

Thanks to Sherwin-Williams, who was now in possession of a huge check for paint plus all the extras—vinyl drop cloths, rollers and pans and handle extensions, two nylon brushes guaranteed to take the work out of painting.

After a tedious afternoon meeting with the staff on strategies to save the paper, which had produced little that was helpful, she had become embroiled with digging through her father's papers that were stored on the third floor. She riffled through old correspondence and memos that spilled over the brim of the claw-footed bathtub that had been brought over from the house when it had been remodeled.

Wading through the third floor was like rummaging in a stranger's attic. None of it, however, indicated that Vincent had had any personal dealings with Georgia Chase, nothing to justify Ethan's ambiguities and her mother's strange venom.

With a sigh, she dropped down to rest on a rolled-up sleeping bag that she'd also found on the third floor.

She stretched her legs, long and paint spattered beneath her cutoff jeans. Wiping her brow with her forearm, she tied her front shirttails into a knot and tucked the tailing ends beneath the band of her bra.

She aimed a stream of air between her breasts. Paint was caked beneath her fingernails, hardly elegant enough for Andrei Gavrilov playing Rachmaninoff on her portable stereo.

She drew a red bandanna from her hair and shook out its damp length. "Now the fun part," she muttered, sighing. "Cleanup."

Below her, a horn honked twice, and she smiled, heaving up from the bedroll. "But first, a pizza orgy. I deserve it."

Still carrying her paintbrush, she opened the heavy metal door at the top of the stairs and skittered down the steps, which were cast deeply in shadow.

"I'm coming, I'm coming."

With her back, she pushed open the outer door and braced her sneakered foot to hold it as she fished in a pocket for several wadded dollar bills that Sherwin-Williams hadn't taken.

"If you'd been any later," she told the deliveryman over her shoulder as she counted out the money, "I would've starved to death."

"Not very likely," Ethan drawled as he stepped into the circle of light and took the strength of the door so that she stumbled out onto the parking lot. "They say the human body can go seventeen days without food. I haven't tested the theory, myself, of course, but Gandhi did. You aren't really going to *eat* this stuff, are you?"

Chapter 9

Tradition was clear in the matter. A person falling in love, when gazing upon the object of their affection, was supposed to hear the deafening rush of a locomotive, the clang of a joyous bell, shooting rockets and, on occasion, an odd calliope shrill or two.

The person was then supposed to go hot and cold all over and revert to preverbal skills involving a lot of stammering and "oh-yessing" and "dear-dearing." This was the way it had always been, and this was the way it was supposed to be.

When Kelly peered up at Ethan, who was balancing her pizza high over his head like a maître d's tray, she felt none of these things. What she did feel was a deep sense of rightness, a sense of dissonance resolving to its place of rest, a warmth, a settling.

Neither of them smiled. With an odd sense of motionlessness they looked at each other. They looked and looked.

His snow-white deck shoes and loose, pleated cotton pants were in marked contrast to his usual Western boots and a Stetson, she thought. His T-shirt hugged the spare flesh covering his ribs, and a frivolous black curl had crept over the ribbing of the neck. Right or wrong, there would never be a man for her but him.

Smiling, she said, "Don't you believe in calling first?"

The lines fanning his eyes crinkled. "Don't you believe in saying hello?"

"Hello, Ethan."

"Hello, Kelly."

Kelly walked a few feet beyond the building and turned full circle. "What happened to the pizza man?"

He was still holding the door. "The pizza man? I'm afraid I had to shoot him. But it was a clean kill. He didn't suffer."

"How very noble of you, Ethan." As she entered and motioned for him to follow her up the stairs, she added, "I suppose now you're going to want half my pizza."

"I'm living on love these days, thanks."

Did she hear the faint clang of a bell?

Turning on the step, she crooked a finger through his belt loop and gave his pants a jiggle. "You'll forgive me for saying so, but you look a little undernourished, Lieutenant."

"Well . . ." His smile slid to one side of his face. "I admit to being in a bit of a slump lately. But things are looking up. I met this really weird lady."

The small space, Kelly found, laughing, was suddenly much too warm. Turning, she stumbled on the step. "Dear, dear."

He collided gently with her back. "I have this effect on people," he said more gruffly. "Some genetic trait, no doubt."

"Passed down from generation to generation."

"Our children will be cursed with it."

It was a deadly game they were playing, Kelly thought, and she wanted to look back and see his face. She wanted to tell him that she had thought about him all day, and what they had done. How could she let Ethan know she had no intentions of sending him a bill for one, unplanned night?

She held her paintbrush with both hands like a bridal bouquet. "You don't waste any time, do you, Lieutenant Chase?"

He leaned nearer her ear until his breath was warm on the side of her cheek. "Not when you've got a case of it as bad as mine. A terrible condition. People have to repeat everything, and you keep losing track of time. You can't sleep, you don't make sense when you talk. But I guess you wouldn't know about any of that, would you?"

Kelly had already put the name "love" to her own feelings, but she could not do the same to his. It was too dangerous to even believe that he meant half of what he was saying.

"You regret it," he said with a sudden hardness.

"No." He had misread her hesitation, and she sought his eyes. "I told you last night—"

His look offered no quarter. "Daylight changes things."

Kelly drew her breath sharply. He was searching for a way out! He didn't have the courage to tell her that *he* regretted it!

She reached for the box of pizza, which he promptly held out of reach. "Yes," she said tersely, taking refuge in a feigned pique. "It makes you hungry."

The pause was a ticking array of disappointments.

He offered her an unpleasant grin. "Then I suggest you get your little fanny up the stairs."

Kelly couldn't skitter up the stairs quickly enough. And she was certain, as she hurried, that he was indulging a lewd excursion up the sawed-off legs of her jeans.

"You can stop doing that, too!" she snapped.

"Doing what?"

"You know perfectly well."

His chuckle was well suited to their sniping mode. "Kelly, you shut the door on a man before he can poke his foot inside."

"It's not your foot I worry about."

With the curve of her right hip, she leaned her weight against the door at the top of the stairs and fell into the room just as Gavrilov was reaching the final crescendo of the Rachmaninoff prelude.

"You'll have to excuse me—" she raised her voice over the rippling arpeggios, glad for the chance to collect her scattered wits "—I was in the process of cleaning my brush. Once it gets hard, it's a devil to mess with."

The door slammed shut behind them.

He looked briefly around. "It happens."

Kelly squinted at him through a fringe of lashes. "I don't have any soap up here to wash out your mouth, Lieutenant, but we can always use paint thinner."

She marched across the drop cloths that were spread from wall to wall. She lowered the volume of the stereo.

Amused, he placed the pizza on an unopened can of paint and strolled the length of the place. He was interested in the scaffold that she'd paid Jerome six dollars an hour to help her erect so she could reach the skylights. He also admired the old-fashioned arched windows that were now draped with sheets.

"Nice," he said.

Of course he would find it nice. She could imagine the boat he'd said he lived on. It was probably some dry-docked relic that would sink the minute it was put on the water.

"You have a real way with words, Ethan," she said, and pried open the box of pizza to remove a wedge.

Catching his eye, she offered him some. When he declined, she stuffed her mouth full while he ambled over to read the label of her CD. She licked sauce from her fingers and gathered up her paint tray and roller and brush.

Chewing, she took them to the water spigot and, stooping, carefully filled the tray with cold water and swished the brush.

"You'd prefer Tom T. Hall or George Jones, I suppose," she said over her shoulder.

"Rachmaninoff in small doses is bearable."

He brought the pizza box as he came to stoop beside her. His legs formed in a powerful wedge, his weight poised forward on the balls of his feet and his face on a level with hers.

"I've always loved pizza," she said with lessening confidence, and selected another piece.

"I've always hated pizza."

"Then I'm afraid I couldn't possible marry you." Appalled by the words she'd just blurted, Kelly wolfed down the pizza.

"Hmm. In that case..." Grinning, he made a theatric gesture out of deciding on a piece and bit into it. "Yum, yum." He rolled his eyes. "Don't you just adore pizza?"

Easy, Kelly. Be cool. Play this straight as can be. Joking about marriage isn't getting the blood test.

"Idiot."

She rose and walked quickly to the center of the room, swinging out her hand in a grand arc.

"This is where I'm going to live after I stop publishing the *Mirror,*" she said. "And before you say anything, I know it's a bad investment. But it's all I have left of my father. I wouldn't get much for it on the market, anyway. Not in this neighborhood."

She pivoted in a slow circle, inspecting the walls and trying to retrieve her earlier enthusiasm. "Yep," she said, more for herself than him, "this is it."

He walked closer. "It's a big undertaking."

"For a woman?"

"For anyone."

He was inviting her into his eyes with their crystals of blue, and Kelly had the sinking sensation that they were merely picking up where they had left off the night before.

She struggled for a fresh sense of balance but found none. "I just play it day by day, Ethan."

Sighing, she nervously untied the knot of her shirttails and ludicrously attempted to smooth the creases.

"It needs an expertise I don't have," she admitted, and continued to convulsively tug at the fabric.

"But you're doing it."

"Not for much longer. The *Tribune* is burying me, you know. Your father's making me look like a fool on this Russo thing."

"Then do something about it."

The music had stopped, and the silence underscored the raw bluntness of his remark.

She fashioned a sarcastic smile. "I don't suppose you have some pearls of wisdom you'd be willing to cast before the feet of swine, do you?"

"I might." With his tongue, he searched for a piece of food caught between his teeth. "If I could find a pig."

They laughed until Ethan, unable to bear the loveliness of light glancing off Kelly's cheek or the unspeakable sexiness of the golden curve of her throat, wanted to catch her up in his arms and never let her go. He wanted to lay his head on her breast and tell her that he hadn't been able to think of anything except her, that he admired her marvelous fighting spirit even when she was certain she could not win, that he already was in much deeper than he'd thought he would ever go.

An urgency like that of his youth began in the hollows behind his knees. By the time it reached his brain, he was clenching his fists.

"If you want to save the *Mirror,* Kelly," he said with an effort to keep from sounding like a fool, "there's a way."

Her lifted brows were their own question.

He said, "First of all, you have to learn what news is."

For a moment she considered his words. Then she marched to the pizza box and closed it. Baffled, she gaped at him over her shoulder.

"I know what news is, Ethan. What in the world do you think we're publishing? Yellow Pages?"

"You're *reporting,* sweetheart. That's all. Say, are you through with these drop cloths? Want me to pick 'em up?"

Distracted, she glanced around and said, yes, they should be gathered. When he began moving through the place, arranging them into the semblance of folds and stacking them into a heap, she trudged along behind him.

"That's what papers do, Ethan," she argued grittily. "They report."

Ethan doggedly kept gathering drop cloths. "Reporting is not the same as publishing news."

"Is that so?" She was stomping now, belligerent as a child. "Then, suppose you tell me how to publish news."

Dropping the armload of vinyl, Ethan faced her with his fists on his sides, waiting for the green flash of her eyes.

"News, my dear," he said as if instructing a slow-witted student, "is a story that dominates the media for weeks, sometimes months. A news story doesn't end with the telling of it, Kelly. It gains momentum with each passing day. The more it's written about, the more it grows."

Bridling, she cocked her head at an oh-well-of-course angle. "Is this one of those pearls of wisdom, Ethan?"

"Success in the publishing business doesn't depend on skill or even on quality. It hinges on public reaction. Until there's public reaction, a story is just a story—a report, an airplane trying to get off the ground on a too-short runway. It can't, because it can't work up any speed."

"I don't understand."

Gone was her facade, Ethan saw. Her eyes were snapping now, wanting to see everything, to greedily absorb it all and turn it to her advantage. Every inch of the lean, trim length of her was poised for action. God, what he would not give to feel such passion again!

"Okay," he said, and walked closer, gesturing expansively with his hands, "take Watergate."

"If I had Watergate," she countered crisply, "my troubles would be over."

"When the *Post* first reported Watergate, though, it was a story. It wasn't major news. Then Walter Cronkite used it on the CBS evening news. It got prime public exposure. It began to gather speed. People reacted. Watergate was growing into a major news item. After Judge Sirica got on the bandwagon, it took off."

The impossibility of her predicament registered, and a cloud passed over her face.

"Yes, well." She nodded slowly as her thoughts clicked. "It isn't very likely that Tom Brokaw will address the toxic-waste dump of Southeast Medical on the network news, is it?"

With a sigh of defeat, she kicked the pile of drop cloths. The hardwood floor was now readily visible. Once it was finished, it would be splendid beneath her white walls and skylights and arched windows.

Not knowing exactly how to give birth to the embryo of his idea, Ethan strode to the water spigot, placed his mouth against it and drank.

She came to stand beside him. When he was finished, she also drank and blotted her mouth with her arm with such a lack of finesse, he kissed a droplet from her cheek.

"You're right," he said, and drew a fallen lock of hair from her eyes, anchoring it behind her ear. "You don't have Watergate."

Nibbling the inside of her cheek, she studied him skeptically. "So, what do I do?"

"What you need is an influential and respected catalyst to get your story off the ground—somebody in the environmental field who carries real weight, someone who will take an interest in what's happening environmentally in Montgomery, Alabama."

"Ethan, who could possibly care about one rinky-dink landfill in Alabama?"

"No one, maybe. But a lot of important people might care about a principled young woman fighting the system."

Kelly could hear the ring of truth in Ethan's suggestion as she inched backward to one of the pillars supporting the room. Yet, as her imagination dealt with the magic of it, a part of her held back. Something wasn't ringing true here. Ethan was very much the expert now, which didn't truly surprise her since he came from a long line of newspaper people.

But experts didn't give away advice for free. And they certainly didn't try to implement the advice. Why was Ethan being so helpful?

"Sure," she said cautiously, "I'll call Ralph Nader tomorrow morning. If I can't get him, I'll just ring up Carl Sagan."

"You don't have to do that. I just happen to know someone. Rather, I know someone who knows someone."

Again he surprised her, and again part of her held back, more than before. "Where is this someone?"

"New York."

She stood scraping dried paint from behind her nails. "Ethan, why are you doing this? Have you ever even *been* to New York?"

"I go to New York all the time."

Looking up, she studied the lines of Ethan's face. Each one, it seemed to her, was a mark of experience, many of them best left forgotten. He had been around a lot; he had lived a lot. There were many things about this man she did not know.

It struck her, then, the reason why he was telling her this. By helping the *Mirror* stay alive, perhaps even become a small success, he would be evening an old score with Georgia that Irwin Pritchard had told her about at Mendino's. Her situation was made to order for Ethan's revenge!

Sadness closed about her heart like a fist. She slumped weakly against the pillar at her back. She wished he had never said anything. She wished he'd never told her about his connections in New York. If she had any pride, she would turn her back and never look at him again.

But where would that get her? Besides, if he were using her, why should she not use him back? That way, he would get what he wanted, and she would get him. For a little while, at least. That's what love did best, wasn't it? Use until there was nothing left?

"All right," she said as she grimly began to circle him. "I'll go along with that for now, Ethan, but I have to tell you—it's been my experience that nothing ever comes for free. If you do this for me, connect me to your connections, what do you expect me to do for you in return?"

With a tread as light and graceful as a burglar, he rotated, following the path of her orbit. She stopped. He stopped. Kelly shivered as if he had heard the dull thud of her suspicions.

"Why do you do that?" he asked, frowning.

The bottom dropped from Kelly's stomach. "Do what?"

"Believe the worst of people?"

"I—"

"Or do you only believe the worst of me?"

Stung, the heat of being unfairly accused clotting her words, she whirled away, her sneakers scuffing their frustration and anger.

"You really take the cake, Ethan, do you know that? For a smart man, you're really stupid. You're the one who can't believe in anything. Tell me what it would take to get *your* trust. The sky's the limit. Tell me, damn it! And don't stand there looking at me like that!"

As she turned, expecting him to be halfway across the room, she gasped to find herself literally swept off her feet. He was holding her so tightly, she could not breathe. She was clinging desperately to his shoulders as his kisses consumed her, and she lay back in his arms, her head that of a rag doll and her body at the mercy of his.

"Say this isn't just some passing thing," he demanded in a passion-clotted voice as he pressed his lips to her breast. "You never say anything about tomorrow, Kelly. I don't know where I am with you."

But she couldn't address tomorrow because tomorrows were never between just two people. Her family, his family—both had to be considered, and she couldn't find the words. He was backing her to the pillar behind them, lifting her up and trapping her between ceiling and floor—pinned like a butterfly to a master's board.

"Ethan, listen to me . . ."

His teeth closed with sweet pain upon the lobe of her ear. His breath, roughened and hot, affected her like a drug.

"Belong to me, Kelly," he groaned. "Be mine. Tell me. Promise me. Commit to me."

What woman had never been distracted from reality by a man's desire? Was she to blame because she forgot, for one lost moment, the direction their paths would take into the future? Was she wrong in overlooking his faults and her own starved need to be treasured?

It was so easy to imagine spending the rest of her life with him. Bearing his children. Giving, taking, sharing.

His hands were everywhere, demanding that she answer him. She slipped her own beneath the loose band of his pants until her palms were pressing the warm flesh, holding him hard against her, arching up to meet the surging rhythm of his hips.

He groaned his pleasure and draped her leg upon his side, her eyes closed as she climbed him and let him know that she wanted to be taken.

"What do you want?" he muttered thickly.

"Everything."

And though Ethan didn't want her this way, not for a few nights, a few months, a few years, he rose up into her like a steel spire, and they were no longer two but a single blend of humanity. In the fulcrum of their joining, in the center where he filled her, it was physical, but deeper, in the mute reaches of the soul, he had to wait for her to meet him.

Slowly, with great effort, she opened her eyes. They were connected in the most personal way two could be, yet there was so much more.

"Only once before did I ask a woman to take a chance on me," he whispered as the glaze of passion overpowered him. "What would it take for you to love me, Kelly? To see me at my worst and still want me?"

Impaled by him, Kelly sought for words, but her only reply was her acceptance of his steady, orbital thrusts. She placed her face into the hollow of his neck and could not prevent the release when he made it happen, or the shattering one that she fell into immediately afterward.

She gave herself over to him, to the way he seemed to know better than she, and when she took him into her own sheltering arms for that one moment of shattered, splintering time when he was at the mercy of himself, she still had not given him an answer.

Later, when the printing presses were grinding beneath them, Ethan smoked and Kelly lay curled against his side.

They were lying on the bedroll that had come in handy for something, after all.

She wore his T-shirt and he wore nothing at all. The warm April night was drifting through the windows he had opened. Sleep was creeping beneath her eyelids, but she could not rest, not yet. And she could not stay the night and alarm her mother.

"Kelly?" He was running a lazy fingertip down her side and up again.

"Mmm?"

"What does Hite think about your plans to live here?"

Kelly's eyes flew open, and she was instantly on guard against an unnamed danger.

"What do you mean—" she tried to sound casual "—what does Hite think?"

"He's in love with you. That leaves me in violation of a principle I've always held dear. I don't take something that belongs to someone else. I'm not doing that, am I?"

"Ethan, I don't love Hite. I mean, I love him, but . . ."

Smoke trailed slowly into the small atmosphere above their heads. "I didn't say you were in love with him—I asked how he fit into your future."

"He's my friend."

"He's my friend, too. But sometimes we do things for friends."

"Really?"

"Yes, like . . . marry them."

Sitting up, Kelly drew her knees to her chin and leaned her cheek upon them, grateful for her veil of hair. "I have no intentions of marrying Hite Pritchard."

He ground out his cigarette and laid his hand on the curve of her spine, shaping her bones with casual possessiveness.

"Then I have a responsibility," he said. "I'll tell him."

"About me?" she asked sharply, lifting her head.

"About us."

He drew her back into the wedge of his body and wrapped her in his arms and legs. The future was opening before Kelly, and when she peered inside, she saw pain for two families.

"You were married once," she said.

"A long time ago. It ended badly."

"What happened?"

"She took money and went away."

"I'm sorry."

He wanted the answer to his question, she knew. He wanted her to say she loved him. But she was walking on a fragile crust of quicksand.

She drew his arms tightly around her. "Ethan, what do you know about my father that I don't? Why was my mother so upset when she heard I'd been out with you?"

Price Masters, Ethan thought, would have had an elegant answer for such words. With unerring candor he would have said, *Look, angel, we were sold down the river long before we were old enough to know—me by my mother and you by your old man.*

But he was Ethan Chase, a flesh-and-blood man, and he closed his eyes. "I wish I'd never said a word about your father. It didn't occur to me then that you didn't know."

She stiffened. "Know *what?*"

Kissing the back of her head, Ethan rose and pulled on his pants. He sat down and reached for his socks.

"I'm not exactly sure when it happened," he told her, staring out at nothing. "If I had to guess, I would say it was a couple of years after your father started publishing the *Mirror.*" He searched for her eyes, found them and held. "This is only secondhand talk, Kelly. Understand that. I don't know anything firsthand."

She was hugging herself, her face chalky with dread. "Go on."

"What I understood from conversations between my mother and father was that Vincent was taking a hefty bite into the profits of the *Tribune*. It was sort of like a political race when neither candidate can claim a majority. It got to the point where both papers were pretty well at a standoff, profit wise. The *Tribune* was afraid to lose its white readership, so my mother played it safe. But your father... Vincent Madison wasn't afraid of anything. He refused to take a racial slant. He was doing really well."

"I knew it!" She sprang to her feet. "I knew Daddy was that good. I always knew!"

"He didn't pull out in front, Kelly."

"But he could have." She hesitated, nibbling apprehensively on her lip. "Why didn't he?"

"My mother made Vincent an offer he couldn't refuse."

Her disbelief came slowly. She opened her mouth to say something but took several steps away instead. Like a pup that cannot understand when its mother has fallen prey to the hunter's shot, she brought her hand up before her face. Slowly she moved her head back and forth. Slowly she inched backward, slowly, slowly.

Ethan knew he would pay a heavy price for speaking this truth. "Kelly—"

She tried to find words, but there were none.

"Hell, Kelly, they couldn't both win."

"But—"

"Vincent agreed to pull back to a decent second place. Damn it, he agreed to stop competing. There, you wanted to know, now you do. And I swear to heaven, I wish I weren't the one telling you this."

Deep in her heart, Kelly supposed that part of her had sensed the truth for years. Babyish memories of bitterness between her parents, perhaps. Whispering between her sisters at night. How many times had she walked into a room and felt the conversation stop? How many times had she seen disappointment in her mother's eyes when she looked at her husband?

So, all the time it was Vincent, not Caroline! It wasn't even that Vincent had compromised himself while she, Kelly, had worshiped him. She could have forgiven him that. But with Georgia Chase?

She sank to her knees on the floor as life came from out of the darkness and sank its teeth into her. She shook her head when he reached out a hand for her.

"I knew this would hurt you," he said.

She battled for breath to speak. "Ah, would you mind terribly if I asked you to leave now, Ethan?"

"Look, Kelly—"

"It's nothing to do with . . . you know what I mean. I mean, what I should do now, I think, is . . . I—I . . ."

Kelly had no idea that she knelt there, frozen in time, until some moments later when she looked up. "What was I saying?"

Despair stained Ethan's face. He wanted to hold her, but she couldn't bear being touched when she felt so tricked, so soiled by the past.

"I understand betrayal by a parent, Kelly," he was saying desperately. "It stinks, it really does. But I'm here for you. I'll wait as long as it takes. Then we can face our demons together. You didn't deserve to be deceived. I understand why Vincent kept it from you, but you didn't deserve it. When you're ready, I'd like to make it up to you."

Chapter 10

If Kelly had been a hell-raiser, her reaction to Vincent's sellout would have been simple. She would have headed in a straight line for Mendino's and ordered one tequila after another until her reflection in Quentin's mirror was a blur. She would have cried on Pat's shoulder a bit. She would have complained about how bitchy life was and how the world was going to the dogs. The next morning her hangover would have been so horrendous, even Vincent's treachery would have seemed mild in comparison.

Unfortunately she had never raised hell in her life. In a series of clumsy circumventions amid vague mumbling, she confessed to Caroline that she knew Vincent had made a deal with Georgia Chase. Afterward she sat very still at the kitchen table, her hands covering her mouth as she stared into space.

Knowing about her father wasn't the same as accepting. Even if the answers remained the same, the questions were different now. The future must be viewed through the filter of a different past. How did she feel? What would she do? How would her relationship with Ethan shift? She needed to think, think, work it out, work herself out.

Caroline brewed a pot of coffee and poured them both a cup.

"I had hoped, my darling," she said as she went through the motions of pouring, robotlike, "that you would never have to face this. I would give everything to spare you, but I can't. I wonder if you would excuse me for a minute, darling? I seem to have developed the most fearful sinusitis. Now, where did I put my antihistamine? No, don't get up, dear. Drink your coffee. I'll be right back."

Once in her room, Caroline quietly beat the air with her fists as tears flowed down her face. The bitter war she and Vincent had waged had outlived him.

"Oh, Kelly, my innocent angel," she wept, and shook her head. "I wasn't enough."

Later, when Kelly explained that she wanted to get away for a day or so and clear her head, Caroline offered Kelly use of her car because, she said, it was doubtful that Kelly's Ford could make the Alabama-Mississippi state line.

"Perhaps not even the Montgomery city limits," Caroline added in a clumsy attempt at lightness.

With misgivings for not telling Ethan she was leaving town, Kelly drew some of her precious inheritance dollars out of the bank—a notable irony, she thought, to use Vincent's money to recover from a wound he had inflicted.

Hardly packing anything except a toothbrush and a credit card, Kelly took Interstate 20 and drove west—no destination in mind, no purpose except to wear out her grief.

The weather was perfect. The sky was full of high, majestic clouds propped on shafts of sunlight. She turned on the radio but didn't really listen. When night came, she rented a motel and ate fruit and bread in her room. She slept fitfully, dreaming of kittens with razor-sharp claws.

The next day she made Meridian and Jackson, Mississippi, where James Meredith had made history at Old Miss. On to Vicksburg, where she turned off the interstate and drove along the Mississippi River.

Parking, she stood high above the muddy, hurling water that had fought its way down from Illinois and pushed inland through sluggish tributaries, staking its claims before it self-destructed in the Gulf of Mexico.

Barges were moving downstream in the dusk. Boats were hooting their mournful horns, waking ghosts and memories of Ulysses S. Grant.

She missed Ethan more than she'd expected. Surprisingly the long hours were spent thinking more about him than how she would deal with her father's legacy.

At Delta Point Restaurant, after staring for some moments at a lovely serving of salmon and creamed asparagus tips, she laid down her fork and asked the waiter for a telephone.

"Where the hell are you?" Ethan's temper blasted when he came abruptly on the line. "I've damn near gone crazy worrying about you! Your mother said you just packed up and left. Damn it, Kelly! You can't just leave. You can't just . . . leave."

It had never occurred to Kelly that she could inflict such a keen wound on a person, or that Ethan would think history was repeating itself.

"I had to lick my wounds, Ethan," she clumsily attempted to explain. "I didn't want you to see me do it. I'm not Patty Lomax, please believe that. I wouldn't do that to you."

"Ah, Kelly." Relief was in his long, dwindling sigh. "I should never have told you about your father."

"I would never have forgiven you for not telling, Ethan."

"Then get yourself home. Why didn't you come to me? We could've talked it out. I could have helped. There's nothing you can't tell me, Kelly."

"We're talking now, aren't we?"

"But you're two hundred miles away. I can't hold you. Look, stay where your are. I'll fly over and drive you home. While we're in the wound-licking business, there're a few things about myself that we need to talk about."

The silence hung between them, weighted with shadows and mystery.

"What things?" She couldn't bear more pain, but she was powerless to keep from asking.

He intuited her dread. "Nothing. Nothing important. Nothing at all."

But he was lying, and she knew it. She could hear it in the breaths he drew, and now she would wonder what he had not said.

"Ethan, if you want out of this—"

"What?"

"I've never placed any ties on you, Ethan. You were always free. You are free."

"Kelly, shut up."

Kelly closed her eyes with what seemed to her an infinite weariness.

"When will you be back?" he asked.

"In a day or so," she said, and pressed back unshed tears. "I have some thinking to do."

"About us?"

His directness always stripped her to bare bones. "Ethan?"

"I'm here, sweetheart. I'm always here."

And he truly meant it, which somehow made her feel worse. "He wasn't a moral man, Ethan," she choked. "My father wasn't—"

"Kelly, honey, I know you're hurting. It's difficult to be generous when you've been robbed, but you mustn't judge him."

"There're codes of conduct, Ethan. The rule is, you don't lie to people you love. You don't sell them out. How can I respect him now?"

"Whatever your father and my mother did was between the two of them. It's over, Kelly."

"But it's not over!" Realizing that her voice had risen, she cupped the receiver and whispered hoarsely, "It's not over. Can't you see that? Your mother believes she can pick up with me where she left off with my father."

"She'll learn soon enough she's wrong."

"You know what I wish? And please don't take this the wrong way. I know your father's doing a good job at the *Tribune*, but I wish...I wish the *Mirror* could blow the *Tribune* right out of the water. I wish I could make your mother regret the day she ever heard of Vincent Madison."

Ethan's laughter was as healing as sunshine. "Don't knock that dream, Kelly. I have the same one with a few variations."

Smiling, Kelly wrote his name on the tablecloth with the tine of her fork. Beneath it, she wrote her own. She foolishly enclosed them both in a squiggly heart.

She said, "I don't suppose your offer to help me get the *Mirror* on its feet still holds?"

He laughed. "I'm way ahead of you on that. I've already been talking it up and looking around for acquisitions."

Kelly dropped her fork, and it clattered loudly to her plate. She jerked around to see if she'd alarmed her waiter.

She cupped the receiver like a spy. "Wait a minute. Hang on, now. What do you mean 'acquisitions'? Like *buy* something? Radio? Television? No. No, no. I'm not ready to start thinking like that."

"If you're serious about keeping the *Mirror* alive, Kelly, much less blowing the *Tribune* out of the water, you have to shed your image. Look, the *Mirror*'s just a small paper. Small's not always bad. In fact, if you have a surefire way to grow bigger, right in front of people, being small could be an asset. But you have to be able to grow and do it spectacularly. The thing is, once you get people's attention, it's imperative to have something to say. You have to keep the momentum, or you'll lose it."

"I guess you know you're scaring me to death."

"It's called playing with the big boys, darling. Or, in your words, blowing the *Tribune* out of the water."

"Oh, God."

"What you have to do first is show enough potential to convince people to invest in you."

"You mean, invest in the *Mirror.*"

"Technically. But, in fact, they would be investing in what they see you, as a publisher, doing with the *Mirror.* Once you get more working capital, you can acquire two or three small papers and enlarge your working base—nothing big, nine thousand circulation or so. The *Sun* in Phoenix, maybe, or the Chicago *Tattler.* Then your investors will get returns on them, too. They'll love you."

Kelly was still one step behind him. "You mean, I'll have to knock on doors and ask people for their money?"

His laughter was not comforting. "Not exactly, but sort of. I can help you there."

She groaned.

"Everything worthwhile, my darling, even love, especially love, carries within itself its own death."

The waiter appeared abruptly at Kelly's table, staring down his nose in offense. "Is everything all right, madam? Is something the matter with the fish?"

Kelly looked down at her plate and blushed. "No, no. Everything is delicious. Just delicious."

Smiling thinly, she took a bite of the fish. After the man had moved on, giving her a suspicious look backward, she hid behind her hand.

"I had hoped, Ethan," she whispered, "to make a profit somewhere down the line."

He chuckled in her ear. "Don't worry. I was born to this. I'll be right there with you, every step of the way."

There it was again: the future, *their* future. Now he was waiting for some indication that she accepted such a statement of fact—some word, some murmur.

She cleared her throat. "First I've got to get myself together. I've got to stop thinking the way *he* taught me to think. Then—"

Disappointment was in his pause and in his sigh. "Come home, Kelly. I want you here. I need you here. I miss you. I can't . . . Kelly, just come home."

After promising to call him twice a day no matter where she was, Kelly drove through Louisiana and into Texas.

In Texas, summer was already burning. The sun hammered down on her car from a cloudless sky. On and on she drove to the desert, where she wouldn't have been surprised to see sun-bleached cow skulls lying beside the highway.

How much easier it would have been to remain ignorant of the truth, she thought. Truth always killed the parent. In the end, the child always left the parent behind to become the parent in another rolling over of time.

Why, Daddy? Why did you hurt me? Hurt Mother? For Georgia Chase, of all people? Why did you take the easy way out and cheat us?

It was when she was halfway to El Paso that Kelly finally ran out of anger. Left with only sadness and scalding tears, she pulled over to the side of the highway.

Who said a parent must be perfect? So what if Vincent made a mistake that lived after him? Would she have done better if she had been a fourteen-year-old boy hitchhiking to

Montgomery from a shotgun house where there was never enough?

"I don't want to hate you, Daddy," she whispered to the past.

She thought of Caroline—all those years she had misjudged her mother, thinking her weak. She owed Caroline an apology.

Alone in the desert, she wept. She wept until she wanted to retch. Finally, after she washed clean, she buried her father beside Interstate 20 and turned around for the long trip home.

"What I don't understand," Kelly argued with Ethan two weeks later, "is why we have to actually go to New York City to interview this... what was his name?"

"Previtz. Simon Previtz."

"You say this Simon Previtz is an authority on the environment. Okay, I'll buy that. Why can't we conduct an interview on the phone?"

Like a comfortably married couple, they were in the stifling stairwell of the Redmond Building, arguing. For the past two evenings, Ethan had been installing hot-water pipes up to the fourth floor. She had been elected gofer, and to offer unsolicited advice.

He stood on a folded ladder with sweat streaming in rivulets down his bare chest. With his lighter, he was firing a small propane torch, and the torch caught with a hissing rush like a dragon's sigh. As the temperature in the stairwell increased several degrees, he stretched up to braze the copper pipe, the stub of a cigar gripped between his teeth and his ribs neatly corrugating his sides.

"A lot hinges on this interview, Kelly." He talked around the cigar, and moved the flame back and forth over the joints of copper. "You can't conduct an interview this important on the telephone."

From her perch on the steps, Kelly scowled. "I don't suppose it's ever occurred to you that I could go broke."

He inspected the seam and removed the cigar to wipe sweat from his eyes. He flashed her a satisfied grin, turned off the torch and started to back down.

"Hold the ladder, will you?" he asked. "And yes, it has occurred to me."

Kelly obediently placed her foot on the bottom rung. "Making this an apartment is costing me more than I figured. And there's no telling what it'll cost to bring new blood to the paper."

"There are a lot of college kids out there who would be willing to work cheaply and hard if they could see the possibility of making a name for themselves. That's what you have to do, Kelly. Bring in new blood and put it beside your old-timers. Diversity, that's the ticket these days. Constantly emphasize it in your story conferences."

It wasn't easy for her. "I still need every cent I can put my hands on right now."

"You have eight thousand dollars," he teased.

She gave the ladder a shake. "Don't remind me, you sadist. Be serious. Two plane fares to New York will put a dent in me, Ethan. After the *Tribune* has me for lunch, the bank can eat my bones."

When his boots were anchored firmly on the floor, he tossed his cigar away and playfully nibbled her neck. "I'd rather have you than a bone any day."

Kelly's punch to his middle was not entirely playful.

"Besides—" his tan made him appear cast in bronze "—did I ask you to buy plane tickets? I'll pay for the tickets. I'll pay for everything."

"On a policeman's salary?" She thrust her weight to one hip like a gypsy. "Do you think I don't know how much money cops make, Inspector Clouseau? Do you think I don't know you—"

Without warning, he stalked her to the wall and trapped her there, one hand braced on the wall beside her head and the other holding the extinguished torch.

"Exactly what do you know, Kelly?" he challenged, and ran the hard pad of his fingertip across her lip. "What d'you *think* you know about me?"

She knew he was in the wrong profession, but she had never intimated as much. Newspapers were in Ethan's blood. It was in his nature to track down a hot lead and hang around the courthouse and wheedle a secretary out of the county attorney's home phone number so he could get the story and write it brilliantly, then get a little loaded in the neighborhood bar after work.

And he was fast. In the time she required to settle down and collect her thoughts, he had hammered out the rewrite of a story that Fred had called in from the street late in the afternoon. He had also edited some copy and written a half-dozen headlines, all with seeming effortlessness.

When it came to surviving media politics, he was an in-fighter. Everything that was work for her was fun for him, and his vision constantly amazed her. With a remarkable economy of words, he had outlined the *Mirror*'s plan for growth for the next five years. He had drawn up a list of people to call.

If they never made love again, if he suffered some dreadful calamity and didn't even resemble the man he was now, she couldn't imagine enjoying anyone as much. She simply... liked him, as well as loved him. He was, incredibly, her best friend.

"I'm not sure what you want me to say," she said. "You're the strongest man I've ever known, that's for sure."

"You're wrong." He was so near, she could feel his sexuality held in check. "I'm weak."

"You make mistakes, but that doesn't make you weak."

"What else do you know about me?"

Kelly nibbled her lip. Thinking was difficult when he was so astride her world, so in command of things she wasn't capable of.

"That you'd get along perfectly well without me," she said.

He didn't reply.

"And I know you're not loaded," she said with forced flippancy. "So why do you keep coming up with things that are going to make me overdraw at the bank?"

His gaze flicked momentarily to her breasts, where her cotton T-shirt was soft and clinging. He kissed the end of her petulant, upturned nose.

"We'll hear no more about who buys what," he said. "Incidentally I'm not as poor as you think I am, Kelly. One of these days, we're going to have a long talk about that."

"But—"

"The king has spoken. One does not dispute the king. Unless . . ." He slashed his throat with his finger and made a *schtick* sound against his teeth.

Kelly had the impression that they had come dangerously close to a serious misunderstanding.

"You have a torch in your hand," she said with deliberate dryness. "What can I say?"

He caught her hard against him and took her mouth in a swift, demanding kiss. Kelly's hands found his face, keeping him bound to her.

"You can say you love me as much as I love you," he said raspily against her lips. "You can say you can't live without me, that every breath you draw is for me, that you eat and sleep nothing but me."

Though it was true, to say the words was the most frightening step Kelly had ever taken. She defied the chorus of voices in her head, shouting that she could be opening a door to pain for many people. She drew her hands over his chest and savored the hard resilience, each ridge of tendon and swell of muscle. He cupped her hips, and she was lifted to the tips of her toes. Was she merely a moth to his irresistible flame?

Closing her eyes, she melted against him.

"You're not a king, Ethan," she whispered as he began drawing her with him to a land at the edge of the world. "You're a man. You're my man, and I love you."

Chapter 11

Mr. Chase, the placard read, and a uniformed chauffeur was holding it high above his head as a flood of disembarking passengers surged past.

One of the hottest Julys on record had the entire East Coast sweltering. As Kelly stepped with Ethan from the American Airlines ramp into La Guardia Airport, she didn't think she ever wanted anything as much as she wanted to get out of her panty hose.

The sudden appearance of Ethan's name on a placard only added a new element to the strangeness of being so many miles from home. She looked from the face of a kindly older man back to Ethan, who was signaling him with a flick of fingers.

"Wait a minute," she said, dumbfounded as the man nodded and, removing his hat, slipped the placard beneath his arm and stepped forward.

"Mr. Chase?"

Ethan was ignoring her tug of his sleeve. He said, "You're Jason?"

"At your service, sir. Madam?" The man bowed politely from his waist, then inquired, "Do you have luggage, sir?"

As confused as she was amazed, Kelly stopped dead in the path of traffic. This was all very nice, being met by a driver and car and knowing there wouldn't be the hassle of finding a cab to downtown Manhattan, but how had it happened? Where had this more cosmopolitan Ethan come from? It unnerved her sometimes, the things she did not know about him—his days at work, great gaping holes of his past.

Even now as he handed over their carry-on bags and discussed arrangements with the driver as if he did it every day of his life, he was carrying a gun.

He didn't like to talk about his job. Did that mean he was in danger? Could he become a statistic like those in the headlines?

His hand urged her forward. Kelly caught sight of their reflection in a sheet of glass—the tall, slightly attractive couple they made, she with her wide-leg linen slacks and soft blouse, her hair twisted into a Gibson girl knot atop her head, and he with his tailored slacks and casual jacket, the strong, capable lines of his face with his black hair sprigging in a number of places.

"I'm not taking one more step," she vowed as someone's suitcase struck her painfully behind the knees and sent her stumbling forward, "until you tell me what's going on. When did you arrange this, Ethan? Who are you, a spending junkie in disguise?"

Laughing, he placed his hand at the base of her spine. "Smile and play nice, or I'll toss you over my shoulder and carry you out of this airport. We'd cause quite a stir, I daresay."

Kelly remembered when he'd hauled her down a hillside in Montgomery County. They'd caused quite a stir then, too.

She sniffed reproachfully. "I should warn you, surprises are not exactly in my nature to enjoy."

He curled his mouth at one corner. "You're not going to worry us both to death about money for the whole four days, are you?"

Again Kelly stopped walking. Again traffic was forced to eddy around them.

"*Two* days," she corrected. "Our plan was to stay two days, Ethan, not four."

"Really?" His smile was winsome and fetching. "I would've sworn it was four. My, my. Are you sure?"

Knowing it was hopeless, Kelly hurried after him when he began walking again. She allowed herself to be steered to the escalators.

"I can see it in the headlines now," she grumbled. "Alabama Vacationers Jailed For Nonpayment Of Hotel Bill."

Ethan blithely led the way to the luggage carousel, where he drew out a cigar and chatted with the driver.

Miffed, Kelly sat with her chin propped on her fist. She was still sulking when Jason went ahead to bring the car around.

A smoke-colored stretch limousine swept up to the curb like a miracle. Kelly snapped a look from the car to Ethan.

He grinned. "Kelly, if you don't want to find yourself spread-eagled against the car, get inside and find some of your wonderful pre-Beatles music on the stereo. Pour me a drink while you're at it. God knows, you've driven me to it."

"That's not funny, Ethan!"

It was even less funny when Kelly discovered there was no possible way to get into a limousine gracefully. She clambered awkwardly into the luxurious interior and sank into a leather seat that was soft as butter and smelled delicious enough to eat.

"Some friend your friend has got, Ethan," she said. "When do I get to meet her?"

"Come here, you little green-eyed monster." Chuckling, he kissed her as the car slid out into airport traffic, picked up speed and headed for the Triborough Bridge.

Ethan had always known it was only a matter of time until he would have to tell Kelly about his other life as the creator of Price Masters. He should have told her long before now, but he had found it surprisingly painful to hear her disapprove of the kind of books he wrote.

Not that he hadn't made worse statements to himself, but it was one thing for him to call his own work trash, and it was quite another to hear the words from her.

Oh, he'd tried to bare his soul over the telephone once, when hundreds of miles lay between them. But he hadn't been able to, and then for weeks they had spent every waking moment planning a strategy to save the *Mirror*.

That was the trouble with lies of omission, of course. Either a person told it all, right up front, or fragments of truth began drifting around like flotsam—all twisted and waterlogged. She wouldn't appreciate his reasons. She would, like a betrayed wife, only wonder what else he had lied about.

It was through Jake Schimmerman, who was also the agent of Mallory Keene of horror-genre fame, that he had gotten the use of Mallory's four-story town house on the Upper East Side while she was in Ireland.

Kelly's breath caught as he unlocked the door and ushered her into the marble foyer. Like a girl pressing her nose against a window to view Camelot for the first time, she moved to the center of the cupola and tipped up her head. An awesome Austrian chandelier hung there, drooping thousands of crystal prisms.

Jason was placing their luggage on the floor, and Ethan extended a tip, his mind more taken with Kelly's awe than how much he was giving the man.

Jason explained he would be at their disposal for the next four days. "Thank you," Ethan said distractedly.

When the door closed behind Jason, Kelly remained absorbed with the startling grandeur of the place. "Who is your friend's friend, Ethan?" she murmured. "Rockefeller?"

"Don't be silly." Another lie of omission added to his growing list of sins, Ethan thought.

Actually he was a bit in awe of Keene's town house himself. An Aubusson tapestry covered an entire wall. The red-and-gold commode against a wall was undoubtedly from Louis XIV's reign, if his mother's knowledge of antiques was to be believed, and on its surface sat an impressive eighteenth-century porcelain figurine.

Kelly was studying the elevator's grillwork cage. With the touch of a lever, he opened it, and she glanced briefly over her shoulder before entering and fitting herself into the farthest corner from the door.

No strip search had ever been more thorough than the way she looked at him, and Ethan felt a trickle of sweat slide down his back. He took the opposite corner, and the cage crept upward.

She didn't speak, and neither did he. Both of them knew, had known from the moment Jason shut the door, how this night would end.

She had come to read him too well, and she suspected that something about him wasn't quite in focus. Her suspicion only served to place an exciting element of danger between them—as if they were two children playing with forbidden fire.

The cage bore them to the second floor. As they browsed through it, their conversation was stilted.

"If things go well and we can make this story work," he said, "all hell will break loose at the *Mirror*."

"We'll have to make the most of the momentum and act quickly. Get our investors together."

"A few really nice receptions at the Harvey House, I thought. We'll wine 'em and dine 'em—"

"Then sock it to 'em. I suppose it'll cost—"

"Don't think about the cost."

The tension was now a fine skein of silver stretching tighter and tighter. Ethan felt his nerves fraying until he could sense every movement of her pelvis as she walked— the languorous way she had of leaning back so that her bones were a distinct impression beneath her slacks.

Her scent drifted out to him, delicate yet creating a riot inside him. Her breasts, when she leaned forward, were such a subtle invitation, he wanted to rip off her clothes and drag her to the floor.

Keene's furnishings of the second-floor library were priceless—the black marble columns that soared up to eighteen-foot ceilings, matchless Rembrandts and an enormous Gauguin on the wall. Only Mallory's admirable lack of personal vanity prevented her from discovering whose place it really was.

The kitchen was actually two kitchens in one, and a dining room that could comfortably seat twenty. Mallory had thoughtfully left out several bottles of wine. Fetching two glasses and a good Bordeaux, Ethan suggested they proceed to the third floor.

They gave the illusion of calm as they stepped into the elevator again, but when their shoulders touched, it was as if fire had licked them. They directed their words to the walls. They looked everywhere except at each other.

Already he was poised for sex. Desire lodged in his throat like a stone. He wasn't totally in control of himself, he thought.

Entering the bedroom, he touched a button, and a discreet glow of light made the white marble of the four-poster bed even whiter, the white satin sheets more lustrous.

The rug was white, and white damask draperies covered the French windows. The walls were mirrored—all very pagan and sensual, tasteful but arranged with one purpose in mind, which they were both sharply aware of.

Ethan was struck by how perfectly Kelly fit into such surroundings. She was a total contrast, yes, with the uncompromising honesty of her green eyes, the simplicity and determination of her face. Yet that innocence was only a counterpoint to the tigress that he had caught fleeting glimpses of in the past weeks. There was in her a long-denied expression of passion, and if the tigress ever walked . . .

The only sound in the room besides their own uneven breathing was the faint hum of the air-conditioning. As if this ritual had been choreographed in some whirling century long before, their eyes met and moved away. They looked at the room, the bed, at each other again. Neither wanted to rush, to lose the magic of the moment.

Ethan felt, bizarrely, as if he were an intruder in his own body. He placed the wine and glasses on a table. He had the horrible feeling that he needed her so much, loved her so deeply, he wouldn't be able to sustain himself or make love at all. Time had slipped off its track and hung suspended, going nowhere.

"If you'd like to shower . . ." he said, and gestured at the bath that he suspected was more elaborate than the bedroom.

She moved softly about the room and removed some items from her bag.

As if his desire for her were a high-powered lens, he saw himself stepping out of his body and leaving the room to find another bath on the floor above. He showered and shaved—a dispassionate onlooker watching a man who faces danger every day of his life but is unprepared for this one.

He saw, not the hardened cop who could tolerate being called every vile name in the book without a glimmer of response, but a man who wilted at the sight of one slim woman. He did not see Price Masters.

He wrapped his hips with a towel and looked at the stranger in the mirror. This was one time he could not force life to heel through the tenacity of his will. He wanted Kelly. He wanted to marry her. But more than that, he wanted something he could never put into words—to be able to believe that they would be all things to each other for the rest of their lives.

When he returned, she was swathed in a towel as big as a bedspread. She was fluffing at her freshly shampooed hair.

Color rose to her cheeks, and she murmured, smiling shyly, "I was hoping to dry it before—"

"It's okay," he whispered, and drew her into his arms. "It's perfect."

She placed her lips to his throat, and he pulled her closer. He kissed her forehead, her eyes.

"Kelly Jean Madison," he murmured as her soft mouth flowered beneath his. "You'll never know how many times I just say your name."

"Say it now," she whispered.

He unfastened the towel that covered her. It slithered into a white pool at their feet. He kissed her wonderful breasts and her taut belly. "Kelly," he sighed. "Oh, Kelly."

With infinite delicacy she stooped, moving down his body with the sleek smoothness of steel to place her lips against the towel and force her breath through. The heat was devastating. Ethan heard a sound of agony in his own throat, and he looked down to savor her lovely, long fingers shaping him. Bending, he scooped her up into his arms and carried her to the bed.

Never had they seemed so perfect for each other as now, so irrevocably right. And in that final moment before he entered her, she took his face in her hands. "Are you going to marry me, Ethan Chase?"

He thought he said yes. He was sure he said yes. He told her how much he loved her, as if he had been born to love her. Did he tell her that?

He lost his sense of balance, and they were both lost for a time, with no place except the one where they fitted together—moving, sometimes stopping to look at each other, entwined, sometimes with his mouth upon hers, upon her, sometimes with her loving him with her hands, with her mouth, missing nothing, not even the tips of his ears. There were no egos now, only the fever, and the knowledge that there was no time to lose.

She arched her back and raked her nails over the sensitive flesh of his chest. The muscles inside her thighs jerked. She groaned, clinging fiercely while inside, with the heat of her, with her incredible tightness, she was seducing the life out of his body and into hers, lapping up his strength, taking his power—a tigress with claws but with a purr like softest silk.

"Promise you'll never leave me," he said. "Promise you won't take money and go away."

Simon Previtz's credentials were staggering. He surprised Kelly by being intelligent about Alabama's problems in general and Southeast Medical's history of waste disposal in particular. His authority was impeccable.

"You were right," she whispered to Ethan during a break in the interview. "He's good. This is going to work."

They were in a tiny office of the Empire State Building, and the space Previtz occupied was crammed full of boxes and mountains of clippings, thick bound computer print-

outs and a secretary who looked like a high school sophomore.

Ethan leaned back to watch and listen. Previtz, once he
was wound up, talked faster than Kelly could take notes. A
surprisingly small man with rather effeminate characteris-
tics, he quoted Karen Pallarito and Janice Somerville and
mentioned telephone calls from the president as if they were
from his great uncle from the Bronx.

He spoke about the "greening of medicine," and he was
well acquainted with the AIDS suit in Kings County, New
York, and how the Coachman Caring owners were indicted
for illegal waste storage.

"You might want to research the *Post*'s articles by Mi-
chael Weisskoph, Miss Madison," he suggested as Kelly's
pen flew across her pad. "Weisskoph claims the state laws
are nothing but a hodgepodge and the federal laws are useless."

He painted a grim picture of disposal gone awry, and
Kelly came away from the interview with a piece that was
almost print ready.

"For the first time," she told Ethan, "your strategy of
putting the *Mirror* on the map, then going public and ac-
quiring a few foundering small papers seems real. I think we
can make it happen. Not that I look forward to getting on
my knees and begging everyone I know to invest, but..."

When they returned to the town house, she telephoned
Montgomery and dictated the piece to Ann Jacobs.

"Give it four columns, Ann. Front page in Thursday's
edition. I'm faxing a photograph of Previtz, and I'll work
up something tonight for a follow-up. But it's your byline.
See if you can put your hands on what the *Post* has done.
What d'you think?"

"About the *Post*?"

"No. About this piece."

"I think we should call the telephone company and have them install a few extra lines."

Kelly laughed. "If only, if only. Right now I'd settle for Albert Russo threatening us for the record."

"He just might when people start ringing his telephone in the middle of the night. Oh, by the way, Maxwell Chase called from the *Tribune*. He wants to talk to you."

Kelly jerked a look at Ethan, who was on the other phone, talking to someone he'd vaguely referred to as Jake.

She covered the mouthpiece and whispered, "What could your father want to talk to me about?"

Ethan let out his breath with a whistle that could have signaled disappointment or foreboding. "He must have found something."

"Found what?"

He shook his head. "I don't want to even think about it."

On Kelly's few trips to New York with her Aunt Eunice, she had been at the mercy of a middle-aged woman who spent the first week of every June with her late husband's mother. Rarely did they get past the redbrick bungalow on the Bayside of Queens.

Under Ethan's tutelage, however, Kelly discovered shopping. He surprised her by skipping the World Trade Center and Fifth Avenue with its F.A.O. and Bergdorf Goodman, Tiffany's and Saks Fifth Avenue. Instead, they browsed through Battery Park City and SoHo. They spent a morning on the Lower East Side and an afternoon on Fifty-seventh Street.

Their most delightful hours were the art galleries and bookstores. It was Kelly's deep love for words that kept her lingering in old shops with quaint signs and crowded aisles.

Ethan seemed content to take a quick survey of stores in general, to get a feel for which titles were hot, he said. He examined window displays and the endless aisles of fiction.

Whenever the clerks would ask "Are you looking for anything in particular, sir?" he would shake his head.

"What *are* you looking for?" she quizzed.

"I'll know it when I see it," was his stock answer.

They were out on the sidewalk, munching bagels, and Kelly aimed her forehead at a display window of Abernathy's, where a clerk was arranging the display of the latest Price Masters novel, *Smothered with Silk.*

"Like that, you mean," she said with her mouth full.

Ten Weeks On The *New York Times,* the handwritten sign said above the dump that spilled shiny new paperbacks with a beautiful murdered woman on the cover who wore nothing but a cloud of blond hair.

"I should get one for Leah," she said. "The woman has no taste. D'you suppose they have an autographed copy?"

Ethan pulled down his sunglasses and leered menacingly at her over their frames. "What kind of person writes that stuff, do you think?"

"An illiterate."

Laughing dourly, he replaced his glasses, clapped his arm around her shoulders and drew her on down the street.

"Yeah, and he probably comes from a long line of illiterates. He'll marry an illiterate, if he hasn't already, and they'll raise a whole family of illiterates."

"You have a warped sense of humor, Ethan. Did anyone ever tell you that?"

All too soon their holiday was over. Though Kelly returned to Montgomery a different woman than the one who had left, the thin line that the *Mirror* walked preempted any talk of marriage between Ethan and herself.

The *Mirror* printed the Previtz interview, and telegrams and letters began to pour in by the hundreds. School children wrote letters. Middle-class housewives called in, and lower-income workmen spoke their views to WSFA-TV's roving reporter.

So many calls swamped Leah Blankenship, Kelly happily did as Ann suggested and had new lines installed. She also hired a temporary operator to answer them.

To counter the attention-stealing Previtz interview, the *Tribune* ran a full-page advertisement thanking Albert Russo for "his enormous contributions to the city of Montgomery."

When Kelly returned Maxwell Chase's phone call, she tried to forget he was Ethan's father and to demand his respect on the basis of what she was accomplishing at the *Mirror*.

Saddam Hussein had a better chance of receiving the Nobel Peace Prize!

"Mr. Chase is out of town for two weeks," she was told.

"Oh?" Relief flooded Kelly. "Then please tell him I returned his call," she said, and happily buried her head in the sand one more time.

Early in August, on the heels of the Previtz-related articles, the *Mirror* made a spectacular eight-thousand-dollar contribution to the medical expenses of two Pierce Creek students who were mending from their bout with hepatitis. Montgomery, already buzzing about Albert Russo and his leaking landfill, began demanding answers from the city fathers.

Due to Ethan's timely notification of the wire services, the Associated Press picked up the story, and the wheel of momentum began to turn.

CNN's affiliate taped a forty-five second interview on the Redmond parking lot, and Fancy Auletta from Channel 13 had her come to the studio for an in-depth interview on "Point of View."

"How did the donation come about, Miss Madison?" she asked pleasantly when they were on the set, seated in two easy chairs with a coffee table between them.

Kelly smiled without missing a beat. "Actually, Fancy, it was quite strange, and I don't take any credit. The gift came anonymously. I don't know myself who was so generous, but whoever you are, wherever you are, two families and all of us at the *Mirror* are grateful that there are still people out there with integrity and public spirit."

After Fancy cut to another topic, Kelly slipped from before the camera to where Ethan was waiting. Taking his hand, she hurried him out of the studio and laughed with glee.

Grinning, Ethan caught her in his arms, whirling around and around until they were dizzy.

"This wouldn't be happening if it weren't for you, Ethan," she whispered as she laid her head on his shoulder. "You made it happen. You worked a miracle."

"You're the miracle," he huskily replied. "I love you, Kelly Jean Madison."

During this time, Kelly was aggressively going after investors. On Ethan's advice, she filled her days with interviews, luncheon engagements and dinner appointments.

Asking people for money was the essential ingredient for success. It was also the most difficult thing Kelly had ever done. Because she had to live in the same town with the people she called on, there would be no place to hide if she failed.

Not everyone responded—perhaps one in ten—but by the end of September, she had persuaded thirty-five people to invest and had raised nearly seven hundred thousand dollars.

* * *

"If you'll stop being hysterical for a minute and just think about it," Ethan told her one evening when the days were beginning to grow shorter, "you'll see it's no good putting it off. We have to do it sooner or later."

Both of them were on their hands and knees. The fourth floor of the Redmond Building literally reeked with fumes as they put the final coat of varnish on the hardwood floor.

This was the last step, and they had spent every minute they could spare from the *Mirror*. The loft was plumbed and wired. The light fixtures were installed. The kitchen was an island where they had hung their collection of copper tubs and kettles.

Kelly sat back on her heels at Ethan's words, every joint in her body screaming for pain relief.

"I'm not hysterical. Well, not too hysterical. I'm just not ready to meet them, that's all. Anyway, you've always said that you don't care what your family thinks about us. Have I browbeaten you into meeting my family?"

"That day is coming, too. Look, it'll be the perfect time. Brad and Janie will certainly be there, and Kevin. The campaign razzle-dazzle will have everyone in a good mood."

"That's my point, Ethan. Everyone and his dog will be there."

"Crowds bring out the best in my mother."

"Sure. We'll just waltz in and say, 'Oh, by the way, we're in love and our two families will just have to be the next Hatfields and McCoys. Get the old shotguns ready and fire at will.'"

Unfolding to stand, Ethan stood scratching his tousled black hair. "Hell, I think I just painted myself into the corner of the dad-gummed bedroom."

Kelly giggled. "Nope, that's the music room. Wait a minute . . . the dining room. Or is it the linen pantry?"

Glaring at her, he rotated in search of a way out. "What a dastardly little wench you are."

Kelly loved him more than she had thought it was possible for anyone to love another person. Especially as he was now, all big and rumpled, the sleeves ripped from an old dress shirt, the shirttails flapping about his thighs, his cowlick standing at attention on the crown of his head.

Swearing, he wobbled on first one foot, then the other as he removed his shoes. She flinched when he threw a sneaker at her only to have it land in a freshly varnished space.

"Hey, look out!" She retrieved his shoe and gingerly repaired the smudge. "You know, you'd make a wonderful politician, Ethan. You have the knack for getting yourself into sticky situations."

With a bare toe, he tested the tackiness of the gloss and came away with a varnished toe.

"Look on the bright side," she taunted mercilessly. "Most celebrities leave their footprints in cement, but yours will be in varnish." Rising, she waved him toward her as if he were a grounded airplane. "Come on, take one giant step for mankind."

"Might I suggest, Miss Smarty Britches," he growled as he tiptoed across the sticky floor, "that you're very close to painting yourself into a corner."

When the knock sounded on the door, Kelly was still laughing and Ethan was clumping around the dry part on his heels in search of a place to clean his feet.

"I've heard of sticky fingers," she howled as she went to answer it, "but sticky feet is a new one on me. Mother!"

A dead zone of silence.

"What are you...?" Kelly snatched a sudden, desperate look over her shoulder at Ethan. Back to Caroline then, to ask on a beseeching breath, "What're you doing here, Mother?"

Not taking offense at the bald inhospitality, Caroline stepped into the apartment with her usual grace. Her hair was tucked beneath a wide-brimmed hat the color of moss. Her dress was a soft faille in the mossy green, and in her hand was a basket that bulged interestingly beneath a checkered cloth.

"I brought you dinner, darling," she said, and paled slightly when she saw Ethan tucking in his shirt and, still barefoot, walking toward them. "You've been working so hard, I thought—"

Kelly reached out in a gesture of pleading to keep from falling through the varnished floor, down through the earth's crust and into its center. *Please, dear God, don't let there be a scene.*

Before she could think of a proper explanation and pray that Caroline wouldn't recognize Ethan on sight, Ethan had reached them. He wiped his hands on the front of his jeans and extended one to Caroline.

"Mrs. Madison," he said with a cordial smile. "We spoke on the phone a couple of times. I'm Ethan Chase. It's nice to meet you at last. Why didn't you call ahead? I would've carried the basket up the stairs for you."

"Oh," Caroline said as she blinked up at his steady, reassuring smile, then looked less certainly at Kelly.

Should she jump between them? Kelly thought wildly. Should she play referee? Try to stop the flying bullets with her body?

"It wasn't heavy, Mr. Chase," Caroline said. "But thank you anyway."

"Well, let me take it for you now. Won't you come in and...oh, yes—chairs. Hmm, well, as you can see, we aren't quite ready for chairs yet. Would you like to look around? Kelly, why don't you take your mother on a tour?"

Kelly jumped as if he'd touched her with a live wire. "What? Oh, yes. Well, Mother, as you can see—" she threw out her arm to include anything and everything "—the plumbing is in now, and the windows are caulked and painted. We were just finishing with the floor...."

"I can see that, dear." Caroline smiled and moved through the place without so much as a breath of criticism for either of them. "I'm impressed."

Closing her mouth, Kelly tried to read disaster in Ethan's eyes, but he, innocent that he was, was grinning and motioning with his hands that she should take advantage of the momentary lull and get on with it.

"Well, I—" Kelly choked and hurried to catch up. "Actually Ethan's done most of the work."

"Well, he did an excellent job."

Kelly didn't trust this calm. A storm was sure to follow. She trailed along while Caroline carefully made her way along the outer edges of the dried section of floor. She asked if Kelly could remember nearly falling out of one of the windows.

"What? Oh, no, Mother. I don't remember that."

"You were such a little monkey. I used to let you girls play up here, and one day I turned around, and there you were, sitting on the ledge with your legs dangling. As a matter of fact, I think that's where my hair turned white."

Kelly could not smile. It would come now, she knew—the name of Georgia Chase, which would shatter the illusion of peace she and Ethan had found for themselves at immeasurable cost.

The silence held as Caroline stopped walking and looked around.

A line of sweat formed along Kelly's hairline. She steeled herself for the ugly intimation. She took a breath, held it.

"Oh, look! You found that old claw-foot bathtub," Caroline exclaimed, and stepped around a folding screen. "You know, when your father and I tore that tub out of the house and installed one of the modern ones, I was never so glad to see anything go. Now, they're all the rage and bring such handsome prices. If you're lucky enough to find them. Do I detect your excellent hand in the plumbing, Mr. Chase?''

Ethan inclined his head to the affirmative.

Occasionally life paid back more than it took. Occasionally it pushed beyond its limits. From the center of her pain, Kelly realized what was happening. Her mother understood. Without words, without explanations that she, Kelly, had no voice for, Caroline understood.

And in that moment Kelly saw her mother through new eyes. A fresh beginning was in the promise of Caroline's smile, and with a faint nod of her head she acknowledged a pact of friendship that would be theirs from now on. If Kelly and Ethan wanted it.

With brimming tears, she reached for her mother's trailing hand. "Oh, Mother."

"You know, Kelly—" Caroline included Ethan with her eyes "—I've been meaning to replace the wicker furniture out in the sun room for ages. What do you think, Mr. Chase? Don't you think it would be perfect on the end overlooking the street?''

Chapter 12

"Press conference," Fred Woodson announced as he swung into Kelly's office, pushed his fedora to a cocky angle and slapped a press kit onto her desk. "Orders from on high, from Miss Georgia herself, amen and amen."

Fred flicked his mutilated toothpick into the wastebasket and promptly replaced it with another while Kelly turned the pages of the propaganda packet just received from Georgia Chase's publicity machine.

"Wow, I'll bet this cost a pretty penny," she mused, noting the fine quality.

She brought up the press party at the morning staff meeting.

"Don't look at me," Ann said, and held up both hands. "I'm snowed. Let Jerome go."

"You think I'm twins?" Jerome attacked his bitten nails with a vengeance and glared at the city editor. "I've got that human-interest thing at Pierce Creek."

"Well, I can't go," Fred chimed in, shrugging. "I haven't finished with the unemployment piece and the defense fallout for Gunter Air Force Base."

"All right, I'll do it." She might have known, Kelly thought, and reached unenthusiastically for the press kit. "What time and where?"

"Seven o'clock," Fred said. "Out in the country." He wiggled his brows and added evilly, "Where the deer and the antelope play."

With that, the entire staff waxed musical. Jerome conducted, and everyone joined in for the final chorus: "...and the skies are not cloudy all day."

Laughing, Kelly covered her ears, but when the merriment died down, she screwed up her face at Fred. "Way out there?"

Fred had shaped an airplane of the press release and now sent it sailing in a flight pattern that ended in a graceful, two-point landing atop Kelly's yellow pad.

"Yep." He tucked a fresh toothpick into the side of his mouth and grinned. "Happy hour."

The sun was beating down from its zenith when Ethan parked off Dexter Avenue and walked to the State Judicial Building. The leaves were turning. Their fragile hold on the trees was giving way, and more than a few were dancing along the sidewalk in a colorful pirouette and bourrée and *fouetté*.

Ethan knew his way around the three-story building that housed the Supreme Court and Appellate Court of Alabama. Here, Judge Pritchard reigned supreme. As boys, he and Hite had often raced over after school and browsed the halls that were sometimes full, sometimes so still that whispers hung in the air and their heels were loud as thunder.

Entering Hite's office, Ethan smiled at his secretary, who was young and slim with her bangs moussed in a Dagwood flip.

"Ethan Chase," he told her, and flashed his badge because she was still young enough to hustle at the sight of it. And also because he didn't want her perceiving how distasteful this visit was to him.

A few moments later, an inner office door opened, and Hite walked out, shrugging into his suit coat and extending his hand.

"You're early," he said, and grinned.

Ethan smiled back and wondered if Hite would still be smiling after lunch. "I was hungry."

They bought sandwiches at the deli down the block and munched while they strolled over to the capitol at the east end of the avenue. They clumsily gave up trying to repair the damage done to their friendship over the years. They leaned on a guardrail and, squinting, watched the tawny Alabama River rolling through the business district.

"Is Georgia gearing up for the big announcement?" Hite asked.

"I suppose so," Ethan said, chuckling, "seeing as how she's only been planning it for the past twelve years. She'll probably make a documentary of the process and put it in the state archives."

They wandered around to the rose garden in the rear of the capitol. A tedious silence passed between them. Hite stuffed his hands in his pockets with his Indian-brave-roaming-the-hills-looking-for-buffalo look.

Finally he asked, "What's up, Ethan?"

Ethan squinted at the colorful fall trees. "I wanted to talk to you about Kelly."

Hite stiffened, immediately on guard. "Why should you want to talk to me about that?"

"Come on, Hite, I know how you feel about her—so do you. What would you say if I told you I wanted to marry her?"

A muscle in Hite's jaw jumped, and his silence was stubborn and articulate. Ethan could feel distance opening between them.

"I'd say that you should stay away from her," Hite said at length, and began walking, scuffing his right shoe on the concrete. "I'd say you should keep your hands off her, man."

"It's a bit late for that." Temper flashed between them like gasoline dashed onto live coals. "I didn't want you to learn it some other way."

Hite was as pale as Ethan had ever seen him. "She agreed to marry you?"

"We haven't set a date, but yes."

Hite drew back his cuff to consult his Rolex. He mumbled something about having an appointment and started walking swiftly away. Turning back, his handsome features drawn with bitter anger, he raised a finger in warning.

"If you hurt her like you've hurt everyone else in your life, Ethan, by God, I'll break your flamin' neck! You know, you really..." He shut his mouth and ground his teeth. "You just make sure you don't hurt her, that's all I've got to say."

With a curt nod, Ethan buttoned his jacket. Hite spun hard on his heel and walked with a swift and correct grace down Dexter Avenue.

For a time Ethan watched, then he glanced down at his index finger, as if by straining hard enough he could discern the tiny prick where he'd opened the skin with a knife blade and mixed his blood with that of his friend.

Pieces of an old song drifted from out of the past: "When a man loves a woman...he'll turn his back on his best friend if he puts her down."

Ethan retraced his way down the avenue, but somehow the sun wasn't quite as bright as before and the river wasn't quite as sparkling. Somehow the trees had lost their spectacular color.

Love, he thought grimly. It changed everything.

For the first time in her life, Kelly was grateful for Debbie and Melissa's obsession with appearances.

"I want to change my image," she told them, and secretly prayed they would rescue her with a crash course in style.

"Oh, God," was Debbie's reaction.

Her older sister, Melissa, was more straightforward with her cruelty. "It's about time. D'you want to look like Kay Graham or Ben Bradlee?"

Kelly said through her teeth, "I want to look like myself, Melly. Only better."

"Hmm." Melissa gave a doleful shake of her expensive head. "This will take some real thought. I don't know...."

"Forget it!"

Kelly dragged everything out of her closet and stood dejectedly before the full-length mirror on her door. She remembered the glamorous entry Georgia had made at Mendino's.

"Don't panic," she mumbled, and took a deep breath of courage. "Just because you're not fancy—"

Fancy! Kelly jerked up her head, eyes wide with the sudden dawning.

She dashed down the stairs to kneel before the telephone. She flipped through the pages of the directory and drew her finger down the list of names in search of Fancy Auletta. The only time she had spoken with the anchorwoman had been behind a television, but she knew a great deal about Fancy through Ethan, and she suspected the same was true on Fancy's end of the spectrum.

"Of course I remember the interview," Fancy said when Kelly hesitantly identified herself. "But I would know you anyway. John and Ethan have few secrets, you know."

Kelly wasn't sure she enjoyed being talked about, yet that was ridiculous since she'd done the television interview with the precise intention of being talked about.

Now that she had Fancy on the line, however, her courage disintegrated like mist. "Ah . . . oh dear, this was a bad idea, Fancy. I don't know how to say it."

Fancy's breath caught sharply. "Oh, God, nothing's happened to Ethan or John!"

"No, no. Nothing like that, no." Kelly shook her head vigorously. "It's just that . . . well, I've got to attend the mayor's press party in two days and—"

Fancy groaned. "Isn't it a drag? I've got to take a camera crew out there myself."

Kelly swallowed her embarrassment at having to learn at twenty-eight what most women learn at eighteen. "What I'm trying to ask in all this mishmash of words, Miss Auletta, is whether you plan to do any . . . uh, shopping and . . . stuff."

Stuff? Oh, brother!

A delicious ribbon of laughter swirled from the other end of the line.

"Dar-ling," Fancy cooed, "I *always* plan to go shopping. I'll let you in on something—I've just gone through my closet and there is absolutely *nothing* in there! I'm afraid I have to start from the scalp and go down. Would you like to go with me? Tomorrow afternoon? I could really use the company."

Collapsing with relief, Kelly closed her eyes in gratitude for the graciousness and tact of Southern women.

"I would love to," she said.

At the Lovely Lady beauty salon, Kelly and Fancy pored for nearly an hour over books and magazines before they decided on the perfect hairstyle for Kelly—all one length, three inches below her ears, parted on the side, sleek, smooth, the epitome of professionalism.

All the time that Raoul snipped, Kelly watched each long lock slide to the floor. Fancy was much more curious about whether Ethan would be moving into Kelly's apartment when it was finished.

"You've been good for him," she told Kelly. "You have no idea how disagreeable he was before. He spent every spare minute on that boat of his, absolutely refusing to go anywhere or make new friends."

Kelly smiled. She wasn't about to touch that one.

When he finished, Raoul whisked the cape from around her shoulders. Kelly stared at herself in disbelief while Fancy leaned forward with a cosmetics brush to dust her cheeks with blusher.

"Well," Fancy said, and stepped back to view the effect, "it's absolutely fantastic. What do you think?"

Kelly burst out laughing at her reflection, which looked more like Debbie. "I think I don't know this person."

"You may not know her—" Fancy winked at Raoul "—but she's a knockout."

It was true. She was as pretty as her sisters, though only God remembered what Melissa had looked like in her original state.

Kelly was certain that Fancy pressed an extra tip into Raoul's palm before they scooped up their things and made a quick exit. Time was running out.

The next stop, Fancy announced once they were outside, was the jewelry store. Oh, oh, Kelly thought, and stifled a wince for her checkbook.

"Go naked if you must, darling," Fancy said with unquestionable authority, "but you simply cannot go to one of Georgia's parties without the right earrings."

Fortunately the jewelry cost only a small fortune, only because the handsome coin-size chips weren't set with *real* emeralds.

Amazing! Kelly thought as she preened before the mirror, viewing one side, then the other. Why had she waited so long? Her hair, bouncing and fresh, gleamed as if caught by a spotlight, and when she tossed her head, the faux emeralds were shot with fire.

"I could really get into this reinvention thing," she said, laughing and looking at her wristwatch. Oh, dear. "Where to next?"

"Where else but lingerie? One cannot possibly commence a search for the perfect ensemble, darling, without new undies."

After a quickie stop at Victoria's Secret, they raced across town to Meadowbrook Plaza, where Lilly's tiny boutique was squeezed between a soup-and-salad eatery, a spiritual bookstore, a telephone outlet and a bicycle shop.

To their dismay, the Closed sign for the elite women's clothier was turned outward.

"Oh, no," Fancy groaned.

"Wait a minute." Kelly pondered the car parked before the entrance. Perhaps the proprietress was still inside, out of sight as she worked on some last-minute balancing of the cash register.

With the daring that came only from having a new hairstyle, wonderful earrings and two months of selling herself to the monied set, she walked boldly to the door and knocked.

She cupped her eyes to peer inside.

A woman's face appeared, and she tapped the crystal of her wristwatch. "We're closed."

"Are you the owner?" Kelly asked.

"What do you need?"

"My friend and I have an emergency." Kelly motioned Fancy forward to the door.

Fancy's face hadn't been plastered on half the billboards in the city for nothing.

Brightening, the woman opened the door. She paused as she was locking it behind her, and she gave Kelly a quizzical double take. "And don't I know you, too? Aren't you Miss...Miss, uh..."

"Madison," Kelly supplied as she glanced around, positive that she couldn't afford even the buttons in Lilly's inventory.

"Of course, of course. You're the editor of the *Mirror*. I've been very interested in the slant your newspaper has taken lately. Actually I'll be amazed if you don't do something really good for this town."

As Kelly placed Lilly on her mental list to receive an investment portfolio, Fancy was, in her inimitable way, getting their needs across with an economy of words: "Lilly, give us the works."

Lilly's brows lifted with understanding. In her career, she had met many women with many tastes in fashion, most of them hideously incorrect. She turned Kelly in a circle as she nodded her approval.

"You've come to the right place, Miss Madison. You have the best possible raw material to work with. What wonderfully long legs. I only need to know one thing."

Kelly let out her breath in a sigh. "We have only two hours."

"My dear—" Lilly threw out her hands with dramatic flair "—God created the world in less."

The Chase homesite, in its origin, had consisted of a stately house of weathered clapboards that had barely escaped being destroyed in the War Between the States.

As a boy, Ethan had played Indian scout with Hite on its ancient windmill. He had learned to jump a horse on the old post-and-rail fence that was now smothered in honeysuckle. He had fished in the same stream that the Union soldiers had once camped beside.

The estate was no longer bounded by the great old hawthorns but enclosed by an iron fence. It was sixteen elaborately cultivated acres with a long flagstone driveway curving beneath an arbor of moss-veiled oaks. To reach the front portico, one was required to pass through an elaborate security system.

Georgia delighted in giving interviews from her country home. Quite often she was photographed in the famous library, standing behind Maxwell's wheelchair, surrounded by leather-bound first editions and photographs of her children.

As Ethan parked his pickup, climbed out and brushed off his tuxedo, adjusted the ruffles at his wrists and looked up at the massing thunderclouds overhead, he mumbled, "Who in their right mind would dress up like a penguin and voluntarily walk into this snake pit?"

A stray raindrop struck his face, and he watched the camera technicians arranging cables for a taping and debating the wisdom of doing it outside.

"Wait a minute, you," a strange voice briskly commanded from the top of the steps when he reached them.

Ethan found himself confronted by a stocky, uniformed woman whose face resembled that of a Cabbage Patch doll. Her inspection was as thorough as a strip search.

"Don't shoot, ma'am," he said, and held up his hands. "I give up."

She placed distance between her formidable thighs. "Present your ID and credentials, sir."

With a sour smile, Ethan read the name on her identification badge: Dolly. If he hadn't been on his best behavior tonight, he would have burst into laughter.

He unbuttoned his tuxedo so Dolly could see the gold shield fastened to his cummerbund. "I'm just here after the facts, Dolly."

Dolly, her nostrils flaring with surprise, snapped her shoes together. A little-girl apology was in her voice. "I'm afraid I'll still have to see your ID, sir."

Ethan fished out his wallet. Her eyes moved across the card until they widened to fill her face. "Why, you're—"

"Yeah." He grinned wickedly. "The black sheep of the family. But you did good, Dolly, real good. I'll see you get a raise." He tapped her clipboard with his fingernail. "Could I take a look at that?"

"Oh, yes, sir."

Ethan swiftly scanned the list of guests: Hite, Judge Pritchard, John Fisher and Fancy, his brother, Brad, and Janie, his sister. Plus everyone in town and half of the South, it seemed. But the only one that meant anything to him, Kelly's name, had not been checked off.

He prepared to move unenthusiastically through the door into the world of high-powered politics, where nothing was what it appeared to be.

"I have only one question, Dolly," he said, and thrust the clipboard back into her hands.

She practically saluted. "Anything, sir."

He touched the bow tie that topped a chestful of ruffles. "Is this damn thing straight?"

Dolly's Cabbage Patch smile was worth a dozen Mona Lisas. "It's absolutely stunning, sir."

Ten minutes later, when Kelly showed her press card and clutched the strap of her smart leather pouch in which was packed her camera, a tape recorder and a pad and pen, she felt like a well-groomed Christian about to enter an amphitheater filled with man-eating lions.

Once inside the mansion, she searched for Ethan's head above a crowd that was like every political group she'd ever seen—the laughter too loud, friends kissing friends they hoped would be useful to their careers, empty compliments tossed away like candy wrappings.

The front-room furnishings had evidently been removed, for the floor was cleared, and the guests walked upon priceless Persian rugs. Streamers and balloons drooped from the crystal chandelier. Massively burdened tables lined the walls, each with a floor-length cloth and finger foods that were constantly being replenished by caterers who came from the kitchen by way of the dining room, also cleared of furniture.

Ethan was nowhere to be found. Fancy and John Fisher had apparently arrived only moments before. The black woman, gorgeous in a metallic dress that was more of a long, tight sweater, waved.

John Fisher made a circle of finger and thumb in approval of her lime green crepe pants and matching cardigan. Fancy and Lilly had sworn it would be appropriate for a member of the press. Beneath the cardigan was an azure-and-lime sequined tank top whose neckline stopped just shy of her breasts.

Kelly tried to see everything at once—the gilt-framed paintings lining the walls, past generations of stern, Confederate-uniformed men with women standing behind their shoulders. But she was more aware of the young, clean-shaven, slim-flanked men who stood around the perimeter, flexing their muscles and suspecting every guest of being a terrorist.

Waiters in scarlet jackets weaved through the guests, balancing trays of champagne above their heads with the skill of high-wire artists. A dais had been erected against the back wall, framed with tubs of orchids and ferns. There, on its skirted floor, was Georgia Chase, stunning in a beaded lavender gown as she stood smoking with her campaign manager.

On a smaller platform nearer the French doors, an eight-piece orchestra was playing. A female vocalist in a dangerously strapless gown was crooning "Georgia."

"I don't belong here," Kelly mumbled to herself just as an intangible force tugged at her senses.

Slowly she turned. Ethan was standing far across the huge room, in an elite clique of men, one of whom was Irwin Pritchard. She recognized the owner of the local television franchise. Hite flanked his father as he talked earnestly with two city councilmen.

Kelly had no idea if their conversations were about the law or the enforcement of the law or the election of a new governor to create law. She only knew that Ethan very much belonged in that cluster of important men. He belonged in the clique the same way he had belonged in New York City.

As if he heard her troubled sigh, he looked across the room to find her. Then he was shouldering his way through the press of people, and she was laughing up at his amazed, boyish grin as he stepped back to take in the total effect of her.

"Baby, baby, baby," he groaned, and drew his tongue across his lip as he touched her hair. "What're you tryin' t'do? Set my eyes afire?"

Kelly had to stand on tiptoe and place her mouth near his ear to be heard over the vocalist and applause and pitch of human voices.

"I'll black both of those eyes if you poke fun." She made her own inspection of him and tweaked the bow tie beneath his chin. "You're all gussied up, too. You dread telling them that much, huh?"

"Sweetheart, you'll never know." He pulled a grimace. "Say, would you like to get out of here?"

"This is a working party for me, Ethan."

"You can sweep out the stables. Look, I'm suffering a case of unbridled passion, and if I don't kiss you immediately, I'll probably have a heart attack and die. Besides, I have something for you."

She laughed. "You can't buy me."

Taking her hand, he began clearing a path for them. An announcer was telling the one about the traveling salesman and the loser of the presidential campaign.

Just as they were surrounded by so many people that they had to shout to be heard, he slipped her hand into the right pocket of his jacket. Kelly's fingers collided with a small box that she recognized instantly as one that would contain a ring.

Her breath scattered before the reality of it, and her lips trembled as she searched his face.

"Our parents had their chance, Kelly," he whispered as he pressed his lips to her hair. "It's our turn now."

The Chase butler, who had been with the family since Maxwell's accident, waited until the master of ceremonies reached the punch line of his joke before he approached Georgia Chase.

As everyone was laughing, he motioned to her. When she bent down, he told her that an important phone call had come.

"Who?" she asked.

"The same gentleman as before, madam," he said.

"I'll be there in a few minutes, Charles."

"Yes, madam."

Georgia leaned toward her campaign manager, who was suffering from a severe head cold. "There's something I have to do, Donald." She gave him a wide berth when he sneezed into a monogrammed handkerchief. "And for pity's sake, take one of Max's pills before you give us all pneumonia."

After making certain her necklace was straight for any chance photographer, she stepped lightly from the dais and passed through her guests.

One of her security guards, catching the quirk of her brow, casually left his station, spoke to another guard and crisscrossed the room so he arrived at the door when she did.

"I'm going to my office, Monte," she told him. "Wait outside the door. I don't want to be interrupted."

"Absolutely," Monte said, and caressed the weapon tucked in a chamois holster beneath his arm.

Once she had left the noise behind, Georgia moved quickly. She pushed through the door that led to an office at the rear of the house. When she entered, Monte reached around the facing and snapped on a light.

"No," she said, and promptly turned it off.

The guard shut the door and spread his hulk across it like Mr. Clean in black tie. Not having wanted to use a cordless phone for this particular call, Georgia lifted the receiver, pushed a button and moved to the window that looked out upon the stables.

A streak of lightning flashed jaggedly across the sky.

"Al?"

"Yes," Albert Russo said. "I'm sorry to call you away from your party, Mayor Chase."

"I'm sure you wouldn't have if the condition hadn't warranted it. What's the matter?"

Albert Russo described a situation that Georgia found unnerving. Upon her advice to call in experts who would prove beyond a doubt that the Pierce Creek landfill and furnace were completely within the EPA standards for air quality and soil contamination, the test results were in. They were more negative than either of them had anticipated.

"The landfill's not actually leaking, is it?" she asked after a few moments.

"That's hardly the point now, is it? We can always close the landfill, pay the fine and dig another one. I was perfectly willing to do that, if you remember. *You* were the one who said to hang tough, that this Madison woman would back down, that it would all come to nothing. Now I've got people crawling all over the books, looking for a cover-up. Hell, the governor of New York called my office yesterday. This is not a comfortable position to be in, Mayor, not comfortable at all."

Georgia sighed heavily. It was always something. "Well, Al, just make sure there isn't anything to find. They can't put you in jail for making a human error."

"What d'you mean, human error? This is your baby, Mayor Chase. You can't just walk away and leave me dangling in the wind. I've been very generous. And you've made a lot of promises."

"I've got a campaign to run, damn it. Do you think I can afford to put ammunition into the hands of my opponent? Now, do exactly as I say, Al. Make sure you're clean on paper, then don't admit anything. If you have to close the landfill, close it, but keep my name out of it."

"That could prove to be costly, Mayor."

Wasn't everything? "How costly?"

"I'm not exactly sure right now."

"Well, Al, I have great confidence that you'll come up with a nice, neat figure."

"I just wanted you to know."

"Now I know."

Hanging up, Georgia moved to the window and watched the lightning turn the night sky into one almost as light as day.

"Everybody's got a pocket," she mumbled as she watched a man and a woman skittering lightly down the back steps that led to the stables.

Ethan?

Annoyed, she fetched her glasses from the desk and put them on. Then she watched her son catch Vincent Madison's daughter by the hand and bring her to a stop. He turned her by the shoulders and talked earnestly for a moment, then drew an object from his pocket.

With a rush of breath, Georgia let her back round in a slump. He was taking the little twit's finger and slipping a ring on it. Now he was kissing her, and the sky, as if in celebration, was putting on its own fireworks display.

"Monte!" she yelled.

Like a flash, Monte was inside the room, his gun drawn and his body dropped into a crouch as he brought his arms around in search of an assassin.

"Will you put that thing away, for heaven's sake!" she hissed furiously.

Monte did as he was told and stood at attention. "Ma'am?"

Calming herself, Georgia smoothed her hair and moved her hands down her sides, which were as free of fat as when she'd been seventeen.

"Get Marlene in here," she said with icy control, for she now knew what weapon she could use to send Vincent Madison's daughter crawling back into her cage.

Chapter 13

Ethan kept finding himself ahead of his body as he slipped
the diamond ring on Kelly's finger. He had waited so many
years for this metamorphosis of his heart, he was afraid to
trust its peace. Fate was always the vagrant in a person's
life—wandering around here and there, waiting for the perfect time to destroy everything.

The rumble of distant thunder validated his unease.

He captured Kelly's face in his palms, as if by looking
deeply enough, he could burn his love into her soul.

"What is it, Ethan?" She laid her hands on top of his
own, pressing her lips lovingly against his palm. "Are you
disappointed that I didn't swoon when you proposed?"

Lightning was playing upon the sequins that covered her
breasts. The wind was pushing the storm closer. It was lifting her hair and tossing it with a bolder and more fascinat-
ing grace than ever before.

Ethan lifted her hand where his ring was twinkling like the
birth of something new.

"I guess I expected to have to slay a few dragons or something." He turned the diamond back and forth, enthralled with its fire. "I would, you know—slay a dragon. There's nothing I want so much as for you to be happy, Kelly, to accomplish the things in life that you've dreamed of. You know that, don't you? By the way, did I mention that you're the most beautiful thing I ever saw?"

She hugged him. "Love is notorious for needing corrective lenses, Ethan."

Turning in his embrace, she looked around them, at the walk twisting between the shrubbery to the stables, at the gravel that was turned to crystal by the approaching storm.

"Things will be more complicated now," she said.

He lowered his chin to rest on the top of her head. "If it were up to me, we'd run away and get married tomorrow."

"It would certainly make for fewer confrontations."

He shook his head. "But it's important that we play by the rules now. What we do from this day on is for our children, Kelly."

She lifted her face for his kiss.

"This is what the world dreams of, Kelly, of that perfect second chance, better than the first."

Ethan took her hand, drew her up the steps of the veranda that stretched the width of the house. Through the walls and closed windows, music reached them, and the undercurrent of many voices. Without a word, he drew her into his arms and began to dance. She laughed when he twirled her and caught her close again.

He smiled down at her. "Did you ever believe in Santa Claus?"

"No."

"I did. I believed in Santa and I believed in romance. 'Just Molly and me and baby makes three.' But then you wake up two days after the wedding, and you wonder if you missed something. Even if Patty had stayed, Kelly, it wouldn't have worked. I know that now."

She dropped her head to his shoulder. She was so finely attuned to his lead, she was hardly more than a whisper in his arms.

"I had my own fairy tales," she murmured. "Prince Charming, for one. Kind of lopsided, I suppose, since I was certainly no Sleeping Beauty. And then I turned eighteen." She peered up at him. "I learned a lot of things at the hands of those two young men, Ethan, but what I learned most was that a person must never separate sex from character. You and I will not wake up after two days and wonder if this is all there is."

"Yes, but you and I don't believe in myths, do we?"

She seemed amazed. "I once told you that you wouldn't be destroyed if I left you. And you wouldn't. Do you know why?"

They had stopped dancing. They only moved sensually in each other's arms, content with the knowledge of past intimacies and the future to explore.

"Because you don't depend on anyone," she said. "It's not the reason I love you, but it's the reason I want to marry you. I believe what you say about our second chance. We've both been hurt, and we worked out our own survival. I wouldn't want to live without you, either, but I could if I had to."

She smiled suddenly, and a fresh peal of thunder rolled in, as if her sparkling eyes were the lightning that summoned it.

"Now—" she laughed "—are you sorry you asked?"

Ethan had never kissed her the way he kissed her now—studying her for a long time, then groping delicately for her eyes, her ears, her shoulders, the promise of her breast until neither of them were smiling, knowing that the order of their existence was irrevocably altered.

The unpredictable chastity of it had them both shivering.

"I love you very much, Kelly Jean Madison," he whispered as he folded her in his arms to close his eyes tightly, tightly shut. *Please be happy, my darling.*

She kissed the side of his neck. "Every day I thank God for you, Ethan."

The kitchen of the Chase mansion was a catacomb of stainless steel, designed to accommodate the family cook and butler, but it was not overburdened by a bevy of caterers for two hundred people.

Islanded in the center was a double range, over which great copper pots and long-handled pans and pewter ladles were dangling. In a nearby pantry were racks of wine bottles. Baccarat stemware sparkled behind cupboards with glass doors. Fine bone china filled another.

Kelly followed Ethan past the army of waiters who were hurrying back and forth like medical teams rushing to the site of a terrible emergency.

"Why am I reminded of a surgical room?" she quipped.

He bent over a cart of pastries and assorted fruits. "Because Frankenstein was put together in this very room. Would you care for a candied apricot?"

He held one poised before her mouth, and Kelly tweaked the ruffles on his shirt. "I think I just lost my appetite."

"Nonsense."

Kelly took the crystal plate he thrust into her hand. He began filling it with an assortment of hors d'oeuvres.

"Wait a minute," she protested.

Blithely ignoring her, he plopped on a dollop of caviar. A waiter hurried forward but stopped dead in his tracks when Ethan looked up with one of his "arresting officer" scowls.

"Ethan, I don't *like* caviar," Kelly said.

"This is supposed to be the best. How about lobster? Smothered in some of this disgusting sauce? This family doesn't know the meaning of cholesterol."

Onto her plate went the lobster, molded gelatin, a meat pie, relish and rolls and a number of other concoctions.

Recognizing his black sense of humor, Kelly blithely placed her leather case onto a counter top, scooped up a pair of tongs and commenced filling a plate for Ethan.

"You really must have some of this . . . hmm, I'm not exactly sure what it is. But do have some, Ethan."

"Why, thank you, darling."

Another wide-eyed waiter inched forward, a crisp white towel laid across his arm and a bottle of red wine and two glasses in his hand.

"Madam?" He tactfully caught Kelly's attention and indicated the wine.

Kelly gave him a beatific smile and asked Ethan, "Have we finished with our selections, dear?"

Ethan raked his upper lip with his teeth. "Well . . ."

With another smile for the waiter, Kelly added tiny pearled onions to Ethan's plate, plus a sandwich and a scoop of nuts. As a garnish, she spooned a liberal serving of glazed cherries over everything.

"What do you think?" She looked at the waiter. "White? No, Red?"

The waiter, poor man, was spared the decision as the kitchen doors swept open to admit a great burst of laughter, two men in tuxedos and a pair of glamorous women who were ushering in a dangerously handsome man who was seated in a wheelchair.

Traipsing around the chair like fairies were three youngsters. The boy and girl were somewhere in the neighborhood of ten years, Kelly thought, and the ruffled toddler, no more than two. She was trying to crawl into the wheelchair.

With a murmur of surprise, Ethan put his plate on the stove and stepped forward.

"There you are!" one of the women cried as she rushed forward and threw herself into Ethan's arms, a swirling blue of chiffon and crepe and flashing diamonds.

"Hello, Janie. Motherhood hasn't changed you, I see."

"Beast," she said, and kissed him.

One of the men stepped up behind Janie and said, "You're being paged, old man. For one of Georgia's photography sessions. Did you think you would escape? Kids, say hello to your Uncle Ethan."

After shaking hands with his niece and nephew, Ethan plucked the baby girl from off the wheelchair and tossed her high into the air so that the girl squealed and grabbed the ruffles on his shirt.

Watching on as the other couple moved closer and sucked Ethan into their circle of gravity, Kelly found herself in an unexpected but familiar position—not all that different from never quite being a part of the inner circle of her own family.

How often had she stood on the fringe and watched others laugh and enjoy being at the center of things? How often had she lost self-esteem when Debbie and Melissa were chosen and she was left, when many of their friends and teachers didn't know they had a younger sister?

But now, something was different. *She* was different. She was loved, and she was in love. At its best, that love touched some quality that was shaking itself awake inside her—reluctantly, yes, but with the promise of immeasurable personal strength, the certainty that all would be well with her in the end. Whatever life dealt from this day forward, she would be all right. Alone, perhaps, but never lonely.

Her pleasure was in seeing Ethan's family fuss over him.

"I want to introduce my wife, Ethan," the younger man was saying. "Vivian, this man whose nose is smeared all over his face once put Super Glue in the toothpaste. I would advise you to be very, very careful."

"Don't pay any attention to Brad," Vivian said, and shook Ethan's hand. "I'm very happy to meet you, Ethan. I've heard a lot about you."

"I'll bet you have," Ethan said, and reached back to bring Kelly forward. "There's someone I want you all to meet, too. I've just asked Kelly to marry me, and she has honored me by accepting."

The silence took a moment to settle. When it did, and Kelly did not stop now to analyze why, it was not an ordinary absence of sound. Nor was it a silence of surprise. The abrupt stillness was something more akin to shock.

"I already know Miss Madison." Maxwell's deep voice finally broke through the awkward caesura as he smiled at her from behind rimless spectacles. "At least, we've spoken on the telephone. I was sorry to hear of your father's passing, Miss Madison. I'm Max, Ethan's father."

It was easy to see where Ethan had gotten his good looks. Though Maxwell's black hair was frosted with gray and the skin was beginning to droop from his fine jawbone, he was not without power.

"Bring the wine, Trent," he commanded easily. "We have to toast Ethan and his bride-to-be."

The waiter obediently placed glasses and a bottle on the nearest countertop to the elder Chase.

"I owe you an apology for not returning your call, Miss Madison," Maxwell said as he poured. "Actually I called several times, but you were out, then I had to leave town again. We kept missing each other."

As he placed the glass into her hand and others were passed around, Kelly wondered if it was tactful to ignore his disability.

"You know," she said, deciding on forthrightness, "if you had one of those long cigarette holders, you'd look like President Roosevelt. I don't suppose you have a New Deal up your sleeve that the *Mirror* should worry about."

His approval was hearty in his laughter. "I'll make you a New Deal, Kelly, if you can eat anything on that plate of yours with a straight face."

"Mother should be here," Janie said as they all clustered around Kelly and Ethan and lifted their glasses.

"This has been a long time coming, son," Maxwell said. "You know I want nothing but your happiness. You both have my blessing and my hopes for a long and happy life."

The waiters gave them all a start by applauding the toast. "To Ethan and Kelly," they all joined in proclaiming.

Looking more like a shy boy dressed up in his father's ruffles and bow tie, Ethan drew Kelly into his side and kissed her lips. "To us, my darling."

"The bad news is," Brad said, quickly bringing the celebration to an end, "that Ethan and I have to get our mug shots, or Mother may have us shot. You would be a widow before a bride, Kelly."

Kelly was only too eager to wait behind for Ethan to fulfill his duty.

Maxwell skillfully drew her into his company as Janie and Vivian and the children drifted through the kitchen to rejoin the party outside. He filled himself a more sensible plate and chatted easily about the house—how it had survived the War Between the States and how his wife's candidacy for governor was changing their lives.

One thing he did not mention was Georgia's fury at the *Mirror*.

"What happened here a few minutes ago?" she asked him point-blank when he had run out of small talk.

She wasn't surprised when Maxwell gave the wheel of his chair a spin and brought himself around. She stooped at his knee, bringing her face to the level of his.

"Am I imagining that everyone knows something but me?" she pressed him. "Am I that paranoid to think that Brad and Janie looked at me so . . ."

The lie tried to find Maxwell's tongue, and Kelly started to rise and forget that she'd asked.

"My dear girl," he said, and drew off his eyeglasses to gouge at his eyelids.

"I didn't imagine it, did I? Please, if it involves Ethan and me, I have the right to know."

"Of course you do." Pain scored his face now—not of the body but of the heart. "But would you do something for me first?"

"Of course, sir."

"Would you wait for me in the library? There's something I have to fetch, and then I'll tell you everything."

"Will you tell me why you called me at the paper?"

His smile was a promise. "Just wait for me in the library. I'll be right along, my dear."

Before she could refuse him, Maxwell was motioning the waiter forward. "Trent, could you escort Miss Madison? Make her comfortable. I'll be there shortly."

"But Ethan—"

"I'll see he knows where you are."

She really had no choice, for she was a guest in this man's house. Fetching her bag, she followed the waiter down the long hall past the mirrors and the back of the stairs where the noise of the party reached out to them.

Trent tapped gently on a heavy oak door to make certain no one was inside.

Once in, he flipped a light switch, stepped back and waited politely. "Ma'am?"

She entered the room, still puzzling over Maxwell's odd behavior. What had Ethan said when Maxwell had first called her? *He must have found something,* he had said. When she'd asked about what he could have found, Ethan had said he didn't even want to think about it.

"Thank you," Kelly told the waiter.

When she turned to smile, he was gone.

* * *

As secretary to the mayor and soon-to-be governor of the state of Alabama, Marlene Pace never left anything to chance. She was the woman behind the woman, and her whole career had been spent enhancing the political life of Georgia Chase.

Rarely did Georgia express gratitude to her faithful laborers, but Marlene never complained. She didn't flinch at Georgia's complaint about her image but took a month's vacation, had some cosmetic surgery and placed herself in the hands of an image consultant.

Ten thousand dollars later, she returned, a corporate woman in silk suit, sculpted hair by Henri, jewelry by Givenchy, shoes by Ferragamo.

"I've been looking for you," she briskly told Ethan as she caught him passing Georgia's office with Brad. "Hello, Brad." She promptly dismissed Ethan's brother. "Ethan, could I have a word with you, please?"

Ethan had never been particularly fond of his mother's secretary. But then, Georgia had not asked his opinion when she hired Marlene fresh out of college.

He gave her a saccharine smile. "Brad and I were on our way to be photographed, Marlene. I only have so many smiles in me tonight. If I use them up with you . . ."

Marlene was not amused. She marched to Georgia's office, threw open the door and waited for Ethan to enter.

In no mood to take on his mother's uptight secretary, Ethan ambled into the room, looked around without seeing anything that interested him.

He removed a cigar from a box on Georgia's desk. "The last time I saw you," he drawled as he borrowed a lighter, too, and puffed briefly, "you still knew how to laugh. But life goes on, doesn't it?"

Without bothering to become insulted, Marlene affixed herself to the side of Georgia's desk and crossed her legs to good advantage. "Yes, Ethan. Life goes on. You just took a rather remarkable step, I understand."

Ethan plucked a piece of tobacco from his lip. "Some spy network you've got there, Marlene. You must give me a few pointers."

"Get to the point, Ethan."

Shrugging off all pretense of civility, Ethan put space between his feet. "No. You get to the point, Marlene. I'm not in a mood for this."

Her smile was a crimson gash. "Good. Do you know what you've done by becoming engaged to Vincent Madison's daughter?"

Ethan considered the white ash of his cigar. "Make your point."

"Your timing is horrendous."

"At least it's mine, darling."

"The mayor does *not* want you making any announcements about joining the enemy camp."

"Oh, wow!"

"She's serious, Ethan. You can do what you damn well please with your career, whatever, but if you make her look bad by openly supporting the political posture of the *Mirror,* I personally will—"

For once, Ethan thought that being a son of a bitch had its advantages. He walked to the desk and placed his cigar carefully into the ashtray. With his lips drawn back from his teeth, he bent over Marlene Pace and brought his face so that it nearly touched hers.

He let his voice drop deep in his throat and, by the sheer force of his will, waited until her insulting smile lost some of its edge.

"You know, Marlene—" he smiled evilly and straightened "—this is a strange age we live in. We've got listening devices now that you wouldn't believe. And you know what else? When somebody threatens a police officer, it doesn't take anything to get it brought before a judge."

She paled slightly, then snapped her mouth closed. "Are you wired?"

Grinning, he stretched both arms into the air. "You wanna search me?"

"Is this house bugged?"

"Well—" he drew his fingers over his jaw "—a person can't be too careful, can they? If I were you, I'd check the phones, just to be on the safe side. And I'd be a little more careful of my sexual habits, if you know what I mean."

Spinning on his heel, Ethan strode to the door, knowing that Marlene was only slightly afraid of him and not really caring.

"You will not complicate this campaign, Ethan," she yelled after him. "I mean it."

He didn't waste the energy to look back. "Stuff it, Marlene. I'm sure you'll know where."

The Chase library, Kelly found, smelled richly of fine wood, good leather and loving care of both. It was a room of history, of lush, paneled walls and glimmering marble-topped tables and bookshelves that reached the tall ceiling, filled with old leather law books.

The floor was also marble, and large Oriental rugs were strategically placed. Logs waited graciously on the hearth, and on the mantel was a row of silver and gold cups, Ethan's football trophies among them.

A grandfather clock ticked peacefully in the corner where it lived with the gun rack. Had Ethan once fired those guns? she wondered.

On the west side of the room, French doors opened onto a patio that was bordered with fall flowers. Opening them a small amount, Kelly stood watching the rain that had finally arrived—heavy gray sheets that obscured the outside lights and made her new clothes feel soggy.

She closed the doors and returned to pick up a piece of Steuben glass. Perhaps she should take a picture of the old room. She certainly wasn't getting anything for the paper at the press briefing.

She sank onto a silk-covered chair near the window and listened to the rain.

"You blew this one, Kell," she murmured aloud, needing the sound of a familiar voice. "You didn't make things better by coming—you've probably made them worse. You spent all that time and money on yourself, and what did it get you? The ring doesn't count—you would have gotten that anyway. I wonder what Max wanted to talk about? Damn it, Ethan, I'm tired of waiting on you!"

From a table, she picked up a leather-bound picture album and idly flipped through it.

Georgia, with patrician features that were as familiar as that of a movie star, was pictured on every page—Georgia as a bride, standing with Maxwell; Georgia shaking hands with someone whose name she didn't know; Georgia and Maxwell; Georgia and Ethan and . . . Ethan's *wife*.

The photograph jumped out at her the way a person's own name in print comes alive. It was natural, wasn't it, to be curious?

She brought the picture closer to the light and strained to see the woman standing in the curve of Ethan's arm. She blinked to clear her focus, and her lips parted in . . . surprise?

No. Shock. She could have been looking at her own reflection. That was it! That was why they had looked at her in such disbelief!

She slammed the album shut and thrust it to the marble tabletop. Shivering, she listened to the rain drumming against the doors.

But she couldn't fall into the sick trap of imagining Ethan's mind so twisted that he had asked her to marry him because of some resemblance to his first wife. She wouldn't swallow that. She didn't believe it.

Yet she was suddenly driven to leave this room and this party. It was clear why Ethan's family had been so friendly, not because they'd liked her, particularly, but because they *pitied* her.

Tears banked painfully behind her eyes. Yet the parts of her that had begun disengaging with the past kept her on track. She did not have to deal with this now. It was her life, and if she wanted to put space between herself and the people here, she was not obligated to make excuses. She did not have to feel guilty.

Taking up her bag, she took one regretful look at her beautiful new clothes and hurried out the French doors. Later, Ethan would find her. Because he loved her, he would understand.

And if he didn't understand? She was Scarlett O'Hara with a lifetime of tomorrows.

Chapter 14

"Where's Kelly?" Ethan strode into his parents' kitchen, his words whipping like a backlash. A swift reconnoiter found his father sitting in the wheelchair, a bottle of Scotch cradled in his lap.

Maxwell lifted his head as slowly as Ethan was abrupt. With a soft sigh, he made his own reconnoiter, starting at Ethan's angry expression, then to the determined space between his feet.

"You must need one of these as badly as I did," he said, and spun the cap from the bottle, offering it.

To Ethan, the kitchen was more like the bowels of an alien spaceship now—headed for the unfriendly limits of the universe.

But his father wasn't to blame, he thought with a guilty twinge. More gently, he asked, "Where's Kelly, Dad?"

"I'm not drunk enough to talk about this," Maxwell said, and lifted the bottle to his lips.

"Dad?" Ethan gripped his father's shoulder and tactfully pushed the Scotch aside with more force than was necessary.

"She's in the library, Ethan."

"What's she doing in the library?"

"I sent her there."

"What's going on here? What's happened? What're you trying to say?"

With a weariness that Ethan understood only too well, his father loosened his bow tie. Their places had amazingly switched, he thought; now Maxwell was the one climbing into a bottle, and he, Ethan, was left to offer the voice of reason.

"I need to tell you about her," the older man said as Ethan was walking to the door that opened onto the corridor.

"About Kelly? What about Kelly?"

"Not Kelly. *Her.*"

"Mother, you mean?"

Maxwell dropped his chin to his chest in a stall for time.

"Damn it, Dad!" Ethan could hardly resist the urge to grab his father by the front of his tuxedo and shake him senseless. Only the memory of Maxwell wanting to do the same thing kept him still.

"Cut to the chase, Dad," he said tightly. "Kelly's waiting."

With shaking fingers, Maxwell unbuttoned the collar of his ruffled shirt. He fumbled in his breast pocket for his wallet. Opening it, he searched through the compartments with a tediousness that made Ethan grind his teeth.

Presently, when Ethan's nerves were wound as tightly as a clock, his father brought out a small folded paper, proffered it.

Ethan gazed down at the code—the designation of a computer document, apparently, and he looked up, waving it. "What is it?"

"If you were to go into your mother's office," Maxwell intoned, his tongue thickening, "and if you were to ask her personal computer for this document, you would bring up an entry that she probably intends to delete." He took another long swig of Scotch and wiped his mouth on the back of his hand. "It's been there for months, apparently. The long hand of fate, Ethan. In payment for my sins."

Returning to where his father was hunched in his chair, Ethan stuffed the paper in Maxwell's breast pocket. "The Scotch is bringing out your dramatic streak, Dad."

With his blue eyes flashing their own brand of fire, Maxwell struck Ethan's hand aside. He gave the wheel of his chair a spin and whirled around like a fighter circling his opponent.

"Would you call sixty thousand dollars 'melodrama'?" he challenged.

For a moment, Ethan stood perfectly still. His brain didn't want to calculate the possibilities of such words. When he remembered to breathe, he turned to stare out at nothing.

"Yeah," Maxwell slurred. "Oh, yeah. Sixty thousand reasons. A nice round figure. A present from your mother's good friend, Mr. Russo himself. A check, can you believe it? You know, Ethan, she didn't even have the courtesy to launder it through the city. She deposited it in our personal account. I wish I didn't know. I wouldn't if you hadn't started me digging."

"I'm sorry, Dad."

"She would've done better to call it a campaign contribution. That way she would have broken only one law. But no, she had to call it 'personal' and lasso me into it. What's 'personal,' for God's sake? Trust is personal, Ethan.

Wheelchairs are personal. Sixty thousand dollars ain't personal, by damn!"

Ethan pinched the bridge of his nose. He closed his eyes and shook his head.

"When I asked you to check it out—" he bleakly sought for an excuse "—I honestly thought I'd be putting Kelly's charge to rest. I knew Mother sometimes drifted into the gray areas, but... what a mess."

Now he would be obligated to go through the Chase family records, which would drag the bank into the picture, plus Russo's bank account. Photostats of the check would be required and all kinds of tax records. In the end, he would have proven that his mother deliberately colluded with Southeast Medical to operate on the illegal side of the environmental laws. She would have betrayed the people's trust. She would have prostituted her own political ethics.

"Maybe it isn't what it looks like," he said hopelessly.

Maxwell's reply was to take another swallow of Scotch.

Ethan patted his father's shoulder. "Don't worry about it, Dad. I'll take care of it. Don't tell Mother and get her started. If she's got to be angry, let her be angry at me. Look, why don't you go up to rest? I really have to find Kelly."

Knowing that Trent would find his father, Ethan passed through the corridor toward the library. He needed Kelly. He needed her because he wasn't the master of his own destiny at all. He was a mixed-up tangle of conflicts set loose by loss and loneliness and betrayal by the woman he was now obligated to deal with. In his love for Kelly, he would find sanity amid the chaos.

He eagerly opened the door and came face-to-face with Hite, whose hand was reaching for the same doorknob.

"Hite!" he said ridiculously, and caught himself up short. "What're you doing here?"

"I was looking for Kelly." The attorney, even in his consternation, was more handsomely self-possessed than a man had a right to be. "What're you doing here?"

"Looking for Kelly."

Hite's lip curled in mockery. "Well, I hate to tell you this, but you just missed her."

"What d'you mean?"

Hite gestured to the empty room and the French doors, one of which was banging gently in the rainy wind. Not sure what Hite was trying to tell him, Ethan took the room in three strides and squinted to see outside.

"She left?" he asked, confused.

"Based on circumstantial evidence," Hite drawled, "I would say so, yes."

"Well, why didn't you stop her, man?" Ethan heeled hard about and headed for the corridor, meaning to make the front door his first checkpoint, the parking lot the second.

But Hite's anger had been building for months, perhaps for years. He grabbed Ethan's sleeve as he passed and jerked him roughly around.

Guessing that some part of him had relished this confrontation, Ethan knocked Hite's hand aside and thrust at his shoulders.

"Back off, Hite!" he snarled as Hite stumbled back a step, "and get out of my face. This is none of your business."

Hite lunged forward, his handsome face contorted with outrage, but Ethan neatly sidestepped him. "I warned you, Ethan! Didn't I warn you not to hurt her? And look at you—you've broken her heart already."

The room, indeed, the entire house, seemed to await Ethan's reaction to such a charge. Ethan was suddenly suffused with heat. He clawed at his collar.

"Oh, you can read minds now, can you, Mr. Big Shot Attorney?" he countered.

Hite thrust his chin against his perfect bow tie. "You don't think a woman runs out into a thunderstorm because she's ecstatic with joy, do you? Some cop you are, Ethan. Some human being."

Was this how it happened? Ethan wondered. Was this how a man crossed the thin line between friendship and enmity? Over a woman?

He said with a deadly softness, "You had over fifteen years in this town, Hite, and you never once told Kelly how you felt. So step aside. Tonight I asked her to marry me, and she accepted. Give it up, Hite. She's wearing my ring."

The color drained from Hite's face, and his lip quivered with offense. "You always did win, Ethan. Even when you didn't try, you always won."

Ethan was more concerned with Kelly than with Hite's problems. Another time, he said with the shrug of his shoulders. He couldn't deal with it now.

He turned to leave, but Hite grabbed him from behind, and when Ethan spun around, he jammed his fist hard into the pit of Hite's belly.

Gagging, Hite stumbled backward into the room, his arms flailing to keep balance, one of them sending Georgia's antique hurricane lamp shattering to the marble floor.

The shatter of glass had the effect of a bell ringing at the end of a round. Like boys, they gaped at the glass, then at each other.

"Sorry, Ethan," Hite said, and folded his arms over his stomach.

Ethan held up his hands and backed away. "Hey, I don't want to fight you, Hite. Go back to the party. Have a drink. We'll forget this ever happened."

Hite shook his head, his hair having lost its careful grooming. "Can't do it, Ethan. I can't let you do to Kelly what you did to Patty."

Lowering his head like a stubborn young steer, Hite gathered his strength. Giving a bellow of rage, he charged, and Ethan took the impact that sent him crashing painfully against a bookcase where dozens of law books crashed down on his head.

Swearing, he regained his balance and hurled himself at Hite, plowing into him as a linebacker would take down his man. Hite was thrown to the floor but scrambled deftly up again. He dropped into a crouch, and Ethan mirrored him.

Their harsh breaths filled the room. Both relished the violence now. From far away came the sound of applause and a garbled voice on a PA system—other voices, nearer but having nothing to do with the small, declared war in this room.

They circled each other like wolves searching for the tenderness of the throat, their eyes glittering, their lips drawn back to show their teeth.

Hite moved sideways, his feet crunching the broken glass. Ethan countered the move and lashed out with a whistling blow that knocked the attorney off balance. Hite went crashing against the mantel, and one of Ethan's football trophies struck the hearth.

Neither of them gave it a second look.

A figure appeared in the open library door and cried out in amazement, "What's going on here?"

Ethan didn't turn to see who it was. He ducked Hite's fist and drove his own into Hite's ribs so that his whole arm went numb. Voices were coming from other parts of the room, but he and Hite saw nothing but each other, style and strategy forgotten. Where Ethan lacked Hite's deftness, he compensated with the technique of street fighting that had meant his survival as a policeman.

Hite lunged. Ethan took the blow full in his face, and his nose gushed blood. "Agggh!" he roared.

Enraged by the pain, Ethan counterattacked with brute force, raining down upon Hite with a battery of brutal jabs to his ribs, his kidneys, his face, anywhere he could punch until Hite, groaning, dropped to his knees and covered his head.

Ethan felt sick to his stomach as blood drizzled into his mouth. Hands grabbed him from behind. "Wait, wait! Take it easy! Back off! Let it go!"

But Hite was on his feet, swinging wildly. Ethan tried to dodge, but he couldn't free himself of his captors, and Hite's fist found his right eye.

"Enough of this!" Irwin Pritchard roared, and was abruptly standing between the two men like a prophet about to pronounce doom. "What do you think this is, the Dark Ages? Ethan, have you lost your mind? I'll have your badge for this. Hite, stop it this instant, or by God I'll thrash you myself."

Hite did not yield so easily to his father. Brad released Ethan to lunge for the attorney. Maxwell entered the room, and two of the waiters along with Marlene Pace. While Ethan watched them, Hite evaded Brad and picked up a chair, hurling it at Ethan.

Ethan agilely dodged, and the chair splintered against the wall. "Son of a bitch!"

"I won't stand for this!" Marlene shrilled, and motioned wildly for Georgia's bodyguards to enter.

The two musclemen darted across the room, but Ethan, confronting one squarely, held him at bay. "I wouldn't do that," he warned, and lifted a finger. "I'll just have to take you downtown, and then you'll have to raise bail." He snapped around to find another man moving in on Hite. "And you, fancy pants," he barked. "Back off!"

Both guards stopped where they were and consulted with each other, apparently deciding that physical force would be a bad idea.

"Ethan—" Maxwell's chair moved across the shards of broken glass "—this is all my fault."

"Forget it, Dad," Ethan mumbled, and said to Irwin Pritchard, "Help Hite."

"I can help myself!" Hite shouted as Ethan started for the door. "And I'm not sorry, Ethan. I won't apologize."

Drained of his anger and wanting only to go to Kelly, Ethan found Hite over his shoulder.

"I don't want apologies, you schmuck," he said with tender sadness as he reached the door. "I want my friend back."

"Not now!" Kelly screamed as she sat shivering in her car, soaked to the skin, her teeth chattering as she turned the key in the ignition only to get a *click* for her trouble. "Not now!"

She slammed the dashboard with her fist and crumbled into a soggy mass of weeping. Presently, however, she accepted, as she always accepted. Gritting her teeth against the cold, she fetched the wrench and climbed out of the car into the storm.

Gasping as the autumn rain pelted her once again, she hunkered down in the gravel.

"Ma'am . . ." One of the parking valets rushed up beneath an umbrella, peering down at her in astonishment. "Are you in some kind of trouble?"

Kelly didn't know what to strike first with the wrench, the valet's shin or the solenoid. "Hold that thing over me!" she screeched.

"What?"

"I've got to climb under the car."

"Under! Oh, ma'am . . ."

"Do you know where the solenoid is?"

His confidence failed. "No."

"Then hold that thing over me."

Guessing she looked ludicrous in the once-smart crepe slacks, her sequined tank gaping and her behind higher than her head, she crawled beneath the fender and whopped the solenoid a murderous blow.

"Oh, ma'am," the man pleaded when she backed out, "let me help you inside."

"Just don't look at me," Kelly said as she stood to a height that was more than his. "And get out of the way before I run you down."

Did she imagine, as she drove out of the Chase driveway, that he waved and shouted, "Give 'em hell, lady!"?

The truth was, Caroline didn't enjoy being Melissa's mother much more than Melissa liked being Caroline's daughter.

There were times, however, when Melissa and Deborah were only too happy to come home to their mother. They had inherited her terror of thunderstorms.

When today's bruised clouds had massed and the air grew chill, Caroline was grateful when Melissa's red car zoomed into the driveway.

"I know, I know," Melissa wailed as she burst through the back door of the kitchen, carrying a huge tote bag on each arm and blotting her smeared eyeliner, "I look like a wookie. My sinuses are killing me."

"I knew it would storm," Caroline said. "Prissy and Mott have been underfoot all day."

Pausing long enough to peer down her nose at Mott, who never failed to flatten his ears at her, Melissa hissed a "scat" and sneezed.

"Don't show your fangs at me, you monster," she sniffed when Mott growled and arched his back. "I'll tear your face off."

Caroline gently shooed the cats from the kitchen and set cups, saucers and napkins on a tray with the silver coffee urn.

"Let's go to the living room," she said graciously. "I've made some coffee."

"Oh, no," Melissa said to the ceiling in a semblance of prayer.

The living room was the largest and airiest room in the big house. It offset the dining room on the opposite side of the foyer. The veranda outside fronted the living room and turned the corner to run the entire depth of the east side.

Caroline and her daughter sat in the shadowy interior with only the light from the foyer in order to watch the rain flooding the yard.

They spoke very little. When the thunder pealed and the world held its breath until the lightning cracked, Melissa cringed, and when Debbie's station wagon lurched into the drive, its lemony lights pushing through the gray sheets, she leapt to her feet.

"Misery loves company," she said.

"The same thing as you, I expect."

"But she'll have the twins with 'er. Kids are so... childish."

"So are some older kids I know. Be pleasant, Melissa."

Caroline hurried to the back door as Prissie and Mott thundered behind her. Doors slammed in the garage, and Debbie herded her boys up the steps and burst through the screen door.

"It's raining cats and dogs out there!" she yelped as the twins ducked under her arms and raced for the cookie jar.

Caroline brought towels to lay over her favorite hooked rug.

Kissing her mother's cheek, Debbie giggled. "I think I hurt the cats' feelings." She stooped to pet the whiskered felines. "It's not really raining cats and dogs, Mott. Don't growl at me."

The haughty tom swept from the kitchen, and the twins struck out after him. "Come on, Mott!" Edward's laughter drifted through the house. "Let's go upstairs and watch 'Lassie'!"

Caroline sighed. "Deborah, you really must do something about the manners of those children."

"I know, Mother. It's just so hopeless. Where's Melly?"

"In the front room, having a nervous breakdown."

"And Kelly?"

"Out."

"In this soup?" Debbie tossed back her damp blond hair and shook out her waterlogged sweater.

"A press conference," Caroline said.

"Ah." Debbie's brows lifted knowingly as they walked into the living room. "She's out at the Chase place, isn't she? I can't believe she's really seeing that man."

"Love makes you stupid," Melissa blandly observed.

Debbie laughed. "I always said, Kelly was just like Daddy."

Pressing her lips, Caroline went to the window and rubbed a circle in the condensation. Another pair of headlights was clawing through the rain and lashing the veranda steps.

"Ah, here she is."

It wasn't until Kelly bounded up the steps and burst through the front door to find her mother and sisters standing in a reception line, that she realized how bedraggled she was. As the door slammed shut behind her, echoed by a blast of thunder and lightning, they gaped at her with open mouths and wide, wondering eyes.

Kelly hesitated, then fashioned a silly smile. "Hi!" she said brightly, and squeezed water from her cardigan. "It's raining."

"Is that a new outfit?" Debbie asked.

Melissa leaned over to brush back a drippy strand of Kelly's hair. "New earrings. That's not like you, Kelly."

"And you've cut your hair," Caroline gasped.

To Kelly, years had passed since she sat in the hairstylist's chair and dreamed of impressing Georgia Chase. She discreetly turned her diamond ring down on her finger and considered the widening puddle around her feet.

Caroline stepped to the linen pantry and returned with a towel that Kelly gratefully took.

"How was the press party?" she asked.

"When I left," Kelly hedged as she blotted her hair, "everybody and his dog was there."

"Not everybody," Melissa said, and opened the door to watch another pair of headlights slash their driveway.

Tires screeched to a stop, and the door of a truck slammed.

"Who could that be?" On tiptoe, Debbie peered over her sister's shoulder.

Three guesses, Kelly thought, and buried her face in the towel until only her eyes showed.

Now she felt stupid for not having waited for Ethan. If she couldn't bear a bit of family gossip about her resemblance to Ethan's first wife, how could she possibly withstand Georgia's bitter resentment for the *Mirror?* And other things?

A fist banged loudly at the door. Melissa opened the screen and gasped, "Good heavens."

Kelly threw the towel over her head and dropped to the bottom stair, her voice muffled. "Who is it?"

"I need to see Kelly, please." Ethan's demand rang clearly over the sound of the storm.

"Ask who it is," Debbie whispered.

Melissa snorted. "You ask."

"Oh, for goodness' sake." Caroline waved her daughters aside. "Mr. Chase, won't you . . . dear me."

Without actually being invited inside or told to go away, Ethan pushed through the door and stepped into the foyer.

Kelly peered through the towel as if through a pair of draperies, and she was as shocked as her sisters.

The sleeve of Ethan's tuxedo was dangling by a few threads to its armhole, and the ruffles of his shirt were spattered with blood. A large purplish bruise the size of a peach pit was distorting his left cheek, and his nose was red and swollen. His upper lip, split on one side, was crusted with blood from his nose, and his right hand was wrapped in the black bow tie that had earlier been around his neck.

Kelly pressed the towel to her lips and came weakly to her feet. *Oh, Ethan! What happened to you?*

"We don't want any trouble, Mr. Chase," Caroline was saying with amazing equanimity.

"There's not going to be any trouble, Mrs. Madison." Ethan shot Kelly a look, then glanced briefly at Melissa and Debbie, who were both transfixed.

He added, "Tonight I asked Kelly to marry me."

Flabbergasted, Caroline lifted a slender hand to touch her lips. "And she did *that?*"

As Debbie and Melissa drifted off in gales of laughter, Kelly found nothing amusing. She started toward Ethan, and he, with a formality that would have been hilarious had it not been deeply honest, drew his torn sleeve up to its shoulder seam and held it in place.

No one said a word as he walked through the foyer to the stairs.

Please, Kelly begged him with her eyes as she inched up several steps, *don't make me look foolish in front of my sisters.*

With the flair of a Rhett Butler, Ethan stopped at the bottom of the stairs. His look up at her was one Kelly could read only with her heart—his confusion over a life that had become so unwieldy, his inability to balance polarities and find his way in the world he had left, his certainty that he would find peace in the rightness of their love.

Kelly did not look away as she once would have done. At that moment there was nothing coy in her. She drew him into her heart through her eyes.

I know, she told him.

In two great strides, he reached her and, bending, scooped her into his arms. Turning, he carried her back down, through the foyer, past the three-person reception line to the door.

Still clutching the towel, Kelly confronted the family who had once pitied her because she was not a beauty queen. Now no one said a word of protest. Who would have dared deny the warrior prince come so magnificently for his betrothed?

At the door, Ethan hesitated, turning to them and smiling as much as his tender lip would allow. "She'll call you."

Chapter 15

"When we left my house," Kelly told Ethan as he handed her up the slippery gangplank of the *Great White,* "you didn't tell me we were coming to the mother of all boats."

Laughter brought pain to Ethan's split lip. "Where did you think we were going?"

"To get something to eat. I know, I know, the human body can go seventeen days without food." She gazed down at her soggy state with a dispassion that made Ethan remember why he'd fallen so hard for her. "I'd rather not test the theory."

"I guess I'll have to feed you, then." He swept out his arm in an invitation of her to climb aboard. "While you get cleaned up, Chef Chase will make an omelet."

They moved across the teak deck whose brass handles Ethan had spent hours polishing, on through the deckhouse with its gleaming wheel, down the steps to the cabins and galley.

Kelly had never seemed more desirable to him. She was swallowed by his tuxedo jacket, and her hair had dried in a charming dishevelment. Her mascara and lipstick had been washed away so that her only color was a healthy glow.

The rain had almost stopped now, but the wind was still high. The water was chopping moodily at the hull as they went below deck, and the *Great White* groaned against the lines holding it fast to the quay. So cozily enclosed were they, Maxwell's news about Georgia's bank account seemed distant and unreal.

If he hadn't been such a mass of aches and pains after his bout with Hite, Ethan told himself as he opened the door to his cabin, he would have remembered that he had left his desk incriminatingly cluttered with diskettes and a hard copy of *Treachery on a Pillow*.

"Oops," he said, and attempted to distract her by stepping past and engaging in a flurry of slamming drawers and scooping up clothes that were strewn about. "More messy than I remembered. Why don't you wait in the galley, darling, while I tidy things up a bit?"

But she was too clever by half and had already detected the clues of piled books, some of them Price Masters titles, the dictionary open on the bed, the thesaurus, the pencils, the wastebasket overflowing with discarded draft.

A puzzled tilt was in her brow. "A messy man doth a messy husband make, Ethan," she mused, and gazed curiously at the open dictionary.

Ethan quickly emptied an ashtray. "A side effect of genius, nothing more."

"A genius with secrets?" She attempted to reach around him to the desk.

Laughing through one side of his mouth, he sidestepped, only to have her reach around the other side. They engaged in a dodging contest for a moment until she became more earnest than playful. Then she took an unfair advantage of his battered body to stoop and snatch an open copy of *Kiss Me When I Die* from beneath the desk.

"My, my," she said as she remained stooped at his feet and turned the paperback reprint over to read the blurbs. "I didn't know you were such a dedicated fan of the genre, Ethan."

Cursing himself, Ethan stomped around her and scooped up the manuscript. Her sour remarks about Price Masters's purple pulp and the kind of people who read it still chafed him.

He dumped the hard copy into a box and clapped on the lid. "You like potato chips in bed," he countered grumpily.

"I like murder mysteries."

"Bad murder mysteries."

Ethan testily tapped the front of the paperback. "Twelve weeks on the *New York Times* bestseller list ain't bad, babe."

Her laughter filled the small cabin, and she shrugged out of his tuxedo jacket, placing it neatly on the back of the chair and giving it a pat. "Touché. Now, what did you put in the box?"

"Nothing."

"Come on. Don't be shy, Ethan."

"I thought you were starving to death."

She coquettishly ground her fist against his jaw. "Do you want me to add some more blood to that shirt?"

He was being much too defensive about the matter, Ethan knew, but he had left himself no escape hatch. Snapping playfully at her fingers, he growlingly shuttled the box beneath his bunk and leaned over to punch a button on the stereo.

Ray Charles instantly began to croon an old Hank Williams ballad.

"Get a move on, wench," he ordered, and slapped her rear. "Shower if you want, and there's some clean sweats in the bureau. I've got to take some aspirin. My nose is killing me.''

She took a last suspicious look around the cabin and moved into the head. Listening for the sound of her movements, Ethan hurried around the cabin, removing every incriminating piece of evidence he could find.

She appeared unexpectedly in the doorway, wearing only her sequined tank top and pair of silk boxer panties. He flinched, caught holding the wastepaper basket.

''Your aspirin,'' she said, and captured his hand to open it and drop two tablets into its palm. She rose to her toes to probe his bruised cheek. ''Have you got any ice for that?''

''My little X-rated Florence Nightingale,'' he said dourly, and peered down the front of her top.

''Don't be cute. I'll find some ice, then I'll make *you* an omelet. You can put your feet up and meditate on your sins. You and Hite are crazy men, you know—both of you. If I live to be a thousand, I'll never forget the glory of having won a fistfight.''

''That's because you never won one.''

''Well, I'm not walking around with a broken nose, either, am I?''

She began rummaging through his bureau drawers, her sexuality so natural and so lovely, his heart twisted with longing. She brought out a gray sweatshirt that would reach her knees.

Dropping the aspirins on the desk, Ethan stripped off his bloodstained shirt and unbuttoned the waist of his trousers, loosened the zipper. He trudged into the head and ran a sink of hot water.

Immersing his head hurt as much as it helped, and when he peered into the mirror and turned his lip wrong-side out, he found the cut caused by his tooth.

He filled a glass of water. With water droplets clinging to his whisker-shadowed jaws and the hair on his chest, he stepped back into the cabin.

There, sitting on the foot of his bunk, Kelly was reading discarded pages of *Treachery on a Pillow*.

Oh, Lord!

Looking up, she shocked him by having tears in her eyes. She surprised him even more by taking the injury upon herself.

"Why didn't you tell me?" she asked, holding up the pages as tears slid to the ends of her lashes and clung there, glistening. "Why did you let me go ranting and spouting all that self-righteous stuff? You had a thousand opportunities, Ethan, especially when we were in New York. I'm so embarrassed I want to crawl in a hole."

Too stunned to move closer, Ethan had never felt more like the dark side of her innocence. "Embarrassed?" He could not articulate what her approval meant to him. "I thought you hated these books."

"Not if *you're* writing them, you stupid jerk!"

Before he could reach out and draw her to him, she had lunged to her feet with a crunch of computer paper and crushed him in her arms.

"Easy, darling," he croaked as he shuddered with pain.

Her embarrassment evolved into instant resentment that prompted her to step back and skewer him with a glare.

"You're not poor!" She pointed a damning finger at his head. "All that time, you let me steam and stew about money."

With his face screwed up in bafflement, Ethan signed for time out. "Wait a minute! I must've told you a dozen times I had money."

Her pout was inflammable, and she wagged her head mockingly. "Oh, you did, did you? What are you worth, anyway? A million dollars?"

"I don't want to go into this now."

"How many of those have you written?"

"Thirteen. Look, Kelly—"

She rolled her eyes to the ceiling. "Thirteen, he says."

The stockpiled troubles of the day ambushed Ethan, funneling into his temples with the pain of a jackhammer. He tossed back the aspirin and washed them down with water. He slammed the glass to the table so that the pencils clattered in their cup.

"A million dollars isn't much money these days. Look, Kelly, I apologize, I really do. I grovel at your feet. Here…" He spread his arms wide so that his chest was bare to his navel. "Run me through with a sword. Lop off my head. Pour my miserable blood into the Alabama River."

With a sardonic smile, she reached over to painfully tweak a curl on his chest. "While you're in such a penitent mood, poor baby, maybe you'll tell me why you let me go to your home and meet your family without warning me that I'm the spitting image of your first wife."

Ethan gaped at her in confusion. "What?"

"Don't pretend you didn't know. Everyone saw it. Even I saw it."

He was flabbergasted. Patty was tall and slim and blond, yes, but . . .

"You don't look at all like Patty," he growled.

"Then you'd better take another look." She shoved her face beneath his and skimmed her hair ruthlessly back to expose her features. She remained that way, her green eyes wide and clear, her fine nostrils flared, her rosy lips pursed in a pout.

Perhaps it was the headache that pushed him over the edge. Perhaps it was the realization that he had wasted so much of his life cauterizing his feelings. Perhaps it was his certainty, Price Masters aside, that men like him didn't deserve someone like Kelly.

Despair closed upon him, and he wrapped his arms around her and let her whimper break his heart. That she clung to him in quick surrender, meshing the angles of her body sweetly with his, was a miracle that humbled him beyond anything he had ever felt.

He drew the straps of her top over her shoulders, and they slithered down her arms. Rising on the tips of her toes, her nipples leaping as she grazed his chest, she offered herself.

He was in agony when he drew her back to the bed and fell with her. She urged him into her with a hunger that hurled him into some dark abyss. They seemed driven to have everything of the other as quickly as possible.

Only when they were quiet and facing each other in the still eye of the hurricane, rocking gently with the boat, was she suddenly shy. She clutched at the spread covering the bed and drew it over them. She kissed the good side of his mouth.

"When will you marry me?" he asked, and turned on his side, propping his head on a fist.

Smiling, she arranged his hair. "Mmm, I don't know, Mr. Masters."

"Hey."

"After the election?"

"I've been looking for you nearly twenty years. I'm not waiting till any election. We'll move into the apartment."

"Yes." She rained kisses on his chest. "When?"

"Whenever you say."

"Thanksgiving."

Beneath the bedspread, she found him, unaroused and docile, a condition that didn't last. Straddling him, gently impaling herself, she was poised to take rather than give.

She had no idea of the pleasure she brought him, Ethan thought. She moved with a purity of purpose that mesmerized him, and he drew his hands down her long arching back and cupped her hips.

"Thanksgiving," she said, her voice husky with her own search for fulfillment.

She closed her eyes and moved quicker then, and more sensuously. With a sharp catch of breath, she trembled, and the muscles inside her tightened. She sank upon his chest.

"Don't keep secrets from me again, Ethan," she whispered against his ear. "No matter how bad it is, promise you'll always tell me."

"I promise," he said with a sudden jab of memory that he hadn't yet told her about Russo bribing his mother with sixty thousand dollars.

Her body molded itself into the curve of his like a spoon nested within a spoon.

"Ethan?" She drew his arm more tightly around her waist.

"Hmm?"

"Nothing could happen to you, could it?"

"What d'you mean, happen?"

"I mean, when you go out every day, that gun you carry. How much of yourself do you risk?"

So. It had finally come—the thing that lovers eventually face when one is an enforcer of the law: death, just around the corner, life changing in the blink of an eye.

He sighed heavily.

"You don't have to do it," she whispered with soft poignance. "I mean, it's not like you need the money. You have your writing, I have the paper." She covered her face. "Oh, God, I told myself I would never ask this of you."

Ethan buried his face in her tangled hair that he loved. How many times in the past years had he wanted to make the change and had not dared to be so honest with himself? How many lies had he told his heart?

She made him see how bound at the ankles he was, always holding himself in check, forgetting that the things that really matter are the ones you don't expect. Was he now ready to sever the great foils of his past and to ally himself with his own expectations?

He found himself in the glistening green pools of her eyes. She looked fresh and young and very beautiful. He had never seen anyone so beautiful and could have spent the rest of the night watching her.

"Could you stand living with a writer?"

Her brimming smile surrounded him like an embrace. "The only thing I couldn't stand is for you to be hurt. I love you, Ethan, rich man, poor man, beggar man, writer. I love you."

November was bitterly cold. The sun sent long shadows across the frosty land, but there was little warmth. People bundled up in coats and mufflers. With the Christmas lights already strung by the city and the department stores putting out their decorations, everyone was saying it felt more like December than the middle of November.

And then, in one of the jet stream's hilarious jokes, the world magically took a new lease on life. Golden warm air descended upon Montgomery and blew gently through its streets. It tugged at the colorful leaves still on the trees and sent them tumbling cheerfully beneath the feet of shoppers who streamed into the shopping malls and children who romped on school playgrounds, mothers pushing baby strollers in the park.

"One of the loveliest Indian summers on record," the newscasters were marveling. "Today's temperature will range in the midseventies."

"We should take advantage of the weather and move now," Ethan said when he called Kelly from his office. "Why don't we rent a big U-Haul and do it all in one fell swoop?"

"I'm game," Kelly said as she laid down the latest figures of the *Mirror*'s growth. Subscriptions were up, and advertising had nearly doubled.

Her only problem was a piece on Albert Russo that she had written the moment Ethan had told her about the sixty thousand dollars.

"Ethan, the piece on Russo is ready. I can't hold off printing it indefinitely. Have you and the prosecutor gotten together?"

In an unspoken pact made when he had told her about Maxwell's discovery, they referred to the investigation as Russo's, never as Georgia's. Kelly knew that Ethan was finding it more difficult to gather evidence for the grand jury than he'd anticipated. She had begged him to bow out.

"It's like a doctor performing surgery on a member of his family. Get Hite to present the findings."

"Hite and I aren't on the best of terms these days."

Then get on the best of terms, she wanted to tell him. If he had loose ends in his life, she certainly had a few of her own.

The *Mirror* was closing in on the *Tribune* now. It was the time to make her move. It was time to wield her blow at Georgia.

But her love for him prevented her from pressing.

"I saw the prosecutor this morning," he finally said with a snag in his voice. "I didn't think I would hate it this much."

Shortly after Ethan's meeting with the prosecutor, one of the nameless informants in Marlene Pace's information network called and told her that he'd just heard from one of the clerks at the courthouse that Albert Russo was being asked to fly down to Montgomery County to give a deposition.

It pertained to an alleged sixty-thousand-dollar check that had allegedly turned up in the mayor's bank account, she was told. Allegations were that the money could be connected to the various clean-air regulations that may have been violated by Southeast Medical Group.

Within minutes, Marlene had relayed this information along to the mayor, who promptly locked herself in her office and called her good friend Irwin Pritchard for some off-the-record legal advice.

In the course of the discussion, Georgia raised her concern about the invasion of privacy by the press, namely, the *Mirror*. She also asked if any out-of-the-ordinary subpoenas had come through Irwin's office in the past few days.

No strange subpoenas, the judge said, and mentioned that he did know firsthand that Kelly Madison had been working on a feature story about Georgia, which had apparently been shelved because more-pertinent environmental issues had taken the lion's share of the news.

Georgia asked if Irwin would, in deference to their long and mutually beneficial friendship, find out if Ms. Madison—"The bitch! Pardon my French!"—was planning to pull such a piece off the shelves during the immediate future.

Irwin said he would be happy to make such an inquiry.

"Please use discretion, Irwin," Georgia added.

"Discretion is my middle name, Georgia, dear."

The next day Irwin called the mayor with what he had learned, which wasn't all that much, he explained, as he couldn't afford to appear obvious. But he did learn that Ethan had had a long meeting with the county prosecutor. Ethan had also gotten a subpoena from Judge Higgins to acquire the bank records of Albert Russo.

"What's going on, Georgia?" Irwin asked. "You can't afford any adverse publicity right now."

When she hung up, Georgia looked at Marlene and felt her age more than she had in a long time.

"My own son," she said, and pulled off her earrings and dropped her head into her hands. "I can't let Ethan do this to me, Marlene. I have to make him back off."

Marlene knew what she had to do. "Don't worry about it, Mrs. Mayor. I promise you, he will not pursue this."

In Marlene's opinion, by stopping Ethan, she would stop the *Mirror*. It was a class case of getting two birds with one stone.

Kelly had never been so nervous about serving a dinner before.

Though Thanksgiving dinner would be small—just Ethan, Caroline and herself—it was the first really serious entertaining she and Ethan had done since moving into the apartment at the first of the week.

She did her shopping at the last minute, wanting only the best and freshest produce possible. She bought a small, lean turkey and crusty brown bread, butter and the makings of a salad, virgin olive oil and fresh peaches and cheese.

Ethan did his share by dipping into his stash of wine and bringing home an armful of fresh flowers. Besides having sent over the wicker furniture, as a housewarming present Caroline gave them a set of French china she and Vincent had started housekeeping with.

Well before noon on Thanksgiving Day, Kelly laid out the china and gave the stuffed turkey its final basting. While Ethan finished some editing and listened to a football game on television, Kelly soaked in a hot bath behind the folding screen.

Promptly at eleven o'clock, Caroline's taxi deposited her on the parking lot. Ethan met her at the side door while

Kelly removed the turkey and placed it on a great hand-painted platter she and Ethan had found at an antique mall.

"Isn't this the most beautiful Thanksgiving you've ever seen?" Caroline exclaimed as she walked through the door and Ethan took her coat to place it on an enamel hook near the basket of umbrellas. "I couldn't wait to see what you've done with the apartment."

Not expecting to be so nervous for her mother's stamp of approval, Kelly wiped her hands on a towel and hurried to greet her.

Caroline had paused in the act of removing her gloves. With Ethan behind her, she moved slowly through the loft, amazed.

"Oh, Kelly," she said on a rush of breath. "What you've done with this is unbelievable!"

"What *we've* done, Mother." Kelly laughingly gave Ethan half the credit. "I'm marrying a creative artist, you know. Ethan has a great sense for these things."

Caroline laughed. "I know all about that. Shame on you, Ethan, for keeping such a secret."

"I know, it's terrible." Ethan pretended a meaningless repentance.

Caroline had to see every new addition since her last visit, and she began with the large roomy sofas and chairs that Kelly had covered with cretonnes and silk shawls. Walls had been created by hanging airy, lined curtains that could be swept aside on the rods that Ethan had lowered from the ceiling.

The wicker furniture that Caroline had sent over had been placed in its own rush-floored section and surrounded with an arbor of indoor plants and ficus. Ethan's and Kelly's books occupied a number of different shelf arrangements, and dozens of baskets lay about, some of them lacily lined and some containing favorite books and knitting and magazines, dried flowers and herbs and pine cones collected from the park.

The bedroom occupied one end and consisted of an old-fashioned canopy bed whose draperies were more practical than decorative. A dozen pillows were arranged at its head.

But it was the cinnamon-fragrant kitchen that caught Caroline's fancy. Beside the island that occupied the center stage where the range had been built in, Ethan had placed a long, scrubbed table and a variety of chairs that Kelly had embellished with colorful cushions. A number of dressers had been placed side by side to form a wall, and these were lavishly burdened with painted pottery plates and fat, squat jugs and bowls, many of them containing dried herbs and flowers. The kitchen sink was a deep white china and looked down upon the street. Rush mats were laid out on the floor.

"I can't imagine a more perfect place to begin a marriage," Caroline exclaimed with delight, and brought out of her bag two jars of lovely marmalade.

Ethan took her gift to the table and opened a bottle of wine. He filled three glasses, and the three of them took a glass.

"To our new family," he said with brief gravity as he lifted his glass. "And to those not yet part of it who hopefully will be someday."

"To our family," Kelly and Caroline echoed as the glasses rang with a clear and certain melody.

Later, Ethan and Kelly drove Caroline home and kissed her goodbye on the steps of the veranda.

"This is one of the happiest days of my life," Kelly told Ethan as they took a longer and more leisurely way home.

She was snuggled into the curve of his side, and they drove through the affluent streets to admire lavish homes and congratulate themselves that they'd created one better for themselves.

Kelly grew solemn with thoughts of Ethan's estrangement from his family.

"Someday we'll all be friends," she murmured. "Wait until the children come. Babies have a way of softening old, hard hearts."

"Maybe our wedding will break the ice."

"Mmm," she said, and twisted around as the siren of a fire truck screamed past them. "If it were left to your dad, maybe. I really like Maxwell, Ethan. He's a good man."

"I know."

When another fire truck bore down upon them, Ethan asked, "Have you got your camera?"

"Always."

"This one's probably news. Shall we chase it?"

"In this car? You can try. But fires on holidays are always so sad."

Ethan hooked a hard left while Kelly rummaged for her Nikon, making certain she had film. The sky had a pink glow now, and traffic was picking up.

"Do you think it's on our side of the highway?" she asked as she caught a glimpse of Ethan's grim jaw.

"It's awfully close, if it's not," he said.

As they raced down Edlestein Parkway, Kelly felt a moment of alarm. She dismissed it as that part of herself that was always assuming the worst.

But the closer they got, the more nervous she became. "I don't like this."

Ethan lowered the window, and they were caught in a whirlwind of senses—the smell of the water-soaked air that was all around them now, the smell of burning, the sight of thick smoke that billowed over the tops of buildings.

As they turned onto Mimosa Street, Kelly could not keep from crying out, "It's too close. Ethan, it's too close."

Neither of them dared say what they both dreaded. Mimosa Street was clogged, lined with cars. People were running toward the Redmond Building, and when Ethan and Kelly could see the parking lot, they saw the two fire engines and police cars.

Kelly didn't realize where the high, keening wail was coming from as Ethan swept into a parking space and jumped out with her hysterically on his heels. He reached back for her hand, looking as if he had been hit hard in his face. Speechless with sobs, Kelly held tightly.

Now the flames were visible—leaping out of the windows, bursting the glass and sending bright orange-and-yellow sparks into the night sky with a deafening roar.

Pat and Quentin Mendino spotted them, and Pat ran up with her caftan sailing behind her. "Oh, Kelly!" she cried. "My God, Kelly. Isn't this awful?"

The heat struck in a wave, and Kelly was so numbed by shock, she hardly noticed the ash and sparks spewing down upon them.

"My desk!" she screamed, and thought in horror of Ethan's partial manuscript. "Your book."

Crazed, she strained at Pat's restraining hand. "Let me go, Pat. I have to save something! Anything!"

"Kelly!" Ethan yelled at her with a savage shake. "It's gone, darling! It's gone!"

But it couldn't be. The firemen on the roof of Allen's Paint & Body Shop, directing the water, weren't doing it right.

"Get her out of here, Pat," Ethan ordered as he gave her over to the older woman and sprinted toward one of the police cars.

But Kelly stayed. With her arms crossed over her stomach, she watched, it seemed, for hours. Sometime during those hours, Hite arrived. When he found Ethan, the past anger seemed not to have ever existed.

Hite returned to take Kelly into his arms. "I'm so sorry, darling."

Had Pat or Quentin called Caroline? Kelly had no idea. She knew only that when she caught sight of her mother, the frail thread that had been holding her together snapped. It was the last thing she knew until she came to and blinked up at one of the paramedics who was helping her stretcher into an ambulance.

"No," she said, and struggled against the strap that bound her. "I'm fine. Let me up, let me up. Where's Ethan? *Where's Ethan?*"

"Easy, miss."

"I think you should let them check you over," Ethan said as he climbed into the ambulance with her and the doors slammed shut.

Weeping with a grief that was worsened by the sight of Ethan's reddened eyes, she clutched his hand. "Oh, Ethan. What'll we do? What's going to happen now?"

He shook his head and looked away, at the driver up front and the lights of the city through his windshield.

Kelly dug her fingernails into his sleeve, bringing him back. "The truth, Ethan. We promised. No matter what."

Burying his face into her shoulder, his shoulders shook briefly then gathered strength until they were a fortress. When he straightened and they were slowing down, sweeping into the canopy of the hospital, he smiled sadly and kissed her hands.

"They told me it wasn't an accident," he said in a strange voice. "Not only was it not an accident, but somebody wanted the arson to be unmistakable. Very obvious."

The horrible truth found its way in the silence they shared.

"But I don't—" she began, and gripped his hands until the feeling left her own.

He shrugged off the grief that kept trying to find his shoulders. "It was a warning, Kelly," he said woodenly. "And, God help me, I think I know where it came from."

Chapter 16

"What day is it?" Kelly asked her mother.

"Saturday."

"It feels like . . . I don't know—Friday. It feels like Friday. Have I lost two whole days?"

After leaving the hospital, Kelly had not driven out to the *Great White* with Ethan. They held hands and mutely considered the evidence of something far beyond their control. Love had made them a prey, and despite love's tendency to cannibalism, it was also part savior. Neither was willing to endanger the other.

She did not resist his insistence that she go to her mother's house. Romeo and Juliet, she thought icily.

"Maybe I should go away," she told Caroline. "How could Georgia have so little feeling for her own son?"

Caroline kept her eyes on her knitting. "I don't think it's that she has no feelings for Ethan. She simply has more for her own ambitions. But you can't be sure that she was behind the fire."

"Of course she was behind it. She had to stop me from printing that she had been compromised. She also had to stop Ethan from taking what he knows to the prosecutor. But she's smart as a fox. By making the arson obvious, the investigators have to include me as a suspect, as well."

After the investigator intimated that she might have torched the Redmond for the insurance, Kelly had promptly called Morris Cavanaugh.

Ironically the Indian summer held, and the day was beautiful. Beyond the window, leaves were dancing along Ferris Street. Children were racing up and down the sidewalk on their bicycles, making the most of their holiday.

The grandfather clock chimed three times. Caroline's knitting needles echoed with a *click, click, click.*

"Try not to worry, dear," she said. "The truth has a way of finding its surface."

"How naive you are, Mother," Kelly blurted, and instantly regretted her sharpness. "I'm sorry. Look, don't pay any attention to me. I just don't know what to do. People are depending on me for their jobs. What do I tell the investors who went out on a limb and gave their money? What do I tell them?"

Caroline removed her reading glasses and took Kelly's hand, which no longer wore its diamond ring.

"The *Mirror* wasn't a bunch of machinery, Kelly. The *Mirror* is the people who create it. You can buy new machinery. You can build a new building. Ann and Fred can have a new desk. But, darling, you cannot buy another Ethan Chase. You can't build love. Ethan's in Gethsemane, darling."

"Do you think I don't know that? My heart breaks for Ethan." Kelly stuffed her hands into the pockets of her corduroy pants and shrank into the bulkiness of her sweater. "The closer I am to him, the more easily Georgia can get to him."

"Are you sure that's why you returned his ring?"

Stunned, Kelly gasped at her mother in horror. "How can you say such a thing?"

Rising, lovely in her ivory skirt and blouse and sweater and neat-heeled shoes, Caroline moved about the room that so reflected her good taste.

She picked up a figurine and caressed it. "Sometimes it's easier to sacrifice oneself for love than to make demands of it." Her thoughts were faraway. "Your talent and mine has always been to sacrifice. If I had to do it over, I think I would have fought your father." She smiled a small, sad smile. "Georgia knows more about love than you give her credit for. If you want to hurt someone, Kelly, you don't go after them, you go after what they love."

As Kelly received the full measure of her mother's wisdom, the ancient truth struck her like lightning. It was love's simplicity that had eluded her! Backing away from Ethan wasn't the way to defeat Georgia!

She blinked at her mother in amazement. "Our weapon against Georgia is for us to be happy."

"Exactly." Smiling, Caroline drew the back of her hand along the curve of Kelly's cheek.

Going into her mother's arms, Kelly drew in the fragrance she loved. How many years she had lost by blindly siding with her father.

"How wise you've become, Mother."

Caroline's laughter was soft. "I haven't suddenly grown wiser."

Kelly stepped back and laughingly shook her head. "Life is all backward."

"Yes. Now, why don't you let Georgia do whatever she's going to do? Leave the insurance company to Morris Cavanaugh, and give your investors a little credit for having made a wise choice. Wash your face, my darling. Go find that man of yours and tell him you want the ring back, that you'll be by his side, whatever happens."

Choices, Ethan had come to realize in the past two days, the really important ones, were not made all at once. They came in pieces, in small, subtle shades and degrees, inch by inch without a man consciously knowing what was happening. Then, all of a sudden, a man knew he had taken the step beyond any turning back.

The sense of inevitability that came upon him as he and John Fisher walked out of their meeting with the prosecutor and found Hite waiting for them on Dexter Avenue was overwhelming. It wasn't possible for things to end any other way than what they were.

The Alabama River was a warm tawny gold. The leaves of Indian summer were rushing along in its current.

"Well?" Hite asked where he waited with his hands stuffed in his trouser pockets.

Fisher laid his hand on Ethan's shoulder and said to Hite, "There'll be a hearing. If all goes as we think it will, Albert Russo will be indicted on six different counts."

"That should make Kelly ecstatic."

In his pocket, Ethan found Kelly's ring, and he slipped it onto the first joint of his index finger.

"At the same time," Fisher said, answering the question that had not been put into words, "there'll be an inquiry made into the mayor's part in the affair."

They were moving toward Ethan's truck, and Hite asked, "So, where're you going, Ethan?"

"Ethan has another matter to see his mother about," Fisher said.

Ethan squinted through the sunlight to where Georgia would be sitting at her desk behind walls that were no longer enough to protect her from him.

"The fire," Hite said as comprehension dawned. "Let me do it, Ethan. You don't want to be remembering this for the rest of your life."

Ethan gouged at his eyes, which were gritty with exhaustion. "No one can do this but me."

"At least let me go with you," Hite insisted. "I'll wait outside."

"Thanks anyway, Hite, but no. Fisher's going. I don't look for any trouble. And about what happened before, between you and me..."

Hite cut off the apology with a slash of his hand. "Look, if you want to talk later, you know where I'll be. Say hello to Kelly for me."

Nodding, Ethan tried to veneer his grief with a smile. He wasn't sure when he would see Kelly again. If he had any character at all, he would never see her. This was all his fault. His experience with Patty hadn't taught him anything.

Ethan and Fisher left Hite and crossed the street. They did not speak. To Ethan, it seemed that his entire life had been spent confronting Georgia or planning to confront her. What flaw did he have that he could not be as other sons were to their mothers? Even Kelly had forgiven Vincent Madison, and if the man had lived, they would have repaired the breach between them.

A fury was building inside him. He wanted to throw back his head and roar a primitive cry for blood. Now he could see how crimes of passion were committed. Only those who were loved could reach into a man's margins of sanity.

He kept the image of Kelly in his mind—Kelly, in slow motion, as she lost consciousness and had to be carried to the ambulance, as she came to his office that first day to accuse his mother and he had not believed her, as he had loved her and made love to her.

He walked into Georgia's outer office, where Marlene Pace looked up from her desk and the two younger women who occupied two smaller desks near the wall turned around.

"Wait here," he told Fisher.

Though it wasn't what Fisher wanted, he complied. Without a word, Ethan passed Marlene's desk, and she scrambled up, hurrying after him in her black corporate suit and flawless figure.

"What do you think you're doing? You can't go in there, Ethan. The mayor has someone with her. Stop it this instant, do you hear? Who do you think you are?"

With a rage that finally burst through him—a wild river forcing through its broken dike—Ethan whirled around to catch Marlene by the collar of her McFadden blouse.

The woman's eyes flared, and her mouth was a crimson gash. She stumbled back. One of her heels snagged the carpet, and she struck a cup of pens, sending them spilling to the floor.

"Oh!" gasped the two underlings.

"I'm your worst nightmare, Marlene," Ethan snarled as he towered over her. "So don't screw with me. I warned you, Marlene, but you didn't listen. That little weasel you went to see at Hardiman's Magneto—you remember the one. You gave him a thousand dollars to plant a device that starts fires, remember?"

"Oh, God!"

"God won't help you now, Marlene. The little weasel is going to testify. He's going to make you famous, Marlene."

Her breath was a long, hissing sound, like gas escaping. "Ethan, please . . ."

"I was going to do you second, Marlene. But hell, why wait? Fisherman?"

The detective came forward.

"You're under arrest, Marlene Pace," Ethan said, and motioned to his partner, who appalled Marlene by bringing out a pair of handcuffs.

While the girls looked on in horror, Fisher slipped them on Marlene's wrists and recited the *Miranda* warning.

Ethan, feeling the pulse at his right temple resounding in his ear, was cold in his self-knowledge. He did not feel as if he were entering the office of the woman who had held him when he was a baby, had bought his clothes and taken his hand at street crossings. He felt only the clarity and freedom that came from making the decision to protect Kelly, no matter what the cost.

One of Georgia's consultants was with her, and he rose, his practiced smile fading as he caught sight of Ethan's stance and the badge clipped to his waist.

Rising in confoundment, Georgia looked from Ethan's face to her door. Fisher's voice was carrying as he informed the secretary of her rights.

"Oh, Ethan," she breathed with more imploring than he had heard from her in years.

Ethan hooked his thumbs on his belt and refused to let his eyes show a shred of pity.

"Mother," he said quietly, and was aware of John entering behind him. "I've come—"

Georgia inclined her silvery head at the consultant, dismissing him. She said, "I know why you're here."

He must have imagined a thousand times, Ethan thought, the satisfaction he would feel when Georgia repented. Everything would have had a purpose then. Everything would have an order.

What he did not know then was that the future is a perfect reproduction of the past. Now he understood, and he reached into the breast pocket of his suit and brought out a folded piece of paper that Georgia recognized as a copy of her bank statement.

He carefully placed it on her desk, and she stood looking at the figure circled in red. He could see the lines of aging in her face now, the skin that was beginning to sag at her jaw.

"Does your father know?" she asked.

"Yes."

She looked up at him with a flash of her old fire. "I'll fight you on this."

"I know."

Georgia removed a cigarette from a silver case and lit it with shaking hands. "You've done what you came for. Please go."

"Not quite," he said, and removed the summons from his pocket and placed it on the desk. She made no move to pick it up. "You're under arrest for the destruction of private property, Mayor Chase, and the intent to do bodily harm. If those charges aren't enough, I can come up with a few others."

Georgia inhaled smoke and blew it out. "I didn't set that fire, Ethan."

"No, Marlene hired someone to do it. And you hired Marlene. Mother, do you think you can go through life playing God? Hurting everyone who disagrees with you?"

Her face was stony, and Ethan wanted to slam his fist into it, to raise some show of regret.

But he saw now that Georgia would never be sorry. It wasn't in her. He would cost her the governorship of Alabama, and she would be sorry for what she had lost, but she would always believe, right up to the end, that she had the right to be above the law because of who she was and what she had become.

It slid off him, then, like a snake shedding its skin—his refusal to accept the earth's terrible turning and his own frailty as a human being living on it. He didn't want Georgia's sorrow. He had enough of his own.

Turning to John, he availed himself of the wordless communication they had developed.

"There's no need for handcuffs," he said, and started for the door.

"Ethan!" Georgia called as he was reaching the door.

Ethan did not turn around.

"There is always room for communication," she shouted.

He said, still without looking at her, "You will not hurt her again."

To Ethan's surprise, Hite was waiting for him in the corridor.

The attorney grinned sheepishly. "I know you said not to come, but I thought I'd just walk over, anyway. I had nothing better to do."

"Thank you." Ethan rubbed at the creases spanning his forehead. "If you don't mind helping John..."

"Of course."

Ethan's steps down the corridor sounded strange to him. He wanted nothing as much as to get away quickly. He wanted to go to Kelly. He wanted to pour himself out at her feet and lose himself in the redemption of her love.

He wheeled hard about. "Hite?"

With his hand on the door, the ebony-haired man looked back. Ethan returned to stand before him, frowning. "You always come to me during the terrible times."

Tears of friendship collected in Hite's eyes. "You're my brother, Ethan. A man has to stand by his brother."

How good it felt to close his arms around Hite, Ethan thought. How good. Kelly would be glad.

Kelly was disappointed when she could not reach Ethan at his office. With her decision made, she was eager and nervous and at a loss for what to do next.

For twenty minutes she drove around town, not really
looking for Ethan but glancing about the streets in case she
saw a familiar span of shoulders, a loose-jointed gait, a
Stetson.

As if her actions were preprogrammed, she wound up at
the Redmond parking lot and pulled into a parking space
fronting Allen's Paint & Body Shop.

No one spoke as she crossed the street. How strange the
site was now, its ugliness incongruous with the Indian summer afternoon.

She was glad Vincent wasn't there to see the half-
remaining walls, his lovely dream gone up in smoke. He was
gone, and so were the three little blond-haired girls who had
posed before the revolving glass door.

That door was a twisted clump now, and she stifled the
impulse to rush about and start picking up debris and putting it in garbage bags.

Picking up a length of pipe, she dazedly picked her way
through the ashes and roasted computer terminals, the
blackened printing press. The water had dried the ashes into
a hard crust that crunched beneath her feet, and the smell
of burning drifted up into her nostrils. At one end, the claw-
foot bathtub was broken in pieces.

She gazed at the cars passing on Mimosa Street, feeling
the same loss as after that horrible night in Terry Benedict's car.

Like an instinct that no amount of living would completely eradicate, the old reassurances returned—her prince,
whispering, *You're okay now, Kelly. Everything will be okay
now.*

But it wouldn't be okay, would it? Nothing would be okay
now. Destruction surrounded her, and at the opposite side
of the lot . . .

Ethan! Ethan was making his way through the debris in his boots and jeans and Western hat. He was looking for her, but the sun was in his eyes. Its brightness was the same golden haze of the summery day, and it made him appear to be in another warp of time, somewhere with a crowd cheering and screaming his name. A page turned in her mind, and she saw the girl making her way toward him with difficulty. Except that she was that girl now, and nothing in her life was as important as reaching that place of resolution in his arms.

Finding her at last, he did not smile. Kelly wasn't smiling, either. Tears were streaming down her cheeks and sliding into the corners of her mouth, not because her hopes had gone up in flames but because time had not won. It had scarred her lovely golden prince, and it had made her afraid to believe.

But she and Ethan had won. Despite the heartache of the journey, despite the pain of the past and the misplaced hopes, they had found each other.

She went into his arms as if she were coming home. "I was wrong before," she said as she flung her arms around his neck.

He stuffed his face into her neck. "You're my woman. I've come to get you."

"And you're my quarterback hero."

There, in the ruins, Kelly leaned back in his arms to see the cost of the past days on his face. He could tell her everything, but for now all she needed to know was that life would never become too much for them to find each other in its debris.

Pushing his hat to the back of his head, he kissed her and kept her in the circle of his arms.

"Some mess," he said grimly, and looked around. "We're going to need one hell of a dustpan."

Spying her ring on the first joint of his finger, Kelly pulled it off and slipped it onto her own finger. She placed her arms around his waist, too. Side by side, they started to walk, leaving the destruction behind.

"It's okay, Ethan," she said, and turned her face to the warm, golden sun. "Everything's okay now."

*   *   *   *   *

AMERICAN HERO

Every month in Silhouette Intimate Moments, one fabulous, irresistible man is featured as an American Hero. You won't want to miss a single one. Look for them wherever you buy books, or follow the instructions below and have these fantastic men mailed straight to your door!

In September:
MACKENZIE'S MISSION by Linda Howard, IM #445

In October:
BLACK TREE MOON by Kathleen Eagle, IM #451

In November:
A WALK ON THE WILD SIDE by Kathleen Korbel, IM #457

In December:
CHEROKEE THUNDER by Rachel Lee, IM #463

AMERICAN HEROES—men you'll adore, from authors you won't want to miss. Only from Silhouette Intimate Moments.

COME BACK TO

CONARD COUNTY

There's something about the American West, something about the men who live there. Accompany author Rachel Lee as she returns to Conard County, Wyoming, for CHEROKEE THUNDER (IM #463), the next title in her compelling series. American Hero Micah Parrish is the kind of man every woman dreams about—and that includes heroine Faith Williams. She doesn't only love Micah, she *needs* him, needs him to save her life—and that of her unborn child. Look for their story, coming in December, only from Silhouette Intimate Moments.

THE DONOVAN LEGACY
from Nora Roberts

Meet the Donovans—Morgana, Sebastian and Anastasia. Each one is unique. Each one is . . . special.

In September you will be *Captivated* by Morgana Donovan. In Special Edition #768, horror-film writer Nash Kirkland doesn't know what to do when he meets an actual witch!

Be *Entranced* in October by Sebastian Donovan in Special Edition #774. Private investigator Mary Ellen Sutherland doesn't believe in psychic phenomena. But she discovers Sebastian has strange powers . . . over her.

In November's Special Edition #780, you'll be *Charmed* by Anastasia Donovan, along with Boone Sawyer and his little girl. Anastasia was a healer, but for her it was Boone's touch that cast a spell.

Enjoy the magic of Nora Roberts. Don't miss *Captivated,* *Entranced* or *Charmed.* Only from Silhouette Special Edition. . . .

Take 4 bestselling love stories FREE

Plus get a FREE surprise gift!

NORA ROBERTS

Love has a language all its own, and for centuries flowers have symbolized love's finest expression. Discover the language of flowers—and love—in this romantic collection of 48 favorite books by bestselling author Nora Roberts.

Two titles are available each month at your favorite retail outlet.

In November, look for:

For Now, Forever, **Volume #19**
Her Mother's Keeper, **Volume #20**

In December, look for:

Partners, **Volume #21**
Sullivan's Woman, **Volume #22**

Collect all 48 titles
and become fluent in

THE LANGUAGE of LOVE

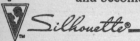

Silhouette®

If you missed any of volumes 1 through 18, order now by sending your name, address, zip or postal code, along with a check or money order (please do not send cash) for $3.59 for each volume, plus 75¢ postage and handling ($1.00 in Canada), payable to Silhouette Books, to:

In the U.S.
3010 Walden Avenue
P.O. Box 1396
Buffalo, NY 14269-1396

In Canada
P.O. Box 609
Fort Erie, Ontario
L2A 5X3

Please specify book title(s) with order.
Canadian residents add applicable federal and provincial taxes.

LOL1192

Silhouette CHRISTMAS Stories 1992

Experience the beauty of Yuletide romance with Silhouette Christmas Stories 1992—a collection of heartwarming stories by favorite Silhouette authors.

JONI'S MAGIC by Mary Lynn Baxter
HEARTS OF HOPE by Sondra Stanford
THE NIGHT SANTA CLAUS RETURNED by Marie Ferrarrella
BASKET OF LOVE by Jeanne Stephens

Also available this year are three popular early editions of Silhouette Christmas Stories—1986, 1987 and 1988. Look for these and you'll be well on your way to a complete collection of the best in holiday romance.

Plus, as an added bonus, you can receive a FREE keepsake Christmas ornament. Just collect four proofs of purchase from any November or December 1992 Harlequin or Silhouette series novels, or from any Harlequin or Silhouette Christmas collection, and receive a beautiful dated brass Christmas candle ornament.

Mail this certificate along with four (4) proof-of-purchase coupons, plus $1.50 postage and handling (check or money order—do not send cash), payable to Silhouette Books, to: **In the U.S.:** P.O. Box 9057, Buffalo, NY 14269-9057; **In Canada:** P.O. Box 622, Fort Erie, Ontario, L2A 5X3.

ONE PROOF OF PURCHASE	Name: _____
	_____
	Address: _____
	_____
	City: _____
	State/Province: _____
SX92POP	Zip/Postal Code: _____

093 KAG